BLUE MERCY

ORNA ROSS

PREFACE

The mother-daughter relationship is one of the most fascinating, complex and under-explored relationships in fiction. There are, it is true, a lot of novel about daughters rebelling against a strict and difficult mother but that is only one side of what is, always, a double-barrelled story.

The Irish novelist, Edna O'Brien once said: "If you want to know what I regard as the principal crux of female despair, it is this: in the Greek myth of Oedipus and in Freud's exploration of it, the son's desire for his mother is admitted. The infant daughter also desires her mother but it is unthinkable, either in myth, in fantasy, or in fact, that that desire can be consummated."

Star would think that a lot of tosh, motherless Mercy would be puzzled, but I agree.

What comes between Mercy and Star is a man. Actually, two men. The women are so focussed on Martin, the father, and Zach, the lover, that they fail to see each other. It was my hope, in writing their story, that it might help us all to more truly see our own mothers and daughters.

Orna Ross, London. 2020.

PART I
BLUE MERCY

An act of mercy that has unanticipated and injurious consequences.
An act of revenge that turns out to be a mercy.
[*slang: Irish*]

STAR

2009

*S*hando pokes his head around the door, his duty check, and immediately is caught by the sight of her pages scattered across our bed. "How are you doing, hon?" he asks, dragging his gaze back up to me. "You okay? How far have you got?"

"Just to her arrest."

The head nods, solemn. "Well done. The beginning will be hardest."

"You do know it's a sham?"

"Star... Please..."

"It is. Already it's contradicting itself, twisting things up."

"Honey, you've only read one chapter."

"She begins with..." I falter over the date we never name. "She says nothing about my arrival that day."

"Arrival?" he asks, face blank and solemn as a priest. "What day?"

"That Christmas. When Granddad died." *That* day, my husband, dear, the one that almost destroyed us all.

"There's loads about that, Star. And there's loads about you. That's why you need to read it."

"You do know it begins with a letter from her —"

"Yes, yes," he interrupts, not wanting me to say "boyfriend". Stupid word for the lover, yes, *lover*, of a sixty-something-year-old woman. "I know it's hard, hon, I do. I do. But trust me, you'll be glad once you've read through to the end. "

Wake up, I want to shout at him. *You're being an idiot. Can't you see what she's doing?*

As always, words fail me. Words were her tool; they never come out right for me.

"I think you could do with a nap now," he says, in his husband-knows-best voice. "Don't you? Read a bit more later on?"

I let silence answer that suggestion.

"Take it in small bites, y'know?"

"I don't have to read it at all."

"Would you prefer to go down to the sitting-room? I've lit the fire down there."

She's brainwashed you! But has she? Or is it me who's got it all wrong?

Doubt drags the words back down, unsaid.

"Look," he says, "I'm going to take the kids out for an hour so you can get some rest. You'll feel better after a nap."

He makes his escape.

I don't blame him, not really. If I could get away from myself, I'd be out of here too.

Time has sliced itself up since my mother died five days ago, and keeps shuffling itself like a deck of cards in my head. Two days in particular keep turning up on top: Christmas Eve 1989, the day Granddad died, twenty years back. And the day out I had with Mom at the end of last year, in Glendalough, when she tried — yet again — to push her manuscript onto me. *Blue Mercy*. By Mercy Mulcahy. How typical of her, that title. Mercy, Mercy, always Mercy. Even now.

I'd recognised the manuscript the minute Mags, Mom's

lawyer, extracted it from her stack of deeds and testaments that morning. The reading of the will was supposed to be our last death-duty and Mags had arrived promptly at 10 a.m. and worked smartly through her list of legalities.

Blackberry Lodge, officially ours at last: tick.

Most of Mom's money, also to us: tick.

Trust fund for the kids: tick.

A bequest each to Pauline and Marsha, her closest friends: tick.

A donation to the Right To Die Society: tick.

Just when it looked like we were done, Mags reached deeper into her satchel and pulled out this: six-hundred tattered and benighted pages held together by two criss-crossed pink elastics. And that damn title staring up at us. Everything in the room — husband, lawyer, furniture, fire — faded for me as she slid it across the polished table.

I paused a moment, then slid it right back.

"Ah, Dotes, come on now." Mags, the least doting woman in the world, had a habit of calling everyone Dotes. I shook my head. If I was ever going to read that thing, I would have taken it from Mom that day in Glendalough. If I hadn't then, when she herself had put it into my lap and gripped my arm turning her big, mother-guilting eyes on me, why would I take it now?

Shan put his hand on my arm, much as Mom had done that day, and started to urge me — "Honey, don't you think...?" — until he saw my face and stopped short.

As well he might.

Mags knew enough to stay silent too.

So we sat, three capable adults, gagged by awkwardness and respect for the dead but mostly by the memories swirling in the sticky silence. Clueless about what to do next, until I, sighing a sigh that even I could hear was petulant, snatched it up, and the other two rounded off the meeting as fast as they could.

Which is how I've ended up here, one chapter in, unable to go on. *Unable*, I say.

I'll go downstairs to the sitting-room fire right now, and toss it in and watch it burn, I decide. I gather up the white pages, I tap the edges to line them up, sideways, lengthways. I pull them back into order, I snap their pink elastic band back on.

If I *were* to edit this book and ready it for publication, as she'd asked, I'd want to tell it my way. Not so much what happened on Christmas of 1989 as all that led up to it.

I, too, can hold a pen.

But Shando says no. It's Mom's book, he says, not mine. My job, if I took it on, wouldn't be to "write back" but to ensure that what she wanted to say was said clearly and fully.

It sounds so fair, so right, so reasonable but she herself said I could do what I liked, so long as I *read* it. "It's your story, too," she'd said, as she was trying to persuade me not to give it back.

She'd sat so erect that day in Glendalough, on that bench in the churchyard, her legs angled both to one side, like a posh lady in a drawing-room. Old and ill and frail, a word I never expected to apply to Mom, but still arresting. The grey hair highlighted to a crisp ash-blonde. She wore it long, too long, some might say, for her age. Usually pinned into a coil at her crown but at that moment folded over one shoulder, falling like a curtain across the prosthetic breast that lurked under the elegant white shirt. The tips of her hair floated across the manuscript, where I'd just set it, back in her lap

A wave of claustrophobia cuts off my breath. Through the bedroom window, a glint from beyond the trees catches my attention. The lake. That's it, not the fire, the lake.

I would take it down to the lake. Down there, I would know what to do.

They have a saying in this adopted country of mine: *when sorrow sours your milk, it's time to make cheese.* A very Irish way of saying: count your blessings. As I make my way downstairs, slowly, like an invalid, I take myself to task, as I so often need to do.

Yes, it is true that my mother has jumped up out of her coffin, waving her manuscript like a traffic warden with a ticket. Yes, my husband has leapt to defend her, turning my mind down worn-out tracks I'd promised myself I'd never travel again. And yes, her passing has stirred up Granddad, has him rattling his old bones in our faces, showing us he isn't dead and gone as we liked to pretend that the horrors of what happened still lurk just under everything else, easily — all too easily — resurrected to stalk our days again.

But it is also true that the same husband is kind and faithful, that we are as happy as can be expected in this lovely home we've created together, where we run our lovely business, and raise our two lovely, long-awaited, children. And that outside the window is our lovely garden among lovely grounds, five acres stretching towards the wilds of Wicklow, the loveliest county in Ireland.

So...

On the porch, I transfer my striped feet into the wellington boots that live by the door. The higgledy-piggledy porch is my favourite room in our house, with our walking boots and trainers, our coats and umbrellas, our backpacks and shopping bags. All the ordinary paraphernalia of country family life, looking almost holy to me today in the steely winter light. *Lovely, lovely, lovely.*

The door clicks shut behind me. It's chilly out, and a small gust of wind whips up. Leaves from a pile in the corner swirl into it, dancing around each other, as if enjoying their freedom, oblivious to the reality that they are half dead already. Above, a last few cling to almost-bare branches. Their doomed tenacity makes me want to cry. When they fall, as they surely will, does that mean their efforts to hold for so long were wasted?

I cross the yard, heading up the back pathway through the trees. Before there was a house here, there was this lake and these woods and the wild Wicklow hills. We have to work hard to keep them from taking over again. They're ready to do it. If we let off for the smallest while our cutting and trimming and weeding, our feeding the plants we want over the ones we don't, in they'll move, to swallow up our house and land. Nature. It doesn't need us at all, but how we crave it.

That's what brings all the people, the hikers and bikers, the day-trippers and weekenders, out here to Doolough. The sound of a different kind of silence to that in their bedrooms and kitchens.

At the lake, I put the manuscript on the ground, kneel on it and lean in to see my reflection in the murky water. I look old today, older than I am. In this posture, gravity pulls my jowls and chins forward. She was beautiful, I am not. Was that the fullness of our story?

She never lost her looks. Most Irish people do, develop in age the distinctive features other Americans and the English charmingly call "potato-head". Not my mother. I think of her again that last day she spent out of the house on our trip to Glendalough. She had only twelve weeks left to live but was lovely as ever in her new, ever-more-fragile way. Knowing she was dying, as we did by then, I'd fixed us a day out together with the kids.

Grandmother, mother, children. Picnic lunch. Gentle tour of the monastic ruins. Soft stroll through the woodlands. All of which we enjoyed. And for the finale, my *coup de grace*, I'd thought: a visit to the nearby churchyard at Laragh, where they've installed a sculpture, a bronze tribute to the story of Saint Kevin, the saint who'd settled on this site and turned it into a place of pilgrimage fourteen centuries ago.

So we drove up there, through the green drowsiness of a summer afternoon, and I settled her on a bench in front of the sculpture, while the children tried to climb and clamber over it. And I gave her the poem I'd photocopied and folded into my bag about the legend of Saint Kevin. Even I could tell it was good, how it asked us to imagine the saint holding out his hand in prayer, when a blackbird came and lay her eggs in his palm, and how he continued to hold his hand up and out for her, still and steady, for days, weeks, all through the nesting season, until her chicks were hatched and reared. It wasn't by WB Yeats, her fave rave, but the other guy, the one who looks like a farmer. Heaney.

She appreciated the gesture, as I'd know she would, and read it aloud for us and we sat in silence afterwards.

"That's one to learn off-by-heart," she'd said, and asked me if I had and when I said I hadn't, told me I must. "Poems have to become like the marrow in our bones to be appreciated," she'd pronounced. "Learn it, Star. Do."

All my life, she'd said things like this.

On that day, in the peace generated by the blackbird story, I was able to let it go, and even able to smile a moment later when I heard her murmuring a line. "It's all imagined, anyway."

I'd thought we were both happy, united for a few hours, by my bringing us both there, to the village where we'd run into such trouble before, after Granddad's going. I'd thought we were enjoying a seemingly small but actually enormous great reward for having managed to make a life that worked, despite all. Silly me. A minute later, she was pulling her own surprise out of her bag, the *Blue Mercy* script, and forcing it on me.

I told her what I'd so often told her before: "I'm never going to read it, Mom."

"You must," she'd said, putting her hand on my arm, giving me her best supplicating stare. And then: "It's your story too, Star."

I *must*. How had she never learned that was the worst possible way to get me to do anything?

My mother was a writer and a thinker and just about the last person anyone would expect to commit murder. Not just murder, patricide. Yet — strange thing — when she said she hadn't done it, nobody believed her.

Now at the lakeside, kneeling on the *Blue Mercy* manuscript I close my eyes to all that, as I have so many times before and call to mind again — like a litany — all the things I've made for myself, for all of us. Things I thought I'd never have: lovely husband, lovely children, lovely home. This place transformed from house of horrors to house of healing. *I* did that. Not alone, but it couldn't have happened without me. My life has not been wasted. I am *not* a bad person.

That's the thought that snaps me into standing, to assert again what should have been my birthright, but which I had to hand-stamp into myself. The right to do what's right for me. *Me*, Mom.

I pick up the hateful pile of paper and pull off the elastic so determinedly that it breaks. I take a page and bunch it up and fling it, unread, into the lake.

It's hard to fling paper. It doesn't carry, there's no satisfactory plop as it hits the water. It just hovers there, hardly touching the surface, wimpily uncertain. There are more than six hundred pages in this manuscript but I will clump each and every one into a paper ball. I will cast them, each and all, upon the lake. I will watch them, bob-bob-bobbing on the lapping shore, slowly soaking up the water that will see them sink.

PART II
STARCLOUD

a region where stars appear to be especially numerous and close together.

MERCY

CHRISTMAS EVE 1989

*E*arly on Christmas Eve morning, hours before Zach left or Star arrived, my father asked me to kill him. I'd spent some of that night in a chair at the end of his bed. At one point, he woke and started to panic, then remembering, reached up to push the button that released liquid morphine into his veins. I saw him lie back into the effort of keeping his breathing going, so hoarse and loud, a sound like the sea pressing through a blow-hole.

"Better," he sighed, as the pain relief kicked in. "That's better."

His hand went up to press the machine again, but I knew nothing would issue from it again so soon. Maybe he believed it had, because he dropped off immediately into a more settled sleep and didn't wake again until breakfast time, when I brought him the bowl of mashed banana and yogurt that was all he could manage first thing.

His eyes clicked open as I came into the room and he said, in a clear voice, "I need a pill."

"What about the pump?"

"No, a pill."

I took the container from its place on the window ledge, shook one pill into his hand. He took the glass of water and gulped to swallow, his whole throat working over it. He coughed, then drank again.

"I need more."

I reached for the jug.

"More pills, I mean."

"You can't, you know that."

"I've had enough now of living like this." His eyes locked onto mine, as they only ever had once before.

"Please."

"Let the one you've just had take effect," I said. *"You'll feel better then."*

"There's no better for me." He put his fingers on my wrist, his grip surprisingly tight. *"Please. Have mercy."*

He gave a macabre grin, maybe at the pun on my name, or maybe because the pill was already beginning its work. Or maybe it was the effort of making the request, of taking my arm, of saying such words.

"You're a clever girl, always were," he whispered, eyelids beginning to droop. *"You'll know what to do."*

And his eyes released me, closed over the first compliment he ever gave me.

So picture us at his funeral, the chief mourners, daughter and granddaughter of the deceased, in our places in the top pew, the back of our black coats to the rest of the congregation, absorbing their jabbing stares. Star's appearance gave them extra ammunition for their loaded gossip: her too-black hair, stiffened into spikes, her bovver boots and ripped tights, her nose-ring and of course, her extraneous fat, five or six stone of it, carried like a soldier carries his pack.

I knew what they would be saying, not Pauline or a few kindly others, but most of them. *That must be the daughter, is it, newly arrived from America? Lord God, the size of her. And what a get-up to wear to a funeral. And where was yer man gone, the boyfriend? What went on above in that house at all, at all?*

The event was organised as my father had decreed. Remains to Stafford's funeral parlour in town. No wake. High Mass in Doolough at 10 a.m. Six priests. *Ave Maria. Be Not Afraid. How*

Great Thou Art. Sitting in the front aisle with Star, I hadn't realised how many people were piling into the church behind us until it was over, when we turned to a full house, crowds bunched around the doors, upward of two hundred pairs of eyes nailing us as we followed the coffin down the aisle. The crowd parted for it, for us, then followed us out into the churchyard cemetery for the burial.

Through it all, Star and I had played our parts, standing and sitting as required, heads bowed, faces blank, though where I should have had a core, I had only space.

Afterwards, continuing under orders, we went to Maguires, the local pub, for a soup-and-sandwich lunch, and it was there, once people had settled in over their soup spoons, that Dr Keane — who had had his eyes on me ever since coming in — leaned across the table where I was sitting with Star and asked if he might have a word.

"Of course," I'd said, pushing my untouched food aside.

Doctor Keane was Jimmy to my father, his oldest friend. Despite their different rankings in Doolough's finely-tuned social scale, they were bonded by their active history in the Irish Civil War, when they both fought to uphold a Treaty with England that others thought a sordid compromise.

"We'll step outside, if you don't mind," he'd said, causing a look to fly around the table.

I put down my napkin and followed him out through the crowd. Outside, he remarked on the cold, pulling his scarf tight around his ancient, scrawny throat. He offered me a cigarette, and when I shook my head he lit one for himself, and started talking about the funeral, praising my father and recounting some memories of their boyhood. When he couldn't put off any longer what he had to say, he threw his cigarette to the ground and, keeping his eyes on it as he squashed it with the toe of his boot said, "The autopsy found something wasn't right."

At first, I didn't let in what he was saying. "If everything was all right," I said, "I guess he wouldn't be dead."

"This isn't a joke, dear." He looked at me over his glasses. "The cause of death was an overdose of morphine."

"But that's not —"

"It's beyond doubt," he interrupted. "The pathologist said she never saw so much morphine in a body."

"The pump? Maybe the pump was faulty?"

"It's been checked. The pump was fine."

"The pills?"

"We don't know. We were hoping you might be able to help us on that."

"Help how?"

"Like I say, we don't know. All we know is what the toxicology reports say. An unholy amount, apparently."

Toxicology reports? Pathologist? Autopsy?

"Oh, doctor, you and Pauline know what it was like for my father at the end. Pain, baby food, sleepless nights... An animal in that condition would have been put out of its misery long ago."

"If I were you, m'girl, I wouldn't be going around saying things like that."

"If he hadn't died that day, he would have died another day soon."

"Aren't you wondering who did it?"

"Did what?"

"I'm telling you that somebody killed your father by giving him an overdose of morphine. And all you have to say to me is that whoever did it, did right."

The nausea I had been feeling all day rose up my windpipe. "I just can't believe that *anybody* did it. Who could have? Who would have?"

"Indeed."

"Maybe... Could he have done it himself?"

"I spoke to him a week before he went. He said nothing that sounded suicidal to me."

He tightened his scarf again.

"I wanted you to be told first; that's only fair."

I thought of the looks exchanged around the table as I got up to leave and realised I wasn't the first to know. Already, he or the pathologist or somebody else had been talking. Maybe that's why there had been so many at the funeral? They hadn't come to pay their respects to the little-liked sergeant at all, but to take a look at the daughter who was rumoured to have seen him out.

After Doctor Keane delivered his bombshell, I had to go back into the pub and stay to the very end, my mind clanging with his insinuations. Star sat opposite me at our table, chewing on her pudgy fingers, and I switched out of the talk too, let the conversation churn around me as we waited, waited, for them all to finish. It was hours before they cleared, but eventually only the freeloaders and alcoholics were left and Pauline, more attuned to the niceties of Doolough behaviour than me, said it would be okay to go.

"I will never, ever set foot in that place again," I said to Star as we walked out together. "Never, never, never."

"Ah, now," said Pauline, coming out behind us, putting an arm around us both. "I thought it all went off grand."

Mikey, her husband, had the car waiting outside for us and Star and I sat in the back. Exhausted, I was grateful for everyone's silence. We drove through Doolough, past the school and the smattering of houses known as the heart of the village, out onto the Avoca Road. Past the high walls of Doolough House. Past the police barracks. As the car drew towards Blackberry Lodge, I said: "You can drop us here, Mikey, at the end of the lane. We'd be glad of the fresh air."

"Are you sure?" asked Pauline. "Do you not want me to come up with ye?"

"Not at all, Pauline," I said. "You've done so much already."

She patted my hand. "You let Star look after you now." She twisted her head round to Star, looking for a response. When it didn't come, she got out of her front seat and folded it forward. I climbed out and we waited side-by-side, trying not to see Star's struggle to extract herself. Why are fat people's exertions always so painful to watch?

"I'll be round tomorrow at one o'clock," Pauline said, to distract us. "I'll bring a bit of dinner."

"Thank you so much for everything," I said again.

"You're sure you're all right?"

"Positive."

Star was out. Now it was her turn for a Pauline patting. "It's great you're here now, love. Your poor mam has been a slave to your granddad's illness these past months."

Star nodded, ambiguous.

"Ring me, won't you, if you need anything," Pauline said, sitting back in. "Even if it's the middle of the night."

"You're too good, Pauline." I closed the door on her. "Thanks, Mikey."

"Thank you," said Star, her only contribution since we'd left the pub.

We waved and they were gone, the chuggy sound of their engine carrying across the fields as my daughter and I turned and walked up the lane back to the house where I was raised. Or reared, as they like to say in Ireland, as if you were one of the beasts of the field. I matched my pace to Star's slower, more tentative, steps — the heavier Star becomes, the less solid she feels, somehow — and we walked up the lane in gathering darkness, two feet by two crunching on the gravel.

The short day was coming to a close; December light, pale as water, was fading fast. We could see the house, as you couldn't in summer, through the trees: tall, white, Georgian, protected by a circle of faithful ash trees, with two chimneys either end of the roof in which jackdaws nested and cawed. Is it an Irish or an American saying, that when it comes to money or possessions, "you can't take it with you"? If you could take anything to the place beyond, Blackberry Lodge would have been it for my father. There had always been questions about how he, a Garda sergeant, could have accumulated the money to buy it.

Eight windows — six in a row above the door, one large long one down either side of it — stared down at us. It was ours now, this house, unless my father had a surprise waiting for us in his will. I didn't want it.

All I wanted was to talk, properly, to Star. Since she'd arrived on Christmas Eve, she and I had had no time together. My father died that night and since then it had been nothing but people coming and going and funeral arrangements and things to do. Now I needed to get her to myself. I wanted to show her Doolough and all the beauty spots of County Wicklow. Our old way of being together had imploded and we needed time if we were to replace it with something new, something better.

Yet I didn't know how to ask, or tell her any of this. Imagine that: lost for words with your own daughter. The breach of adolescence, the generation gap is no secret but it's like other women telling you about their birth pains. You only dimly perceive what you're being told, until your own experience smacks you into knowing. And Star and I had complicating factors, if ever a mother and daughter had. Her refusal to discuss that was making other talk impossible.

I ushered her through the back door, followed in behind her. Beneath those dyed and gelled spikes, just below her hairline, was a birthmark about a square inch in size, the shape — if you closed your eyes and tilted your sight a certain way — of a five-cornered star. When she was a baby, I used to kiss that mark after every feed. *I did my best, Star.* I wanted to scream at the spine so hunched against me as I followed it into the house. *I did my best.* Even as I was thinking it, I despised the thought. The anthem of the failed mother.

Instead I needed to find words that might reach through that anger of hers and persuade her to stay on. She'd said she was leaving in the morning but I knew if we were to salvage anything to take into a shared future, I had to get her to stay.

In the kitchen, I put on the kettle and had an idea. I'd show her some of the family photographs and letters that I had found in my father's bureau. Draw her in, then ask her to stay on, at least for a few days.

I went to fetch them from the bureau in the sitting room while she made tea. I'd been meaning to sort them, arrange them into albums, another one of those endeavours I'd not got round to doing. Caring for my father had been a round-the-clock job.

Now I laid them out on the table in front of Star. The first one that caught her eye was one of Daddy and me at the beach. Me, aged seven or eight, in a hoop-striped swimming costume with a frilly skirt piece, standing in front of a sandcastle. My father, already old, sitting upright on a plaid rug behind me, his shirt buttons undone, showing grey hair across his chest. Both of us squinting into the sun.

"You were so cute," Star said, her voice wistful, as if she was looking at her own memory, not mine. "Who took this?"

"It couldn't have been my mother. She was long dead by then." My mother had died when I was three.

"It's so sad that you never really knew her."

I nod. She'd been saying that her whole life long and yes, my mother's absence must have affected me, but it's not something I've ever felt directly; you can't miss what you've never known.

Had she lived, would my father have been different? I don't think so. Nobody could ever rein that man in. I have only one image of her, more imagination than memory. I see us as two shimmering figures of fear, one small, one adult size, standing in front of him.

"Star, won't you stay another day? I could do with some help tomorrow, clearing your granddad's things."

"You should have thought of that before you told me a pack of lies, Mom." This was the nub of the latest injury. My father had told her that Zach spent some time here before she arrived.

"I'd just like you to stay on now for a couple of days. Now you're here."

"Oh, yes, *now I'm here*."

"What does that mean?"

"What if I hadn't decided to come, Mom? How long would I have had to wait before you'd have got in touch with me?"

I braced myself for the attack but when it came, it wasn't about him. Not directly.

"Not a word, nothing, for months. I had to fly 6,000 miles. I had to hire a car in a strange city, not knowing who'd be here when I arrived. And if I hadn't come...?" She broke off, her jowls shuddering with anger. "I get why you ran off, just about, but what I don't accept, Mom, what you can't really, in all honesty, expect me to accept, is what came after."

For a moment, I was tempted to do what she was doing – to let myself think of nothing but *me-me-me*. What would I say to her?

Cut me a break, Star.

Don't ask any more of me than you ask of yourself.

Move on.

Let me and Zach be.

I didn't say any of it, of course. Star was American; I, for all the years in Santa Paola, was still of Ireland and in Ireland, in my day at least, the national motto was: "Whatever you say, say nothing".

And I was the mother, trained into biting my tongue. Daughterly anger we might survive, but maternal self-pity would kill us off. I'd let Zach go so I could make a play for Star. I would do everything in my power now to heal our breach.

But how? "It's all so complicated," I ventured.

"Complicated? To pick up a telephone and call me? To tell —"

"I didn't think you wanted to hear from me. You said —"

"We both said a lot of things that day, Mom."

In fact, I'd said very little. It was she who had ranted and raved before stomping out of the house, but this didn't seem like the time to say so. It felt so forced, this anger of hers, so unable to see anything beyond itself. What about all the years before my unintended mistake, day after day after day of mothering and giving? Did that not count for anything? Should that not be weighed against my sin?

And what of her sins, worse than anything I'd done. Was all this anger an attempt to deflect from that?

Oh, Star, my daughter dear, go easy on me. Go easy, or you might come to regret it.

Next morning, we sat in her little hire car. She had allowed herself to be persuaded to stay one more day by the prospects of a trip to Glendalough. It was a morning that the Irish winter occasionally throws up, just when you despair that the ceiling of grey cloud above has turned solid. A day that seemed to have wandered backwards out of springtime, with a clear-blue sky and golden light. A gift of a day.

I breathed deep as we drove, trying to inhale some of its tranquility and unwind. Our little car was climbing, engine whining as we negotiated the bends further up, and up. More accustomed to an automatic, Star kept crunching the gearstick. As we topped the crest, a bog-plain opened out, tufted peat and raw earth stretching on all sides for miles.

"What do you think of the scenery?" I asked.

"Sure, it's pretty."

It was the wrong word for the ruggedness of Wicklow, but we were together, my daughter and I, taking a day trip.

"What time do you think we'll be back?" she asked.

"I'm not sure. I thought we'd make a day of it, have a spot of lunch?"

"I have to leave in the afternoon."

"Oh."

"Mom, don't give me 'oh'. You know. I told you."

"But not where you're planning on going."

"Mount Mellaray Abbey."

"What?"

"A monastery in County Waterford," she said.

"I know what it is. It's well known." An enclosed order of Cistercians on the bare, windblown slopes of Knockmealdown Mountains. "Star, are you sure?"

"I'd better tell you. In March, I'm going to be confirmed."

It was so long since I heard the word used in this context that for a minute I failed to recognise it. "Confirmed?" I repeated, puzzled. Then I realised. "Confirmed as a Roman Catholic?"

"Yes. I've been going to Mass and taking classes."

"Since when?"

"Since... Oh, a long time."

Star was baptised for the same reason her father and I got married: because, in the 1970s, nuns and priests and Christian Brothers provided what was considered the best public education in America. We couldn't afford to pay school fees, but we wanted the best for our darling, so we decided to capitalise on our Irish Catholic backgrounds. We married and had Star baptised Maria Bernadette, the name she took through school and college and out into the world, though to us she was always Star.

And though she got plenty of Jesus, Mary and holy St Joseph at school, at home we counterbalanced it with our secular view of life.

She'd moved on from the church as she moved on from pretty much everything we gave her, to become angry and rebellious. A punk rocker for a while. A surly challenge to her teachers. How could somebody like that sign up for the Roman Catholic Church?

Her father would have cried to hear it, and I couldn't help but think it was just another way to get at me.

"I'm always surprised when young people sign up for organised religion," I said.

"I'm not asking your permission, Mom. I'm just telling you."

"I didn't mean..." I let my explanation trail away. It wasn't important. "You'll be interested in where we are going then," I said, as we began our descent into a sheer-sided, wood-covered valley, down towards the two elongated lakes that gave this ancient settlement its name. "Glendalough was once the Christian capital of Ireland."

We parked in the lot by the lake and as we emerged from the car, the mountains seemed to have closed in around us and the quiet was palpable, inescapable, underlined by the distant, humming rush of Poulnapass Waterfall. I felt its peace settle in me, felt my blood slow, my muscles unclench.

Star was finally impressed. "Wow! This place is something."

We set off. My daughter is no walker. Because of her size, she was propelled not by her legs but by her belly, her steps somehow delicate as well as full of effort, as if the force of gravity was precarious for her. I knew each pace brought her discomfort and that, in a few moments, her forehead would be lined with a sheen of sweat. Yet it was good for her to walk, surely? Not to give in to her disinclination? I fell into a slow step beside her.

Groups and couples passed us in their colored rainwear, their faces ruddy with fresh air, nodding and smiling. I took her up the back way, through the ruins, the remains of cloisters and chapels left over from the monastic heyday.

"That round tower is sure something," she said, as we stood at the base of it, looking up. "What was it for?"

"A beacon for pilgrims. A bell tower. A refuge when the Vikings came to plunder."

"Hard to imagine plundering Vikings now. It's so peaceful."

And it was. That's why I write it out here. I want to record how Glendalough worked its magic on us, how Star and I laid down our differences for a while, how we walked around the sacred stones put down by monks a millennium before to mark out their holy ground and sat for a long time after in comfortable silence. How, on that morning before she left me for good, before the police came calling, before I knew the worst, she and I were happy among the graves of Glendalough, almost at peace with one another.

Until, on the way back, I made the mistake of driving us home through Laragh.

"Laragh," Star murmured as we passed the road sign. "Laragh…?"

"Yes," I said, thinking she was asking directions. "If you drive on through the village and turn —"

"Laragh? Isn't that where Dad came from?"

I had forgotten she knew that. I had half-forgotten I knew it myself. "Yes, it is."

"Oh, my God, Mom, you are unbelievable!" She jerked the car to a stop, making the car behind us blare its horn.

"Star!"

"Don't you think, Mom," she said speaking slowly, like I was a child. Or an idiot. "Don't you think I might be interested in seeing the house where my father grew up?"

"Gosh, honey, I don't think I even know where your dad's home place is. Once before I tried to find it, from his description, but I couldn't be sure…"

"But not to even *say*."

"I'm sorry." Sorry, sorry, sorry, sorry…

She interlaced her fingers on the steering wheel, rested her forehead on them. Then: "Were you never in it?"

"No. No, your dad and I left Ireland very soon after we met. I never knew his parents."

"Didn't you ever come back?"

"Not together. I don't think he ever did."

"Why? I've never been able to understand that. What had they done to him?"

"He never told me. He flatly refused to talk about them."

"You should have made him. Maybe if he *had* talked…"

This is a new riff on her old refrain, her father's failings were always my fault.

"All right then," I said. "Let's see if we can find anything."

I directed her to turn at the bridge, near the old mill, and we drove up to the house that I believed might have belonged to Brendan's family, parked the car a little way beyond, walked back to look at it. A bungalow, low and squat, without a single attractive feature except the shrubbery.

"The garden's pretty, isn't it?" I said. "Even at this time of year. Somebody in there has green fingers."

"I think we should go in," Star said.

"Absolutely not. I'm not even sure it's the right house and even if it is, they could well be dead by now. And even if they aren't, what on earth do you think we can go in there and say? 'Oh, hi! I was married to your son, the one who left when he was eighteen and never contacted you again. This is your granddaughter. Nice to meet you.'"

"But, Mom, they don't know whether he is alive or dead. Whatever happened, that's just not right."

"I know, honey. But going in there and putting the heart crossways in some old person is not going to give your dad's story a happy ending."

"They might not even know I exist."

"It's too late, Star."

"No. Don't say that. I hate those words."

"If you want to do this, you'll have to do it another day. On your own."

"Or on my own, now."

"Okay. Give me the keys and I'll wait for you in the car."

She rummaged in her bag, handed them across. I turned and began to walk back down the hill. I hadn't got far when she called me. "Stop. Wait."

I turned.

"Maybe you're right," she puffed, as she caught up.

"You could write to them first. That might be an approach."

"I probably won't even do that. As usual I'm a funk."

"You just want to know more about him." I took her arm. She let me and I gave it a squeeze. "It's natural."

But that only set her off again. "Why didn't you tell me more when I was growing up, Mom? Why did you keep it all from me?"

"Star, I've admitted that was a mistake. I did what I thought was best."

"It wasn't."

"I know. You've said. And I'm sorry."

Over and over: the same thing. Was she never going to let it go? These reproaches were the flip side to the excessive love she used to lavish on me when she was little: "I love you, Mommy," holding my head in place with her two little hands, so I couldn't look away from her.

Twice in my life I had wronged her, she believed. The first time with her father and in her mind, our recent travails were connected with that. A connection she would never explain and I could never fathom.

I realised I was going to have to say something, take hold of the subject we were both avoiding. "This isn't just about Brendan, is it?"

"Mom, don't. I'm warning you, just don't."

"I gave up Zach for you, Star. It's finished, forever." There it was, out in the open.

She snatched back her arm.

"Why does that mean nothing to you, Star? Do you know how hard that was?"

"Okay, Mom, that's it. This sham of a day is now officially over."

"I know it's hard for you to talk about it, honey. But we have to. Please."

"Dr Aintree told me this would happen."

I was hardly listening. Amanda Aintree was her therapist, a good doctor. A good woman. I was regretting what I'd just said about Zach and trying to find persuasive words that might work.

"She warned me, told me you'd try to annihilate me again."

That snapped me to attention. Amanda would never say a thing like that, would she? "Annihilate you?"

"We are driving home now, Mom, and then I am going to pack and leave as planned."

"Annihilate you, Star? You have got to be joking. *Annihilate?*"

On the drive back to Doolough, she turned on the radio and refused to talk. Once we arrived back at the house, I said to her, "Will you help me clear away your granddad's things before you go?"

If I could get her to hold off until darkness, she might stay one more night. I might get another chance in the morning. She didn't want to help but she could hardly say no, so we set to it, working through the house with black plastic sacks, separately and in silence, like burglars.

My father was a hoarder. He hadn't smoked for years but he'd kept all his old pipes in a shoebox. Of footwear, old and new, I counted seventy-eight pairs: wellington boots, walking boots, best shoes and second-best and long past their best. Wardrobes and cupboards were emptied of clothes and knick-knacks. Ornaments and pictures, brass plates and candlesticks, holy water fonts and ancient bedside lamps were boxed for charity.

As the shelves and drawers emptied and the bags and boxes filled, I felt them separate from their owner, become pure junk. The blue woollen hat he wore when fishing was repellent, greasy at the edges, but most of all, redundant. Dead.

It took us over two hours, to clear out everywhere except my bedroom and the parlour. "They've already been sorted," I lied, suddenly shy of bringing her into those two rooms that Zach and I had made our own.

She took a carriage clock as a memento, along with the photograph of my parents on the cliff. I brought out the last of the bags and, when I came back into the kitchen, I was shocked to find her beside the stove, crying. Star never cried, not any more, or not any more with me.

"Darling?" I crossed the room, put my arms around her shoulders, and she let me, just about, her spine stiff as a tree, but only for a few seconds before shimmying away, dabbing each eye dry with the back of her wrist. "Oh, Mom…"

"It's okay, Star. I understand. You have to go." I knew what I had to do now was to keep talking, fill the space between us with meaningless sound, hums and burbles and fuzzy static to get us through to goodbye and beyond. "And thanks for helping with the clearing. I needed to get as much of Granddad out of here as I could."

I imagined myself stripping further back after she was gone, taking up the carpets and polishing up the wooden floors. I fed myself that vision in my head and I liked it. Painting every wall white. Turning this place into a new blank canvas.

"It's too cold to go down to the gate," I said, knowing that if I did, I'd break too. "I'll wave you off from upstairs."

I left her then and went up to the spare bedroom. This was my favourite room in the house, a gable-end room with a window on three sides. I went to the one that overlooked the drive. It was only four-thirty in the afternoon, but the day had already faded to dusk. I could barely make her out below, head bent to the soft rain that had started to fall, one hand holding her coat together, backpack in her heartbreaking, chubby grip. She threw it onto the back seat and waved up to me once, unseeing. Then she folded herself in behind the steering wheel.

The car lights came on, front and back, and the red vehicle slipped down the lane. Moran's dog, who hung around every part of the neighbourhood, went running after the back wheels — *bark, bark, bark!* —until the car sped up and he relinquished it.

I watched on. It turned the corner, out onto the road and I

followed its lights as they blurred and faded into the endless Irish rain.

Tea, I thought. I couldn't face food but a cup of tea might help. I went down to the kitchen and turned on the kettle and that's when I spied the hammer, sitting under the corner table since I'd nailed a sprig of holly over the kitchen door a week before, my feeble effort at Christmas cheer. Its two curled fingers, the side used for prising out nails, seemed to twitch, to beckon me across.

I picked it up, tapped its flat head against my palm, felt the weight of what I was about to do. Pulling my mind shut — no more thoughts allowed — I went to the room my father called "the parlour". Stripped of his ornaments and furnishings, but still his. It would take a lot more than a quick clear out for it to be purged. The fireplace was black-empty and cold. I remembered him standing there in front of it, in 1982, after I'd brought my daughter home from America to see him: the sarcastic expression, the bitter words: "Well, well, well, look what the cat brought in!"

I let the hammer swing, hard and fast, into the TV screen. *Smash*. Shards of glass went spiking through the air. Smash again. The glass cabinet this time. I regretted that Star and I had cleared the glasses and ornaments from the shelves a few hours earlier; I would have loved to unleash myself on them.

Thump. I brought the hammer down on the little side table but it only made a dent. I threw it aside, running out of the room, through the kitchen, out the back door. It was now dry outside and not cold, not for December. The security light came on, spotlighting weeds that cracked through the gravel, tough survivors.

Jerking open the bolt on the shed, I grazed my knuckles. I sucked on the pain, my tongue moving across bone and blood as I hurried on, hurrying, hurrying with a wild throbbing hurry that kept thought at bay. In the corner of the shed, I found what I was looking for: the sledgehammer. Its heavy head pulled me down as I ran back inside, leaving the shed door swinging.

I smashed the coffee table and the sideboard. I smashed the fiddly occasional table that always wobbled, making us fearful for the lamp. I smashed the lamp. I turned my back on the piano — that I couldn't destroy — and when I came to the bureau too, I hesitated. My father's most precious piece of furniture: bought in Paris, his only relic of his time in France. All through my childhood, I'd watched him sitting at this desk to write, or do what he called "the books", the accounts that measured his income against his expenses, the largest of which — as he never failed to remind — was me. *Tea: one shilling and six. Butter: two shillings. Eggs: one and eight. Sausages...*

Smash. The lump hammer put a deep V into the desk's top and the back fell open. As it did, a torrent of paper tumbled out. Money. Notes. Old pound notes and fivers and tenners and twenties, one of my father's secret stashes. He had them all over the house: in a biscuit tin under the floorboards in his bedroom, inside an old plant-food container on a high shelf in the back pantry, and no doubt in lots of other places that I knew nothing about.

It wasn't the money, though, that had made me pounce but the notebooks falling from their secret compartment at the back of the bureau. The big one — long and thick, with a red hardcover, born to be a shop ledger — landed first, hitting the floor with an unforgiving thump. And five smaller, black-covered notebooks came tumbling after. His journals.

Seeing them splayed across the floor prodded a memory: his bent back hunched over, his thick fingers clasped around a skinny pen. I reached for the big notebook, opened it, flicked through. The familiar handwriting marched through the pink ledger lines, as though they weren't there and my pulse, already pounding, skidded at the sight.

Traces of him were all over these pages. Not just his writing, but the dog-ear corners he'd turned down, which meant he must have read them back. And other marks. Some kind of oil all over one page, an ink spill on another. Even those pages that seemed clean would have been brushed by his hand trailing across. His DNA could be reconstructed from these, I thought, and I knew then that I'd found what I'd been looking for, even though I hadn't realised, until that moment, what I was engaged on was a search.

August 6th, 1914. "War has been declared," he wrote, in his clear, well-trained handwriting. That was his reason for beginning to write, knowing he was about to become part of recorded history, as he resigned his job as a butcher's assistant in a Parisian meat market. "*Ma patrie*," he wrote, rushing to sign up though his country was Ireland, not France. He had lived there less than a year at that time and he was only sixteen years old.

Not that any of that made any difference. Ireland, England, France; young, middle-aged, old; Europe, Russia, America; men, women, children: all were caught up in the bloody mobilisation, the mass movement towards the biggest war the world had ever known. Was that what damaged him, made him what he was? Maybe this notebook held the answer?

I touched the inside cover where he'd stuck his conscription card and medical records. They slid free, the glue dry and dead. It would have been against regulations for him to keep this diary, but he was never one for regulations, my father, not for himself. A policer only of others.

What would it do to me to read these? The thought set my heart fluttering around its cage of ribs, as if he were still alive to catch me, but down I sat in the middle of the devastation and opened the big one. Hand on my chest, I started to read: *August 6th, 1914. War has been declared. I went down to the conscription office this morning, with a pair of jokers I met on the train…*

· · ·

It was quite a while later — I have no idea how long — when the doorbell rang. My thoughts flew immediately to Zach. Could he have heard that Star had left and decided to come back to me?

The bell rang again.

No, not this time. I had made my choice and we both knew what it meant. Zach was gone, this time forever. Whoever it was, it wasn't him.

I pushed myself up from the floor and tiptoed my way through the debris, the large notebook in front of my chest like a shield. Anyone but Zach or Star was an unwelcome intrusion. I had a sudden, painful ache for home, for California, for the width of its ocean and the height of its trees, for a blast of its big breeziness to come and blow through the cramped spaces of this house.

The bell rang a third time. When I finally opened the door, I saw from the faces of the two policemen standing there that I hadn't done myself any favours by delaying to answer.

"Detective Inspector Patrick O'Neill," said the one who wasn't wearing a uniform, flipping a badge in my face. "And this is Garda Shane Cogley."

They came in without being asked. I tried to steer them towards the kitchen but the inspector — with what detective instinct? — headed straight for the parlour. He pushed the door open and the three of us stood in the threshold, taking in the destruction, the money all over the floor.

"What…?" The inspector asked, turning world-weary, mind-made-up eyes onto me. "What in good God's name has happened here?"

Without further preliminaries, he told me he was investigating the murder of Martin James Stanley Mulcahy, the full name, as if my own father was somebody I barely knew. And that he wanted me to come down to the station to help with their inquiries.

"You're not serious?" I said.

"Just a few routine questions."

Garda Cogley snapped his notebook shut and put it back in his pocket.

"Do you need to inform anyone?" the inspector asked.

I shook my head, dazed. "There's nobody to inform."

"Your daughter…?"

"No, she's not here."

"Is that so? And when will she be back?"

"I'm not sure."

"We need to know, Mrs Creahy."

"Mulcahy."

"Mrs Mulcahy." His look told me that this was not the time to ask for Ms. "We need to know her whereabouts. She'll have to be interviewed."

"She's gone traveling around Ireland. Sightseeing."

"When did she leave?"

"A few hours ago."

"Is that so," he said again, this time with more menace. "You didn't go with her?"

"No, I stayed to look after my father's affairs."

"I see." He took an exaggerated look around the devastated room, lifted an ironical eyebrow. "Right," he said. "Let's be going."

I've been writing this book my whole life long, waiting to be able to give it the beginning and the ending I want, coming back in every so often to tinker and edit and move sentences about, hoping — yes, I do know what I'm doing, even as I recognise its hopelessness — that somehow, giving it attention might work magic, make Star willing to read it.

And now my own time is coming and it looks like it's not going to happen. I can't believe it.

I'm coping well with everything else, happy to have quit the treatment that was worse than the disease. I'm managing my pain and my sleeplessness and even my disinclination to eat. I still think of myself as living, not dying. I know that every hour contains a multitude of moments and the closer death comes, the longer I seem able to linger in each one.

That's a blessing.

I'm ready to go, accepting of everything, except this: I cannot speak to my own daughter, she cannot speak to me. So I'm drawn back here again to this book, this explanation or excusal, back, back and back again, like Fitzgerald's famous boat pushing against the tide, to visit and revisit the great gnarled rock that Star and I dashed ourselves against.

And it's not just Zach, I find every time I sit down to write, it's also Daddy. Everything that happened in those days leading into Christmas 1989.

Writing about it, here, now, I can see that I was not quite sane in those days after my father died. For two decades, I had carried him around in my head and in coming back to Ireland to nurse him, the picture I held in my head of a broad, red-faced bully had been reduced. Age and illness turned him to little more than skin shrouding bone but when he died, I couldn't accept that either version of the father I carried in my head — the young or the old, the fearful or the frightened — was gone.

The strong arms that used to reach so readily for the strap, gone? The sour smell of his sickroom breath, gone? The size 13 feet that had to have shoes and boots specially made, gone? The shrivelled genitals and the wispy, grey fuzz around them? All gone, gone, gone. I knew it but something about it was unknowable.

So when Mr Inspector told me in the station that he was arresting me for murder, a part of me was unable to take it seriously. What I replied, according to *The Wicklow Gazette*, which took a personal interest in my trial, was: "You must be joking." But, already, another, deeper part of me was whispering something that didn't really want to be heard.

Establishing values other than, better than, my father's; pulling together the pieces he'd ripped apart in my childhood, making myself whole again: these were the aims that had guided my life since I ran away from him at sixteen. I had traveled far in my effort to escape — more than 6,000 miles — but, even at that distance, he held me. My body was in Santa Paola, California, but my thoughts stayed in Doolough, County Wicklow; regurgitating what had been, what should have been, what might have been. Each I-wish twist and if-only turn of my mind only tightened the tie I longed to loosen.

Then, when his health failed and I was needed, I came back to Doolough to tend him. To try to find the closure my Californian friends recommended. He was no easy patient and I admit I thought often of the time to come, when he would be dead and I would have survived him.

It didn't seem too much to ask, to be given some years after he was gone. I'd thought that would be enough, that it would be over then, that I'd have peace at last.

Wrong, Mercy. Wrong, yet again.

PART III
STARDUST

(something which causes) a dreamlike or romantic quality or feeling.

STAR

CHRISTMAS EVE 1989

*M*y mother opened the front door of Blackberry Lodge and, on seeing me there, rubbed her eyes as if the Virgin Mary had landed on her doormat. Fury slapped against my ribs, knocking away the good intentions I'd nursed on the plane all the way across the Atlantic.

It wasn't surprise that had Mom laying it on like a bad actor. I was expected. What she was trying to do was hide the reflex response that kicked in whenever we met again after a time apart. That slide of her eyeballs away from the sight of me, the conscious tugging of them back.

Oh, she tried her hardest to hide it, and she just couldn't help it, but whenever my mother looked at me, what she saw first was my fat. My excess flesh was her shame. Public evidence of her failure to win Greatest Mother of All Time Award. Or was it something else entirely? Was she really alone here with Granddad as she'd said?

"Hello to you too, Mom," I said, as she continued to boggle.

"Oh, darling, I'm so... Come in, come in."

She reached for my backpack, but I held it. "Wait," I said. "He's not here, is he?"

"No, no." Another flicker of those flickering eyes.

"Mom?"

"No. I told you on the phone." Again she put out her hand and this time I let her take it.

I followed her into the hall. "Mom, just because I've come... I want you to know, this doesn't negate anything I said before... Every word of that still stands."

"Okay, darling. I understand. But can I just say that—"

"Is it something new, something you haven't said already?"

"I want to say sorry, Star."

"No. No more sorries. No tears either, if you don't mind. And no more explanations."

She flinched. "I understand," she said, but I could see she'd be off again, first chance she got. She wouldn't be able to help herself.

She led the way down the hallway, towards the kitchen. It was strange to be in Granddad's house again. Its old-house smell came back to me from my previous visit, now overlaid with the tang of disinfectant.

"How is he?" I asked.

"A bit low today. It's great you're here."

Last time, Granddad ran us out of the place, telling us never to come back, but she spoke like I was an ordinary granddaughter on a loving sick-call. Oh, that desire of hers to play happy families.

In the kitchen, she put on the kettle and sat down opposite me. Before it was even boiling, she'd started again. "Oh, Star, I do need you to know how deeply sorry I am. I never, never ex—"

"You're unbelievable, Mom. What did we just say out in the hall?"

"But if we don't—"

I held up my hand. "Do you want me to go? Because I will."

"All right, all right... Calm down."

She got herself busy with cups and tea bags while I took off my coat and searched in the pocket for cigarettes. As I shook one from the box, I heard myself let out a sigh so long and so deep it sounded like the last breath I'd ever take.

She turned. "Oh, darling, how are you? Are you okay?"

So I told her, my hands shaking. "No, Mom, I am not 'okay'. I'm livid. I want to bulldoze houses and cut down trees. I want to set fire to all the fields and dump poison into all the rivers. I want to hurt everybody, everybody, in the whole wide world and see if that makes me feel any better."

"Oh, honey..."

"Don't worry, I won't do it. I'll just plod on. But inside I'm seething."

She looked at me, stricken.

"Seeing as you asked."

We sat in silence for the rest of the tea, then she took me in to see Granddad, into a horrible sickroom, that smelled of death. And he was a death's head, grey and shrunken, above a frail body. On seeing me, he said: "Well, well, well, look what the cat dragged in." The words he'd used the first time he met me, four years before. Did he know this? It was impossible to tell what my grandfather knew.

"Is she..." Cough. Cough. He broke into a splutter as he raised himself onto the pillows and eyeballed me. "Is she about to take herself off?"

"What are you talking about, Daddy?" she said and she whispered to me: "Don't mind him. He doesn't know what he's saying."

But I wasn't fooled. I'd seen the red flush of fear flying into her face. I spoke to him instead. "I'm not sure what you mean, Granddad."

"The boyfriend's done a runner."

So it was true. I'd known it but I still couldn't believe it. She'd had him here. Here!

"Boyfriend?"

"Yeah. A long streak (he pronounced it 'strake') of a yoke with a baldy head. She'll be leaving to take after him, no doubt. Always a one for running after the boyos."

She cast her eyes skywards, like he was talking nonsense, but she knew I knew. Underneath that ever-polished front, she surely must have been squirming.

Here. After all that had happened. After all she'd said. So much for sorry.

"Oh, Daddy, what are you on about?" she said again, in the same false voice. "It's time for your meds."

"*Shocking it is, the way she throws herself at him and he young enough to be her...*" *But another burst of coughing seized Granddad's old-man frame, giving her the chance to fuss about him and ignore the tension.*

When he came out of it, he was still talking. "*I'm the great burden, of course. Well, I never asked her to play Florence Nightingale, so I didn't.*" *Cough.* "*I never asked you, neither.*" *Cough.* "*Well able ... to look after myself. Always was.*"

"*Shouldn't you be resting, Granddad?*"

"*Rest, is it? Oh that's what you'd all like to see.*" *Cough, cough, cough.* "*Me ... going ... to my rest...*"

"*Oh, Daddy, stop that old nonsense.*"

I went over to stand by his pillow. "*She's poisoning me,*" *he said to me, his bony finger jabbing the air.* "*Together with himself. They're after the house. You'll be my witness now if I go early.*" *Cough.* "*You make sure you tell the world.*"

Again, she tried to get me to join her in an eye-roll. "*Star, would you hand me across that vial of pills. Thank you. Now, Daddy, here you are ... come on now, up you sit.*"

"*I can do it...*" *Cough. Cough.* "*...Myself ... So I can.*"

But, at the same time as he was throwing out the defiant words, he was letting her place the two tablets between his lips, and swallowing them down, docile as a child. As she settled him back on his pillow, and tidied the locker and straightened the bedclothes, his eyes rolled closed.

"*He'll be all right now for a while,*" *she whispered.* "*Do you want to come through for lunch?*"

"*No,*" *I said.* "*No. I think I'll stay here with Granddad for a bit.*"

Put that in your book, Mom, why don't you?

MERCY

1964

*O*n the night my daughter was born, I stood at the window of an adobe that her father and I shared with five others at that time, watching the sun radiating purple beams through patches of silver New Mexico sky. The earth was palest yellow, the color of a lion's mane, flat and treeless, naked except for a smattering of sage. Across the plain, Taos Mountain seemed on alert, as if it knew what was happening to me. In the sky, a strange cloud formation filtered the rays, iridescent and full of significance, like direct messages from above.

And behind me was everybody, everyone we lived with then, circled around our big, communal dining table. Our housemates —Madeira, Zane, Emma, Jade and Quicksilver — together with Buff and Jalope who'd moved in two days earlier and would stay as long as they were needed. And Snakeskin of course, my man, smoking a toke to relax, playing cards to distract himself. We were Snakeskin and Lightning, now, had been for more than a year. New Mexico beatniks. No longer Brendan Creahy or Mercy Mulcahy from the county of Wicklow in Ireland.

On the floor of our communal room was the child's paddling pool in which I was about to give birth, full of warm water. Jade, who had been a midwife in her other life and studied underwater birthing in France, was going to help deliver the baby. We had laid in plenty of food and they each took turns to cook, except for me. "Mama Lightning" was excused from all duties except rest.

Zane had borrowed a car, in case anything went wrong. But nothing would, I knew it as sure as I knew that Taos Mountain would not fall down.

For thirty minutes, I'd been pacing around and around the perimeter, stopping each time at the big window that faced west, timing my way so I'd have my contractions there. Snakeskin looked up from his card game each time I passed, to show me he cared.

"You okay, Mama?" he'd ask and I'd nod, happy he wasn't any closer, wanting to keep the baby to myself as long as I could.

I had expanded to twice, to ten, to a million times my normal size by pregnancy. I'm not talking about my enlarged belly, but inside. I was changed, we all knew it. I was a fruit, ripe with knowledge. I had become the one the others came to with their problems. *Me*, Mama Lightning!

My cramps clutched me again. I struggled to the window, this time only making a pretence at looking out. Thunder clattered in the clouds and a shriek of lightning tore across the sky. A jack rabbit ran through the sage. Across the plain, rain started to fall — slant and stretched — the kind the Pueblo people call "Long Walking Man". We were still bathed in sunlight.

"Sunlight," I said, turning to the others when my breath was returned to me. "The baby will be called Sunlight." That would give him or her a piece of my chosen name in theirs.

Another pain came, too quickly, bending me over. When I looked up again, night was surging across the sky from the east and Jade was beside me. "It's started, hasn't it?"

I turned to find Snakeskin. He was at the table, talking. I waited until he lifted his head so I could connect with his eyes. Only then did I answer her: "Yes, it's started."

He got up, smiling. What a smile that man had. I let it bloom across my skin, feeling as I always did when he smiled, like he had just covered me, and now also the baby-to-be, in wild roses.

Yes, yes, I know. Lightning, and Snakeskin, and long rain and wild roses. I know.

But back then, we were proud of such things. Our men wore goatees and berets while our women danced in black leotards and played tambourines. We let ourselves sing and say what the wage-slaves feared to think. We were open, or thought we were, to peace and sunlight, to sex and drugs and complicated love, to any kind of living that wasn't the kind we deemed a living death.

And it was this edgy, complicated man who had spirited me away.

I had known he would the moment I saw him, back when he was just plain Brendan Creahy of Laragh, Co Wicklow. We met in Molina Dancehall, one of those Irish arenas of pleasure thrown up on the side of a road in the middle of nowhere, summoning every young person for miles. Boys on one side, girls on the other, bottles of soda pop — we called them "minerals"— clenched in our fists, the sweet fizzy liquid sucked through straws. At sixteen, I was one of the youngest there, having sneaked out the window of my cramped bedroom and walked two miles on a dark country road to attend.

Looking back, I can't believe my daring.

I'm not going to sully these pages with any more than is necessary to help you understand my father and what went on in his house. I don't want to tell you the worst, precisely because it was the worst, it wasn't everyday. I want a representative event, one that stands out vividly enough for me to remember how it felt, yes, but that also gives a sense of what it was like to live here with him, day after day, back then.

Here is the one I have chosen, from 1959 or thereabouts. I was eleven or so, arriving in from school, as I did each day, to my dinner place pre-set on the kitchen table. Mrs Breen, my friend Pauline's mother, cleaned our house and cooked our meals and every morning, her last task before she left was to lay the table for me: a glass for my milk, a side plate for potato peelings, a dinner plate wrapped in foil, with a smaller foil pack on top. It was a Wednesday, so the large foil contained a plate of bacon, cabbage and potato, to be heated over a pot of water on the cooker, and the small, two chocolate biscuits.

I let my schoolbag slide to the floor, opened the biscuits and began to eat them first, putting my feet up on the table to enjoy them better. I could feel my gut, ahead of my conscious thought, fluttering as if it had been colonised by a battalion of butterflies wearing boots. It wasn't until I had both biscuits demolished that I allowed the excitement full form in my mind: I was going to have a bath.

I'd been thinking about this for days, promising myself the next time he was on day shift I would do it. Doolough, in those days, had not progressed to showers, and baths in our house were permitted only on Saturdays, or on once-in-a-lifetime occasions like First Communions or Confirmations, and then only in three or four inches of water, just enough to do the job. Having a bath necessitated asking my father's permission to turn on the immersion heater, controlled by a big red switch in our hot press that I was not allowed to touch. He kept the bath plug in a hiding place in his bedroom to make sure.

In my bedroom, I had a bottle of green bubble bath given to me at Christmas and I wanted to use it and to heat enough water to cover myself entirely. This was, I had discovered, the proper way to take a bath, the way that most people, people who did not have to live with people like my father, did it. I filled my head with an image that allowed room for no other: just me reclining under hot water, covered in bubbles, like a model.

I crossed the room, opened the door of the hot press, pressed the red switch to *On*, my heart taking a flip at the sound of its click. Emboldened by my daring, I then had a look in all the cupboards I was usually forbidden to open. At the back of one, I found the rest of the packet of chocolate biscuits. For the first few, pleasure outweighed guilt, but then the two emotions began to swap places. Yet even after the worry rose so high that I was no longer enjoying them, I kept stuffing them into myself, knowing they would be missed. What was I at?

Then came my dinner, or as much of it as I could manage to put in on top of the biscuits. After washing and tidying up, I put my hand to the immersion tank. Hot. I took two towels and went upstairs in search of the bath plug, a search that would require a forage into forbidden territory: his bedroom.

There was no visible sign of my father in that room, except for an indefinable, personal aroma. Fear was thick in me as I went around to his side of the bed. He might well decide to drop home from the barracks as he sometimes did, especially today, as school had closed early. If caught, I would bring upon myself unimaginable punishment, yet on I pressed, compelled by something stronger than fear.

His bedroom locker was one place kept free of Mrs Breen's housekeeping. In it, bundles of papers and letters were jumbled with reading glasses, a screwdriver, some golf tees and a golf ball, a whisky glass full of copper coins and other debris. Under a stack of *Ireland's Own* and *Reader's Digest* magazines, I found it: the bath plug. And beneath it: a brown envelope torn in one corner. I peeled back the tear a little. What impulse led me to open the envelope, heart banging against its cage? It was as if I knew before I knew.

My father's magazine was full of pictures of half-naked women. It would be considered innocent now, the sort of images that have become everyday, delivered to our breakfast tables in tabloid newspapers. A dark-haired girl in a leather hat brandishing a cocktail glass, her sweater pulled up. Another reclining naked on a fur coat, fabric carefully arranged to cover her pubis. Another lying in the bath, soaping herself, leg bent to block a view of anything too blatant. Anatomically innocent, but its intent the same as all porn, and it was the intent that held eleven-year-old me riveted with shock.

I was at an age where I was just becoming aware of breasts. My own were budding and I had started surreptitiously eying the bulges beneath the blouses and jumpers of the females around me: teachers in school, sixth-year girls, neighbours at Mass. I had never seen anyone else's naked before and now here was a profusion of them in every variety. It wasn't just the nakedness that fascinated me, as much as the look on these girls' faces. Saucy, as one of the captions said. Yes, they were girls, but girls of a different species. They had allowed somebody to photograph them like that because they liked it: "Hi. I'm Sophie and I've always wanted to be a nude model."

Something I was just coming to know about women and men was writ large in this magazine, in my sixty-one-year old father keeping it in a brown envelope in his bedside locker. I wanted to put it back, pretend I'd never seen it, but I also wanted to see more of it. I wanted to know everything it had to tell me.

Magazine under my arm, I went into the bathroom and turned on the taps. The water gushed forth, steam rising from the hot tap. I opened the magazine out on the shelf at *Miss September*, the centerfold, a kneeling beauty who was using the top half of her bikini to cover where the bottom should be. I put a bottle of shampoo to hold open one edge, a cake of soap the other. Then I remembered the bubble bath and went to my bedroom to find it.

As I searched through the shoebox at the back of my wardrobe where I kept all my precious things, a noise outside in the corridor made me jump and my heart started to flap like a bird caught in a room. I turned my ear up, urgently, to listen. Nothing. Nothing, you silly. Only the old house creaking. I found the bubble bath and hurried back to the gushing taps. Nudging the half-open bathroom door, I saw that it hadn't been nothing. No. It was my father.

My father, bent over the bath, turning off the taps.

As he sensed the door move, he swung round. He was dressed for rain, in his official policeman's cycling cape and pull-ups. The chinstrap of his cap dug into his jawline. Level with his head, on the shelf beside him, was Miss September, her chin thrown back, her protuberant breasts on offer, nipples pushing out of the picture.

The water had stopped. Silence was flooding the room and in it, just for one long, still-held moment, our eyes connected. Then I turned and fled.

I want a representative moment, I've said, and in some ways, that one was not. He never responded. No beating or other punishment, no verbal lashing even. Nothing. That was a one-off. I'd no illusions that's how I would be if he knew I was sneaking out to Molina dancehall.

"If my father catches me, he'll kill me," I told Pauline, the first time I did it. She took it as a figure of speech, but I was working on a logical ratio. Given that, being five minutes late home from school could bring on a beating that might last ten minutes, sneaking out a window to a dance was surely putting my life in danger. I could feel the blows and the form they would take if I was caught.

Yet I went, not just once but many times. Something bigger than our sensible selves kicks up in adolescence, or in a certain type of adolescent. I cringe now when I recall the ferocity I brought to those teenage romances that were really rebellions, assertions of self. By the time I'd met Brendan, I had already experienced a series of them, each blazing through me with its own particular and ridiculous fervour. I'd like to deny it now, pretend I was never like that but back then, how I stoked those yearnings, each boy a funnel for the thoughts and feelings I was not allowed to indulge for their own sake. Passion's passion for itself.

So there I was that night, risking. I knew not what for the dubious pleasures of the dancehall, my teenage-girl radar scanning the room. Brendan must have felt my burning eyes on him, because he turned — cigarette still in his mouth — to face me, and his eyes, half-closed to the rising smoke, popped open. I was regretting my choice of dress: a sleeveless number, covered in big red roses and cinched at the waist with a red belt. Too sweet and wholesome a look to attract a boy like him — but no, it was okay. He let his cigarette drop and walked across, confidence and admiration firing from the smile he'd switched on.

Skinny and heavy-chinned, Brendan wasn't the best looking guy in the world — or even in Molina Dancehall — but, oh, that smile of his. His teeth were white and perfectly aligned, unusual in Ireland at the time, but it was more than that. It was how the smile chased away the edgy moodiness while latching onto you, as if you were what drove his bad times away.

He spun me out onto the dance-floor and pulled me into his arms. Within an hour he was telling me how he hated Wicklow and the whole godforsaken, damp dump of a country we lived in and I was telling him things I had never told anyone, not even Pauline.

Next day, I met him at the end of our lane where he was waiting on his Honda with two helmets. Yes, he had a motorbike. And a leather jacket. And a guitar.

He taught me how to drink Guinness and how to roll a joint. He took me on a picnic and fed me food from his hand. He brought me to the cinema and spent the two hours watching me instead of the movie and afterwards told me how he had loved seeing the lights and colors on my face.

I loved how he was astonishing himself with the telling. All the telling. There was nothing we did not tell each other. Or so it seemed to me.

So when — just three months after we'd danced our first dance — he asked me to go with him, to climb onto the back of his motorbike with all I owned and leave soggy, miserable Ireland once and for all, I went.

I went because I wanted him, and because of the miracle of him wanting me. That was the pull, but also there was the push of the daily chores for an ungrateful father, the cooking of dinner and the hanging of laundry that I was now expected to do, since I'd turned thirteen. The studying for my Leaving Certificate at his kitchen table while he dealt out his complaints or read out from his notebook: *tea: one shilling and six. Butter: two shillings. Eggs: one and eight.* The cost of food, of feeding me, in the pounds, shillings and pence of those days.

Brendan was my breakout clause, doing for me what I couldn't do for myself.

At my request, the birthing pool was brought closer to the window. Jade called him over. "Snakeskin! It's time."

He and I got naked, except for a tank top over my breasts, while the others formed a "circle of love" around the two of us in the pool, with Zane playing guitar and the rest singing along, beating hand-drums, or pots, or rapping spoons. Every so often, one of the girls would get up to boil a kettle of water and carefully tip it into the water to keep us warm.

What Jade had promised me came to pass: I had birth pains, but in the water they were bearable — more than bearable: effective.

Essential.

The day faded to darkness. The stars came out to shine. "I've changed my mind," I said to Brendan between two sets of contractions. "Let's call her Starlight."

Sounds were rising in me: universal, female sounds, my breaths becoming gasps, whimpers turning to wails. Soon all I could hear close up was my own pulse; my breathing and crying were distanced from me, somehow. I dissolved into nothing but mother-body: source, vessel, channel, bringer, giver.

Jade mopped my brow, Emma brought me drinks of water and glasses of iced tea, Brendan held my hand in his. I loved that hand, its gnarls and whirls, its too long nails on thumb and index finger, the better to pluck the guitar. It had been two years since we left Doolough, with nothing but his motorbike, some clothes and trinkets and twelve pounds, eight shillings and ninepence between us.

First came a short stint in London, but we quickly gave up on England, where it was so hard to be Irish so we sold the bike and flew to New York on the proceeds. A Brooklyn summer was followed by our best time, when we bought a VW van, painted it up and kitted it out with bed and camper stove. Down the East Coast we drove over the course of months, picking up bits of work as we went. Cape Cod, the Carolinas, Sarasota, across to New Orleans. Brendan drew pictures and strummed songs, including some of his own, on his guitar. I wrote poems in a brown, leather-bound notebook. Then we drove back to the coast and northwards again, as the returning sun grew too hot for our Irish skins.

Just as we were wondering where to go next, we saw a report about groups of what the journalist called "beatniks" convening in San Francisco. The next day we set off west for California, via New Mexico. It was on a wet afternoon, plump with rain freezing towards snow, that we arrived in Taos, with an introduction to a friend of a friend.

We drove up a long dirt road lined with olive trees, as instructed, to be told that the friend was long gone but that we were welcome anyway to stop the night. Almost a year on, here we still were. And now, giving birth to a child.

"Not long now," soothed Jade. "Not long."

My skin stretched, tauter than skin can be stretched, and I screamed with the searing heat as it ripped. The head was through. Then a slither through the soreness, followed by a cry, weaker than the cries I'd been letting, something altogether more faint and fragile that turned the whole room towards it.

"A girl," Jade said, with her serene smile.

She placed her on my belly. The baby's eyes were glazed but she looked at me and I looked at her, both of us astonished. What the look held wasn't of my world, but of hers, the one she'd more recently left.

Snakeskin was observing us, proud but lost. The outsider, for once, and not liking it.

The cord was cut by somebody, I don't know who, and I pulled the baby in closer. The rapid rise and fall of her breath made my insides clench.

"Look," Jade said. "She has a birthmark."

We looked. On the back of her neck, just below a fringe of dark hair lining the base of her skull, was a wine-colored smudge, about the size of a bean, but five-sided. Almost like a star.

Madeira took up her guitar and started to play, a song of Joni Mitchell's, a favourite with us all.

"You are golden," I whispered in the baby's ear. "My stardust."

MERCY

1990

*T*he world was back to work. I had a lawyer, a no-nonsense woman called Mags Halloran, hired the Irish way, through someone Pauline knew who knew someone. Mags was the only girl in a farming family of seven whose widowed mother had struggled and saved and steered them all into college. Each year in August, three of them took a week off their high-powered jobs in Dublin or London or New York to go home to Tipperary to help save the hay. This was the robust approach Mags took into the milieu of Dublin law, where she was known as "a character".

Short and squat, Mags wore calf-length skirts, flesh-colored tights and flat shoes of a kind usually worn by women twenty years older. Her dull-white blouses gaped under the bust, exposing dull-white flesh. I never met a woman who made less of an attempt to be attractive. Mags liked to be underestimated.

My case worried her from the start. She came to Doolough Barracks and sat opposite me at the table in the Day Room to explain that I might not get bail. The serious nature of my alleged crime, the strength of the circumstantial evidence, and the location of my home and business in another jurisdiction — all these were against me.

"Anything in my favor?"

"You tell me. Any previous?"

"Of course not."

"So we'll go with good character, respectable, *yadda, yadda,* unlikely to offend again, *yadda, yadda...* If they go for it, they'll want a substantial surety, though."

"If?"

"Not going to lie to you, Dotes." Mags called everybody Dotes. "We're fifty-fifty at best."

"And if not? I'll have to stay here in the barracks until the trial?"

"More likely to relocate you to Mountjoy, I'd say."

"What sadist decided to name a prison Mount Joy?"

"A more pressing question: do you have the funds for bail? And for legal fees? They're going to want to be sure that you're not going to go skip-a-dee-doo back to the States. And of course" — this with a cheeky grin — "the services of a good lawyer never come cheap."

Later, after it was all over, I wondered why I didn't go skip-a-dee-doo. It seems to me now that nobody would have cared, except perhaps Dr Keane. The Irish justice system knew I was no danger to society.

Mags had brought a copy of *The Wicklow Gazette* to the barracks. I was their front page story, the pun on my name proving irresistible of course. *MERCY KILLING? RETURNED EMIGRANT ARRESTED FOR MURDER.*

A news story on page one continued onto page three and, in the middle of the paper, a double-page spread analyzed the event, complete with a large photo of my father in his uniform, taken at his retirement do. And a smaller, blurry photograph of me, in my convent-school uniform. Where had they got their hands on that?

The reporter had talked to everyone he could find: to the police who said an arrest had been made; to old school friends who said they just couldn't believe it of me; to a neighbour who said I'd been estranged from my father for years before coming back a few months ago; to Dr Keane who said he was confident justice would be done. To everyone except Pauline or Star or Zach or me, the four people who were in the house the day he died.

"Could have been worse," Mags said. "They're going with the mercy angle. That's good."

"Why? Why is that good?"

"We may need to use that ourselves."

"I didn't do it," I said.

"Right. Let's get you filling these forms then."

She took them away with her and eight days later, I was taken, in the back of the police car with Garda Cogley, to Dublin's Four Courts for my bail hearing. We arrived to a glut of reporters huddled around the entrance, like animals awaiting a feed. Notebooks and pens, cameras and microphones poised to devour, they closed in on the car. "Your waiting party," said Inspector O'Neill.

I shivered. I was wearing my most respectable outfit, as instructed by Mags, a brown linen suit, but it was too light for the Irish spring.

"Do you want me to try round the back instead?" Garda Cogley asked his boss. "See if we can avoid them?"

The inspector nodded, his nod as curt as the rest of him.

Garda Cogley swung the car through some narrow back streets, then got out to tap on a steel door. Inside, another cop opened it a crack, listened, looked across at us in the car and nodded.

We were led through a warren of back rooms and when I saw Mags, waiting for us outside Court Two as arranged, I felt like she was an old friend. She led me through further corridors, updating me as we walked. Pauline's bank manager cousin had arranged a mortgage on my father's house and farm to put up the bail and it had come through in time.

Good news then. We took our places in court. After a twenty-minute sitting, bail was granted on condition that I surrendered my passport. Mags could now drive me to the train. I was a free woman until the trial, so long as I kept to their rules.

"Prepare yourself, Dotes," Mags said, as we walked back down the long, narrow corridor that led to the exit. "They'll be out in force by now."

She was loving the whole thing, stomping about in her tough-cookie shoes, steering me through the crowd, her hand on my elbow, as the cameras flashed and the questions were thrown at us: "Is the trial date set?" "What are your plans?" One of them called, "Did you do it?" Could he really have expected me to turn around and say, "Well, yes, actually, I did"?

Some of the questions were for Mags. "Did she get bail?" "What's the plea?" As we pushed through, they moved with us, all together, a multi-headed monster. Mags had her keys ready and, as soon as she had unlocked the car, she leaned across and opened the passenger door for me, but not before they came crowding over, popping questions like machine-gun fire. As we sat in, they pressed their faces to the windows, but it all had a forced feel, a going-through-the-motions of what they felt they should be doing.

Mags revved the engine, not too gently, and they parted to let us through.

She dropped me off for the 1.30 p.m. train back to Rathdrum and, from there, I took a cab to Doolough. As I walked from the cab to the front door, the windows of Blackberry Lodge looked down on me from beneath their eaves. Was anyone who lived in this house ever happy? I wondered. Did children ever play here, giggle through fun and tricks? I couldn't imagine it, but maybe the lack was in me.

What I would have liked to have done was get the house ready for sale. Not so much for the money, as for the activity. Fixing it up, dealing with estate agents, the coming and going of potential buyers would fill my days, but my bail conditions meant I had to stay put, with nothing to engage me except, maybe, writing. The notebooks. Would I finally get an answer to the great, grisly enigma that was my father? The thought that I might propelled me forward.

I went in the back door to the kitchen. A blast of warmth from the stove greeted me. Pauline. The house was back in order, the broken furniture chopped for wood, all the rooms cleaned and vacuumed and polished. The kitchen and sitting room still felt bare, cleared of his furniture and paraphernalia, but he was still there. His smell, but something more than that in the air. Part of him would remain here forever unburied, I thought.

I picked up the kettle. I would have a cup of tea. My father always drank coffee, a relic of his years in France, but tea was Mrs Breen's pick-me-up and I always thought of her as I filled a teapot. She tackled her work like she went at her prayers, steadily ticking off the cleaning and the cooking and the washing up just as she pushed each bead of the rosary through her fingers, all the way round till she was back where she began, only to start over again. Between each chore, like the little chain between two rosary beads, she'd have one of her "nice cups of tea".

Nothing gave Pauline's mother more pleasure than the sight of a meal for me and my father well cooked on its serving plate, surrounded by its subordinate dishes of vegetables and gravy and two kinds of potatoes. Except perhaps Monday evening's ironing stack — sheets and pillowcases and tea towels end to end, corner to corner — admired from across the rim of a nice cup of tea.

When I was young, I feared domesticity. I did what had to be done but I never gave myself over to the tasks. It wasn't until later in life, until I met Zach, that I really came round to appreciating the virtues, the life-saving properties, of cleanliness and order. I needed it now, that understanding, together with all the other practices Zach taught me, that had worked so well for me before. Eat and sleep well, write and free-write, balance work with play. Meditate. And walk daily, even if going outside feels like stepping onto a stage.

All eyes will be on me now. I am the most exciting thing to happen in Doolough for decades, maybe ever. Not that anybody will actually say so, or say anything worth saying. It will all be in the looks, or the absence of looking.

All right, Zach. I hear your voice in my head and you're right. All this *is* just resistance, all this under-eating and over-analysis, this longing to either hunker up at home or else fly far away from here again. Where will any of that leave me, except frightened to the bone? Your practices, together with writing about what really happened; they are what will save me but I hardly know how to start. Any style I pick seems to unpick itself. It's too hard, this scraping up of the past to make it fit the present.

If I can get myself to follow his routine, it will flow free again, I know. I'll try but…

Oh, Zach, without you, I'm not just alone, I'm incomplete. I get through the day, I put in the hours, I live out the minutes, but I want to be what I was when we were together.

Each morning now, I will have go to my father's bathroom upstairs and take off my clothes and step into the same tub I used when I was a girl. I will hear the same water gush from the taps, see the same green light falling in through the opaque glass from the trees outside. As I think of turning off the water and picking up the soap to circle it under my arms, between my legs, over my body, and sliding down to rinse off and feeling the water, hot and soapy, closing over my face, is it any wonder I shudder?

I don't understand any of it, I never did. But if I can manage to write it down — what's happening now, what happened then, what I want for our future— then maybe Star and I might get beyond his shackles if she reads it some day and comes to understand.

MERCY

1968

*B*efore Star was born, Brendan and I had thought we'd
be able to keep on living as we had in the commune.

"Babies don't eat much," I'd said. "And, for a long time, I'll
be feeding him or her myself."

But, of course, it wasn't about food. Once born, Star needed
all kinds of things we couldn't afford: a stroller, clothes in ever-
increasing sizes, educational toys. And then there were all the
needs marching down the tunnel of the future towards us:
bicycles, bedroom, school, summer camp...

The drink and drugs and sexual shenanigans of the
commune no longer seemed the same to us either and, from their
perspective, as Zane said, we'd become "a pair of downers".

Whether, and then how, we were going to leave began to
occupy all our conversations. We'd whisper our plans to each
other in bed at night, so the others wouldn't hear. We considered
Ireland. We'd both been away long enough to become nostalgic,
not for our people, but for the place, the ancient mystery of its
landscape but his homesickness was too flimsy a feeling on
which to build a new life and, anyway, Ireland had even fewer
jobs than Taos.

In the end, we settled on Brooklyn again. Brendan would get

a job and I would take care of Star. It wasn't what either of us wanted, but what we wanted for ourselves was no longer the most important thing in our lives. So, one morning, we drove away with Star in a cot in the back of our VW. We drove straight to New York — no more meandering — into a two-room apartment, a hasty ceremony in a registry office and a job for Brendan, selling advertising in *The Evening Metro*.

We bought him two suits, some button-down shirts and a pair of shiny black shoes. We bought me an apron and oven gloves. Snakeskin and Lightning were put to rest and I found myself with another new name: Mrs Creahy. Off we set into our new ways, new days. Brendan would leave our tiny apartment at six in the morning, to be in the office for eight while I clung to the mattress until whatever time Star woke me with her crying. She always seemed to be crying. This, according to my childrearing manual, was due to feelings of insecurity. To alleviate them, I should immediately answer these cries with comfort. Once she knew she was loved, she would grow secure and the crying would pass.

So I wrapped my time around her needs: for cuddles, for food, for sleep, for baths. Having brought this little scrap into the world, I was determined to do right by her. I bought a baby sling and carried her everywhere, her little body tucked high and tight on my breast, massaging my heart with the rapid rise and fall of her lungs. I would keep her there — *Look, no hands!* — as I cleaned and cooked and baked bread, up to my forearms in flour.

In the evenings, after giving her supper and bath and bedtime stories, I would lie down with her until she dropped into sleep. Often I fell asleep myself, beside her, to be woken by Brendan coming in, looking for dinner. Exhausted, we ate in crankiness or silence, in front of the television. He watched *Mission Impossible* or *I love Lucy* while I looked on at us, shell-shocked.

He began to say things like: "It was about time we grew up, anyway."

Then: "Everybody else has been working their way up. We're way behind."

Then: "All those wasted years. I can't believe we stayed there so long."

"We've had things other people have never known," I would reply. "I wouldn't change a day of it."

For me, it was simple: up to 1961 we did that, now we were doing this but Brendan had to keep comparing and make Taos the loser. So we settled ourselves on opposite sides of the argument. I came to stand for New Mexico, its big skies and warm pulse, and whenever Brendan criticised something about our lives there, I would complain about New York. How the cold was so damp and bitter. How my skin, which had been the color of honey, had turned grey. How people were separated from each other in their little apartments and offices, but mostly in their minds, bustling by each other on the street, locked in thought, all unseeing, only the steam of their breath showing they had warmth inside.

I became the advocate for another way of living. "We would have been all right," I'd say. "We could have lived on like that, dancing to the hum of the planet."

He would look at me like he never thought that way, but I understood. Brendan Creahy, father and provider, had to reject Snakeskin, rebel and vagabond. That much I got, but because he'd been "working" all day — doing activities that yielded dollars — while I was "off" — doing activities that were unpaid, cleaning our home and playing, stimulating, feeding, training, walking, talking and minding our child — he expected, when he arrived home, to pull off his tie and his shoes and to be served dinner.

And at the weekends, or sometimes after work, to go for a few drinks with the boys. Was I really saying he didn't deserve that much?

Well, no, I wasn't. I was worried though that everything outside the house was more interesting to him than anything in it. And when he was home he escaped into TV. The rest I could rationalise, but that drove me nuts. He'd never watched TV his whole life long, yet now our routines — when we could talk, have sex, go out — had to fit around the schedules.

What was that about?

For Star's second birthday, we drove her to a motel in Truro, Cape Cod, for her first ever vacation. That's what we called it, though Star felt no need to be somewhere else. It was we who needed to get away from what we had become. I'd chosen the destination, a seaside village where, a lifetime ago on our travels, we'd slept on the beach, under the stars, in two sleeping bags zipped together to make one. We both knew exactly what I was trying to resurrect, but it was all going horribly wrong. I was navigating from the back seat and had got us lost.

Brendan looked back over his shoulder at me. "We're not on the right road."

"Oh, no," I whispered, looking up from the map. I was whispering so I wouldn't wake Star, asleep in her little car seat beside me. "Please don't say that."

"It's not what I say that counts, Merce. What does the *map* say?"

"It says … um … oh, shit, I think we took the wrong exit."

"For God's sake!" Brendan banged his two palms against the steering wheel. "What in God's bloody name are you doing?"

"My best, maybe?" I tried to keep the wobble from my voice.

"Oh, great, now the bloody waterworks."

"Stop shouting," I hissed. "You'll wake her."

It had taken me ages to get her off to sleep, reading to her, waving toys in front of her face, taking her onto my lap and rocking her off, then slipping her into the car seat. I was exhausted myself. She'd waken so often in the night, broken

sleep left me stupid and helpless during the day. She'd walk
around the house, jettisoning toys, juice, building blocks,
clothing, toast and I followed, half the time on my knees.
Bending and picking, wiping and cleaning, tucking and clearing,
like a servant.

No, servants get paid. Like a slave, one of those immigrant
women who gets locked up in a house by tyrannical employers,
except the tyrant was Star. Or, rather, the poverty that didn't
allow me to buy some help. Or the husband who didn't want to
understand, who interpreted every attempt to talk about it as a
criticism of him, who didn't get that while I might complain
about the housework or baby chores, another part of me was
stunned that I'd been entrusted with this child, this object of
beauty, this crown jewel of a daughter.

Look at me, I'd think. I'm driving her to the store, I'm lifting
her into the tub, I'm feeding her in her high chair. *Me. On my
own. I'm allowed.*

It didn't seem possible. It seemed like something bad must
happen. That must be why I was always issuing warnings.
"Don't do that!"
"Be careful!"
"No! Bad fire!"
"Get down, honey, get down NOW!"
"Mind the edge."
"Come back *here*!"

With much sighing, Brendan got us back onto the right road
and eventually to the hotel. In the bedroom, closing the curtains
against the glare of the day, we spread ourselves on the big
double bed and let ourselves play with her. Her favourite toy at
that time was a letter-board that used to make animal sounds
when she struck the first letter of their name. It was a bit too old
for her, she didn't know her letters yet, but she loved to bash the
squares indiscriminately and hear the sounds. *Moo. Quack. Oink.*

Her enjoyment and the half-dark, muffled peace of the hotel
bedroom soothed us.

"I'm sorry, Bren," I said, after a time.

"Me, too. Give me a kiss." So I did. A long kiss.

When we'd finished, he threw himself back on the pillows, body rigid.

"Ahhhh!" he shrieked and I laughed, knowing what he was going to say next. "Struck by Lightning!" Something he used to say a lot, once upon a time.

I laughed again and shimmied in close. "Snakebite," I whispered in his ear, and offered him my neck.

"Sssssssss!" went Star's toy, just as Brendan's teeth nipped my skin. She had struck the snake box. We burst out in a duet of laughter and Star smiled her toothy smile, gurgling up into our surprised faces, not knowing why she suddenly had our attention but liking it.

"Who's a clever girl?" I said, though she hadn't done anything clever at all. And then we found we couldn't stop laughing — at the silly coincidence, at Star's adorable smile, at the satin coverlet so silky against our bare legs, at the good feelings now filling the room, at the daft names we used to have and the naïve people we used to be. A laugh filled with tenderness for our daughter and our own younger selves. For youth itself, its carefree ignorance.

I was so happy in that moment, that's what I remember, now, sitting here in Doolough. Parenthood might be tough, but we were surviving. Beneath the squalls and storms of living, despite Brendan's dead-end jobs, even with my poor domestics, we still had love to give each other and our little girl. I was proud of us for that.

After a while, we went down to the poolside. We had it to ourselves. The sun was low in the sky, the evening glowing orange and still warm. Brendan put Star's water wings on her chubby arms while I lay on a sunbed, watching them. He swung her up onto his shoulders and climbed down the little ladder into the glinting water and this released a memory in me, of my father holding me like that on his shoulders, walking us both into the water, at some beach. "Ready?" he asked me, his voice smaller in the wide outdoors than it was in the house and, without waiting for an answer, he walked us in, me on top, him below. I held the sides of his head under me, unsure of my grip, frightened he'd go too far, that the water would come right up over his head and then over me.

I shook my head. This was 1968, I was here with Brendan, it was Star's anxiety I was feeling. He was gently lowering her into the water, holding her out in front of him like the figurehead of a ship and she was loving it. "More," she whooped whenever he stopped, and off he set again, her chubby little hands slapping the water.

And then. And then. The breach.

"*Aaaaargh!*" Brendan went, a roar as he went down.

I don't want to recall any more of this now, the story I repeated so often afterwards. How I heard the terrible cry and saw him twitching in the water, then flaying, his face contorted. How I saw Star's face sinking under the surface, and quicker than thought, I was in the pool with them, water to my thighs, grabbing her. Even now, still, I can feel her costume, wet and cold against my chest, and see Brendan thrashing forward, face down, spectacularly splashing until he was just as spectacularly still. And hear the silence that followed, and in it the slap-slap-slap of the lifeguard's bare feet on the tiles, as he came running towards us.

PART IV
STARSTRUCK

the person or act that gives the most heralded or impressive performance in a program.

ZACH

CHRISTMAS EVE 1989

*D*earest Mercy,
   I'm leaving this on our bed. The written word is always the best way to get your attention, isn't it, so maybe this might work? It's our last chance.

Nothing good will come of this, Mercy. Asking me to go will not appease Star. We must do what we should have done in the first place, and simply speak our own truth to her and let her tell us how she feels. She is neither as stubborn nor as vulnerable as you think, and too old to be treated like a child.

As for your father, is he really the obstacle you claim? If he was gone, you say, wistfully… If, if, if…

It does no good for you to keep telling yourself that you don't deserve these things that life has thrust on you. Deserve has nothing to do with it. Deserve is an illusion. Does a father deserve to die? Does a daughter deserve to rule?

You're always quoting writers at me, Mercy, but long ago I gave you the only words you need to hear. I wonder if you remember? It was a line from The Talmud: "If you add to the truth, you subtract from it."

I remember how you tried to understand. You tilted your lovely chin, the way you do. Your ear went down to nearly touch your shoulder and the other ear turned to me, really trying to listen. Always trying. I love that about you.

But, Mercy, why is it so hard for you to hear?

This is our last chance, we both know that. I can't save us on my own and if I leave again today, this time it really will be forever.

Don't do this to us. To me, to yourself, to us all. Get out of your own way, Mercy. Let us live.

Here's another Talmud line for you: "If not now, when?"

Zach

MERCY

1973

 uzzzzzz.

"Yes?"

"It's Iris Cunningham."

"Come on up."

I pushed open the door and a tang of must prickled my nostrils. An old carpet, pattern worn to grey all the way up. The bannister looked sticky and I avoided touching it as I climbed up the flight of stairs, and around and up again, and again a third time. I came to the blue door, as he'd described over the phone, and found a homemade, cardboard sign, inscribed unevenly with black marker: JOSEpH PLoTKIN, PsychoTHerApIst.

I was about to turn and sneak back down, but the door was ajar and a voice called out, "Cm'on in." A billy-hick, Southern drawl. I hadn't expected that: my thoughts had been of somebody urban and urbane, with a dark beard and spectacles. Instead, I found a fat man with bushy, black brows that met in the center, over two bulging eyes set too far apart.

He was seated in an armchair with wooden arms and didn't get up.

"Miss Cunn-ing-ham?" His drawl made three separate syllables of the name.

"No, er —" I'd momentarily forgotten my alias. "I mean, yes."

"Well, now…" He raised one half of his unibrow. "Which would it be: no or yes?"

"It's 'Ms'," I said, recovering. "Not Miss."

The unibrow wilted, returning to its rightful place. "Allright-y ma'am. I'll try to remember that."

He reached under his chair and brought out a clipboard with a plastic pen dangling on a grubby length of string. "Maybe you'd fill out this here form for me." A registration form: name, address, details of payment methods.

"I'd rather not sign up just yet. I'm … em … I'm talking to a few therapists before deciding who to go with."

"Oh. Allright-y." He returned the clipboard to the floor. "So what appears to be the trouble?"

"It's not me," I said. "I'm here about my daughter."

He nodded. "Go on." Go *aw-h-nnn*.

I buttressed myself, launched into the explanation I'd prepared. "She's taken to saving trash in her bedroom. Pieces of paper from school. Juice cartons from the playground. Her friend's discarded lunch wrappings. All sorts of garbage and junk."

"Uh-huuh."

A long silence.

"That's it. I want to know why she's doing this. I want it to stop."

He folded his fingers into a steeple under his chin. "What age is she?"

"Six."

"And how long has this been goin' on?" *Aw-h-nnn*.

"For months now. At first, I hardly noticed. She just wanted to keep whatever she had touched. It started with price tags from new clothes, for example, or a piece of paper with a single mark on it, or wrapping paper torn off gifts. I didn't understand it, but it seemed harmless."

"So you indulged her?"

"I ignored it for a while, but it's been getting progressively worse. It's turned into anything that has been touched by anyone she knows. It's not normal."

"But you continued to indulge?"

"I don't believe I'd use the word 'indulge'.

Another silence.

"It's turning into anything she sees. Trash from the streets and school, as well as home. It can't go on."

"I see. A moment, please."

He bent over his notebook and began to write. I looked around me. He had made some attempts to brighten the room with a pot plant and two scarlet, velvet screens to corner off the interview space. I peeped past them at a counter kitchen, with miniature cooker and fridge, occupying one corner and the bed in the other. Did he live here as well as using it for clients?

"Do you think you might be able to help her, Mr Plotkin?"

"I do believe so, ma'am. But I'm going to need more."

He wanted to know everything, not just about Star, but about me. I answered all his questions, told him about being widowed and coming to live in Santa Paola. With Brendan gone, Brooklyn had nothing to hold me and by 1964, it seemed like California was the place for beats and all the assorted refugees from 1950s conformity. Artists, rebels, gays, outcasts, seekers and wounded soldiers: California was calling us all.

So I set out to go where Brendan and I hadn't reached, to San Francisco. And I loved being there. I found us a place in a shared apartment in a three-story brick building, half of the second floor between five of us, all artists except me. The walls were covered in murals and drapes of Indian cloth, the huge mantel was covered in religious artefacts and candles and I went about half-hungry in order to pay rent, seething in a cauldron of bereavement.

I was now a single mom, alone in the world except for the bohos of San Francisco, who found their way to our place. Fury aside, I enjoyed that time, especially in the early days, when one of our roommates, a sculptor called Matt, looked after us well. But Matt began to press for things I couldn't give, and stopped babysitting for me, and it all became too expensive and anyway, the paint and art supplies were a danger to a toddler.

So I packed us up again and came down south to this coastal college town, to a more suburban existence. Santa Paola wasn't "the city that knows how" but it was sunnier and more child-friendly, with good public schools. I found us a roomy apartment close to Westcliff Road, and Star and I settled into being Californian.

It was a good place for a lone mother and her child to draw together the tatters of a torn life. That was how I now described myself to the new people I met, and how I described myself to myself. Poor, lone, widowed, bereaved. Cast out by heart disease and circumstance. Poor me and my poor little girl, with only each other. I see now how I clung to the hardship in my head. I'd made myself a bed out of self-pity and I lay down in it day after day.

Our real-life, non-metaphorical bed was a single, iron-steaded, ancient monstrosity that Star and I had to share, against which I was forever bumping and bruising my shins. I would lie in it, with her asleep beside me, still as I could so as not to disturb her, my fingers clutching the lumpy mattress. If it wasn't for her, I told myself, I'd give up, thrown in the towel, quit, surrender. What that meant, I wasn't quite sure, but I knew that most days what got me up was having to answer her cries, even if that meant being tired later; having to produce healthy food for her, even if I couldn't care what I ate myself; having to dress her up pretty, though any old clothes did me; having to brush her hair when it was matted, though my own looked — in Doolough parlance — like I'd been dragged through a bush backwards.

Nothing in my life had prepared me to be both carer and provider. My choices were limited. I had a couple of part-time stints stuffing packs to redeem coupon offers, another calling telephone owners to offer them complicated discounts. And one sitting at a table in a dark hotel basement, asking people what they thought of a chocolate advertisement or an unnamed brand of margarine. For the most part, though, I cleaned and I served, the female fallbacks.

The worst thing about that kind of work are the managers. Bartenders and waitresses serve, pot-boys scrub, but all managers do is try to keep down staff or keep up profits, usually through getting petty about something like ketchup bottles. There's not much that's wholesome in work like that, even before you add the personality failings. The ones who think you're available for a grope. The ones who act like your pay check comes out of their own pocket. The ones who get a kick out of making your evening a little bit tougher than it needs to be.

But I did it, didn't I, Star? I carved out a good life for us in the gentle town between the mountains and the ocean. Back then, it was just about possible to keep a decent apartment and a car and a child on such jobs. It meant scrimping and saving, recycling and salvaging, and help from friends if you wanted treats or luxuries but at least you could do it in those pre-Reagan days. It would be impossible now.

California was good to us. The Golden State, how I miss it now. It has the highest mountain in the US, the most extraordinary bird, the biggest vineyard, the plumpest oranges, the hottest desert, the tallest waterfall, the oldest living trees on earth. It's a waking dream of noise, smog, beach, sky, mountain, fog and open, hazy, golden light. It's nostalgia even while you're living it. Never was a place more put upon by fantasy but for me, for us, it delivered. The ever-present ocean, the spectacular sunsets, the Redwood pines, the dependable mountains wrapped in raiments of snow or mist. I made them ours.

At weekends, my friends and I would take you out to the wilderness, to enjoy the gift of year-round sunshine. Coming from Ireland, a country that often did four seasons in a day, I loved the consistency of Santa Paola's climate. Two seasons, wet and dry, with subtle variations that arrived, on schedule, each year. We moved there in November and those first sunny winter days will stay with me, always. Wind full of dust and dried-up leaves and the parched land seeming to listen for the rain that, when it came, was nothing like an Irish downpour but more a gentle baptism, wafting in from the sea in mild and mellow veils, followed by days of softer sun and cooler air. Quickly, in a matter of days it seemed, the brown hillsides turned to green.

I didn't know that first year that this was Santa Paola's false spring, tricking plants into budding, or even blossoming out of season and people into throwing off their clothes. In January, the real rains came: in torrents, not from the ocean this time, but from the clouds directly above cracking open like eggs. Around us, dry riverbeds and arroyos raced with water but, unlike Ireland, between each downpour we had blue skies and warmth again.

By the time the last rains came in April, in fitful squalls, real spring had arrived with its blaze of color. Then it was the long, hot, dry season, greens gradually bleaching again. In May, the first desert winds came sweeping down the canyons, like somebody up there had plugged in a giant air heater. It ripped off palm leaves, sometimes even branches, and shifted the mountains closer. Inland was baking-hot, desert-hot, headache-hot, but in Santa Paola, we had our kindly fog bank. Throughout the summer it sat there, offshore on the water, about 1,000 feet thick. As night fell, it would move in, filling the spaces between our homes and in the morning, as the sun climbed, it would obligingly roll back out to sea.

Most of this I told to Joseph Plotkin, leading up to asking him the question I had to ask. Despite my efforts, ensuring Star was clean and healthily fed, brought out at the weekends when I felt like sitting her in front of the TV, sending her to the best school and all the extra-curricular activities I could afford, might this behaviour of Star's be a reaction to having a working mom? The newspapers were full of such warnings at the time and I couldn't rid myself of the feeling that I was doing something wrong.

"Maybe, maybe not." His unibrow frowned. "I'd like to fill some gaps, ma'am. Can I ask you about your sex life?"

"I don't see how…"

"Oh, believe me, it's gonna be relevant."

I felt the way I imagine any woman, alone in a room with an unknown man and a bed, would feel.

"Do you have a boyfriend?" he prompted.

"No."

"But you have a history?"

I shrugged.

"Please, ma'am. I need to hear it."

"There hasn't been anybody serious since my husband."

"But there have been men?"

"Yes."

"Women?"

"No!"

"How many men?"

"I'm not sure."

"Approximately."

"I've never counted. I really don't see…"

"Please, Ms Cunningham. If you and I are going to work together, you need to trust me to do my job. If you would…"

There had been a few. After Brendan was gone, it comforted me to see admiration in a man's eye. Flirting was the closest I came to fun, and casual encounters — slipped between work and Star — suited me well. Joseph Plotkin was waiting.

"Em… About eight."

"How long again since you lost your husband?"

"Four years."

"When asked a question like this, a significant percentage of people lie or underestimate. It is important that you tell me the truth."

"I have."

"Okay. Good. Now, tell me what sex is like with these men."

"It depends on the man, I guess."

"Can you identify any pattern? Anything at all?"

I shrugged.

"It's important, ma'am. Take your time."

In the shopping precinct on the street below, faint voices were bidding each other hello and goodbye, having ordinary conversations. What was I doing, trapping myself in this room?

"It's been easier with them than my ex— my dead — husband," I said.

"Easier? Do you mean sexually?"

I nodded. "I loved my husband very much; he was a very attractive man. But —"

I could hear him breathing, noisily and damply, through his mouth.

"Were you incompatible? Sexually." He just loved saying that word. "Go o-on, Mrs Cunningham. Did you enjoy sex with your husband?"

I shook my head, hot with shame.

"I see. Would that be lack of orgasm? Lack of desire? Or lack of pleasure?" He sounded like a laconic waiter listing off the dishes of the day. Each syllable was drawn out until it was almost a word in itself: or-gasm, dee-sire, pleas-uuure.

"Maybe," I whispered into my lap. "I suppose. Sometimes."

"Which?"

"All, I suppose. I didn't think about it too much at the time. We were happy together."

He nodded, as if he'd come to some conclusion. "Ms Cunningham, I need you to come across to the couch," he said. "I want you to lie down and close your eyes and relax."

"Why?"

"I want to ask you about your parents."

"What have my parents — or my sex life for that matter — got to do with Star?"

"A great deal, I'd say."

This was my worst fear. But how? What evidence was he going on?

"Look, I..."

"Ms Cunn-ing-ham, don't fight shy now. You are doing very well, very well indeed."

"I really don't see..."

"If you don't feel able to continue, we can stop here and take it forward next week. But you do have" — he glanced across at the clock on the mantelpiece — "twenny-five minutes left."

The clock ticked at me. He stared at me with those baleful fish eyes, like he was begging me to take him onto dry land.

"All right," I said.

He led me across to the couch. I lay down. The bed smelled of body. He *did* sleep here.

"So... Your daddy. Tell me all about him."

"I don't know what to say."

"He's alive?"

I nodded.

"What age would he be?"

I did a quick calculation in my head. "He's seventy-six."

"And you're fond of him?"

"I never see him. He's in Ireland."

"That's not what I asked, ma'am."

"Em... Not especially."

"What about when you were growing up?"

I hesitated.

"Did he beat you?"

"Only... Not... No."

My nostrils had shrunk to pin pricks. The room was airless.

"What happened between y'two? Feeling? Touching?"

The air evacuated the room. I cannot fill my breath.

"Miss Cunn-ing-ham?"

In the street, lunchtime was upping the activity: voices and cars bustling. He was making a note; the scratch of his pen was loud. "What have you just written?" I asked.

"Mrs Cunn-ing-ham. For a girl, her father is the primary male bond. Through him, she learns how to respond to other men."

"What does any of that have to do with Star?"

"Just about everything, ma'am."

Could this be true? Could my father's poison, despite my best efforts, have leaked through and tainted her?

"I don't understand how."

"It is complicated, surely. We'll have to unravel the points of connection."

"How?"

"Get you into a state of relaxation. Get you visualisin' and re-writin' your outcomes. First you'll be cured, then you're gonna find your daughter's fixed up, too."

Rewriting my outcomes, I liked the sound of that. "Really, Doctor?"

"Well, now... In this business, we don't give no guarantees. The mind is a mystery, Miss Cunn-ing-ham, but in your case, I'd be confident of a positive outcome. Yes, ma'am."

I lay back down. He was not a doctor. Why had I called him Doctor?

"So ... you ready to go? Close your eyes there."

Behind my eyelids was a night sky splashed with orange.

"You breathe deeply now. That's it. In through your nose, out through the mouth. Deep breaths. Now relax your muscles, let your body grow real heavy. Yes, ma'am, that's it ... very good. Now. I want you to picture in your head what I'm describin'. Your daddy has walked into your bedroom and he's comin' close to your bed. You see that?"

"Yes."

"Under those bedclothes, you're naked. You can see... Miss Cunning-ham! Snakes alive, ma'am, you can't jump up like that!"

The door. Where was the door? I couldn't see the door.

"Miss Cunning-ham, puh-lease. Lie back down. To leave without completion could be dangerous."

I stood, dizzy, getting dizzier. "Can't. Can't."

"You are over-reactin', ma'am. Now, I'm thinking this is likely what's causin' your problems. If you don't lie down now, it is over for you."

I put my hands over my ears.

"Yes, ma'am. For you, and for your girl." His dead fish eyes fixed me in a stare. "For y'all. Forever."

My vision cleared. The door emerged. I did what my instinct had told me to do at the start and fled.

MERCY

1990

*L*ate February in Doolough. I stand by the window, looking down on Blackberry Lodge's front lawn, remembering, remembering. In one hand, I've a coffee cup and in the other, rolled into a scroll, a letter from Zach.

Half a page. Less than one hundred words and not one of them a word I need.

Dearest Mercy,
I have found a place where I can be. You were right about the
West of Ireland. I spent the New Year on Inishmore and am now
in this village in Connemara, below a mountain I've befriended.
I climb it every day, but never to the top.
I hope all has come to pass as you wanted — that your father
departed and your daughter arrived and both of them — and
you, of course — are at peace.
Yours sincerely,
Zach.

"A mountain I've befriended". It sounded so phoney on paper, though I knew that in the presence of his six-feet-two of sleeked muscle, in the hold of his piercing eyes, in the force-field of his presence, it would sound real and true.

This letter was so abrupt, it hurt. I'd prefer not to have received it at all. But why was I surprised? Long ago, he'd told me he was wary of words. It was the only thing he ever said that made me wary of him. We were in Santa Paola Central Park at the time and I'd replied, "The man who is wary of words is wary of life," which made him sit up.

"Do you really think so?" he'd asked.

"I was paraphrasing someone."

"Who?"

"An English writer you yanks probably have little time for. Doctor Johnson."

"Of dictionary fame?"

"Yes. He once said the chief glory of any people is its writers. I agree."

"Doesn't it depend on the writer? Lots of writing just feeds our false sense of self. Words can deceive, the written word most of all."

I staggered, stopped to argue. Our first disagreement but it felt vital that he should understand how, to the young me words were, as my favourite poet WB Yeats put it, the only "certain good". The lodestar of human achievement. Especially the written word that allowed us to reach across place and time. Growing up in Doolough, books had saved me, showing me there were other ways to live, other kinds of people, other principles and ideas. To me, only words were capable of encompassing it all, able to touch head and heart and soul, altogether, all at once.

"It's a matter of balance," he explained, when I offered all this, like a speech from a lectern on the value of literature. "Words *can* be good but our babble's grown too loud in our culture. We so rarely turn off our thoughts or our talk. I believe what this world needs right now is more silence."

Zach was only a student then, just setting out on life. How did he know so much? We started to stroll again. As we walked, I was conscious, as always, of the stares of others. Were they admiring us? We made a handsome couple. Or were they wondering about a thirty-year-old woman being with this guy who was barely out of boyhood.

We stopped again, to admire a magnificent flowering bush. I couldn't remember what it was called. "I know the name," I said. "I know it, I just can't remember it. It's on the tip of my tongue…"

"What does it matter what humans name it?" he said. "Be quiet so you can look at it."

I quieted down. And immediately remembered it was a hibiscus.

Halcyon days.

No hibiscus in Doolough, in dead February. Down on the lawn, I see a robin digging up worms. The grass is green, but the rest of the world — the trees and the sky and the mountains and slivers of lake — are grey, grey, grey. It's ten in the morning but the electric light is still on overhead and my desk lamp also lit. I'd forgotten how long and low-hanging an Irish winter can be, with its fifteen or sixteen hours of darkness, and the day so grey when it finally does arrive. So damp and cloud-congested, that it feels like planet earth has a head-cold.

My writing is drowning in detail, but all I seem to hold from my early years is an intense but undefined embarrassment. Me, blushing and shuffling through my days, especially when with my father in the presence of others. I was ashamed, but of what exactly? I can remember slipping out, up to the mountain or down to the lake when the house was too full of feeling, my face burning, my feet tripping over the stones. I rummage through my child's mind and find nothing but a swirl. Only Pauline and her mother stand out, clear. The rest is blotches, blotched.

I do have memories of this house, especially of the kitchen. I can conjure up the border of walls, the solidity of the big kitchen table as I rode around it on my tricycle, the warmth of the fire, the cold gusting in the back door, the grey light looming in the low window, everything tall and over-hanging. But it's like a finger-painting slathered out, the strokes too broad and all smudged.

I tilt my head back to drain my coffee. End of break. How ordinary life remains, even when extraordinary things are happening. Here I was, awaiting trial for murder. For patricide. Yet life still came down to breakfast, lunch, dinner; work, rest, exercise, family, friends, acquaintances. Most days I struggled through, with loneliness ever knocking at my poor defences but I had moments too when the shadow of what lay ahead, the possibility of prison, concentrated my appreciation of daily things. A robin's bobbing head. The aroma of the coffee. A walk down the lane to the road and back.

And writing. Time to get back to it. On the long desk behind me, the papers and notes and jottings that made up my life and my father's and Star's are spread, in a fan of files and folders. My fifteen minute break was over and if the writing wasn't done early, it wouldn't be done at all. Later in the day, my mind would wander, to my father's behaviour in his final days, to the impending trial, to the whereabouts of Star, and indeed, of Zach. My courage would disintegrate, my thoughts and memories congeal but now, I had good morning energy to take me through.

I went across to the desk and placed Zach's letter with the other papers. I couldn't afford to think any longer about his meagre words and what they might mean. If he was here, he would order my days. He would know how to cope with this trial that's ahead. He would make it so I would find something other than grey in this deep Irish winter, something besides darkness in sixteen-hour nights. With him, night time was my best time, not my worst.

Oh, Zach, soul of my soul, come back to me.

MERCY

1978

I met him when I was almost thirty and Star was eleven. He was on his college spring break. Yes, yes, I know. But in my defence, Zach Coleman was no ordinary nineteen-year-old.

My job back then was waitressing at Honolulu Bar and Restaurant on the ocean front. It had a stream running through it, dissecting the building and we had to run forwards and backwards over the little bridges, without bumping into each other. The bartenders wore bright green shirts spattered with orange and blue palm trees and we, the floor staff, wore green halter-neck tops over faux-grass skirts and a yellow flower behind the ear. It was Lindie, one of the other waitresses and also a single mom, who saw Zach first.

"Mine!" She elbowed me, as soon as he walked in. We had a mock rivalry running over good-looking punters.

I looked to the door. Tall, young, a small beard, and dark hair long and straight, like Jesus. "Not so fast, Missy," I said. "I do believe it's almost eight-thirty and time for your break."

She looked at her watch. "So it is. *Nyah*, he's only a tadpole, anyway. You're welcome."

When I brought him across the menu and he turned his eyes

up to me, the joking stopped. His eyes were the deepest grey I'd ever seen, the color of the sky around a new moon. He did look like Jesus. And he had the kind of presence I imagine Jesus to have had.

All through the requests from the other tables — a to-go box for table six; three more beers for twelve; ketchup bottle on eight, empty; two high chairs, please; ten picky Europeans with their hold-the-gravy-extra-cheese-burger-without-pickle-no-salad orders playing havoc with Honolulu's order system — I felt him there.

Europeans were always the most work for the least return. Spoiled by their high-wage welfare states, they were unaware of how we relied on tips to make up our wages. Jim-Bob, our manager, allowed us to "grat" them, add a tip to the bill without them realising, but not too much. Not enough, I figured as I ran round for them. Whenever I looked across, I would find the grey eyes looking at me. Each time, I held my own look a little longer but each time it was me who drew my eyes away.

At last, I was able to go to him. I went across and lifted his plate.

"Was everything all right for you, sir?" Everybody over fifteen was "sir" or "ma'am" in Honolulu.

He nodded.

"Can I get you anything else?"

"Nothing, thank you." Nothing but you, his eyes seemed to say. Or was that just wishful thinking?

"I'll get your check then?"

He paid, his tip generous, and I watched him leave, the tallness of him swaying past tables, leading with his left shoulder and then with his right. Moving with soft, sleek grace, like a dancer. Or a big cat. A dark, silken panther. Then he stepped through the beaded curtain and was gone.

I was never going to see him again.

Don't be silly. He'll come back in.

But what if he doesn't?

The thought was enough. I found myself running into the back and, grabbing my jacket, I passed Jim-Bob's booth on the way out. "Hey, where do you think you're going?"

"I'll be back," I called, without stopping.

He came out to shout after me. "Where are you going, I said?"

"Female emergency, Jim-Bob. I'll be back in no time."

"Female emergency, my sweet Fanny Adam. You come back here, girl. You come back here now. If you go out that door, you needn't bother..."

I kept going. I only needed a couple of minutes. I had no idea what I was going to say to him and by now, he might well be gone, disappeared into the dark. The thought gave me a spur of panic but, when I got outside there he was, standing under the canopy, as if he knew I'd follow. Or maybe just sheltering from the rain?

"Hey!" he said, as I drew close. "It's you."

"Seems so." I was suddenly shy.

"That's so great. I was trying to work out whether to go back in or wait till you got off."

That's how he was from the start, my Zach. At first I didn't trust it, this openness of his. I thought that he was doing the thing some guys do. The frank thing, the disarming thing that says, it's okay, you're safe with me, but you're not.

"What's your name?"

"Mercy."

"That's pretty," he said, something Americans say every time. What they really mean is, that's unusual. "I love your accent. You're Irish?"

I nodded.

"I'm Zach." He put out his hand. "Zach Coleman."

I took it, felt an energy, like the cells of our hands were dancing round each other.

"I'd love to go to Ireland," he said.

"Really? Why?"

"Who wouldn't? Hey, maybe you'll take me?"

I laughed.

"Why not? It would be fun. You could show me round. What part of Ireland are you from?"

"Wicklow."

Silence. He had no idea where Wicklow was.

Again he filled the space, simply and directly. "Do you want to go get a coffee?"

"I can't. I have to go back to work."

"No, don't."

"Don't?"

"Come with me instead."

"Sure, I'd love to. Except, if I do, I lose my job."

"Maybe you will, maybe you won't. Anyway, there are other jobs."

I laughed. "This one suits me, actually."

"It's not worthy of you."

"Pardon?"

"Why do they have to dress you like that?" He made a face but with a smile that took the offence out of the words. "I saw you, the way you did everything. You're too good for them. Don't go back."

"You don't know what you're talking about."

But he had taken my hand and was tugging me gently and I was letting him. We walked out into the rain and, for once, because of the small rebellion of running out to him and the way he was looking at me, even the rain felt different, like liquid silver. We found a coffee house and I started to talk and I told him everything, even about Star. I never discussed Star, certainly not with men I'd just met, but Zach knew all about her before we'd even kissed.

Ah, the kiss. It came four hours later, when I'd stopped talking and started to listen and we'd left the coffee house and were walking, aimlessly down a side street I'd never walked before, avoiding the rest of the world. I was drunk on the knowledge that I was doing something I shouldn't and Zach was drunk on me.

I haven't mentioned yet that, in my day, I was considered beautiful. I could give you the details — shade of hair, span of waist and bust and hip, quality of legs, texture of skin — but that's nothing. You have to see beauty to know what it means. Beauty is in the eye of the beholder, they say, but what if you are the beauty? Then, it's the look in a man's eye coming at you, telling you more than you want to know. It's the dislike they deal you for desiring you. It's a sideshow, that's what beauty is. It doesn't write the book or raise the child or learn the knowledge. Beauty belongs to the beholder, not to the object that's beheld.

One good thing about it, though, is that it wises you up early to men and what most of them want from a woman but, like everything about him, Zach's way of looking at me was different. His eyes were two clear mirrors and I actually liked the me I saw reflected in there.

So, yes, the kiss. His lips were warm, tentative at first, then searching. I remember wondering how so young a man could know how to kiss like that, then recognising that it wasn't him, it was him-and-me-together, then letting all thought go... It was a tender kiss, with a fluctuating rhythm, like a finely drawn violin duet and, after our lips parted, we were locked into each other in a new way.

He ran the back of his forefinger gently along my jawline. "My, God," he said, staring at me like I was a newborn baby. "You're stunning."

The kiss sent us swinging down the four blocks to his apartment and up his stairs. All felt natural and easy, even through the usually-awkward bits like finding the keys and getting the right one to fit the lock. Once we were inside, it were straight into the sliding off of fabric, the little tussles with each other's buttons and the first glimpses of each other's skin. I was in it, doing it, too, not just the observer. Soon everything was off,

off, off and we were down to the clear, open bareness of each other.

It was too much for him. In minutes, he was gone. "Oh, shit," he muttered into the base of my neck. "I'm sorry."

"Sorry for what? We're just warming up."

I wasn't being kind, I was pleasured by his pleasure. That was as much as I hoped for in any sex encounter and as much as I usually got. Until that night.

Zach's desire rose again quickly, as I knew it would, but this time he was determined to wait for me. He stayed my hand, he stared me down, he noticed everything and asked me questions and knew very little about what to do. So I had to get involved, to show him. And somehow, in the showing, I found my own way with someone else for the first time.

Then we were off together, surfing wave after wave of astonishment, rising and dipping with desires and discoveries, until the first birds sang a false dawn and beyond, until the real dawn was almost rising and I really had to go.

Kate, Star's night sitter, would be awake, expecting me to be there. I was sometimes late home from Honolulu, but never this late, and I didn't want to meet her — or worse, Star — beginning their morning with the sight of me arriving back.

He drove me home in his car, a Ford Falcon, through hushed and dusky half-morning light. The streetlights were still on. Their flash, along with the hum of the engine and his sated silence, made me drift. With the steering wheel in his hands, he appeared older, like a fully-fledged man, handsome and solid. Someone I could stay with, someone whose kindness I could allow.

What had just happened between us seemed to hold out a promise I hadn't asked for and wasn't even sure I wanted. Yet I felt I could maybe grow to love this. To love him?

No. I snapped myself awake. I did not hear myself think that. A slip of the mind, and a damn-fool one. It was our very first night, I didn't even know him twelve hours ago. And he was just a boy: nineteen years old, for Chrissakes.

The car braked; we were outside my house. The lights were all off in there, nobody up yet. All the houses around were dark, the whole world, except us, slaked in the half-life of sleep. A question was pushing up in me and I had to ask.

"That wasn't your first time, I hope?"

"I'm nineteen!" he said, indignant. As if nineteen was aged. "But," he said, brushing back my hair and touching my face again with his brand of honest tenderness that was half-frightening, "it was the first time I realised what all the fuss is about. The first time it was so completely, fantastically amazing." He whooped. "Actually, thinking about it: yes, it was my first time."

That was my Zach, charming and disarming, right from the start. What could I do but, there and then in the car, offer him seconds?

All is change and change is all, Star. That's the conclusion I've come to as I look back at our young days. Days and doings felt solid back then in a way that they don't now. With you, it was more obvious. The day-by-day changes that take a child from six to seven to eight are more evident than those that take its mother from twenty-four to twenty-five to twenty-six. Now, I see that life is always far more fluid than it feels while you're living it.

Certain events loom out of the murkiness of memory, grown clear-cut through repetition. The day you didn't get the Molly Dolly part. How my heart tumbled over itself to see you coming out of school that day, planting one foot in front of the other, straining to hold your walk as if nothing was wrong.

As soon as we got into the car, you collapsed into tears.

"You didn't get it?"

"No," you sobbed. "No."

"Oh, honey, I'm sorry."

"I have no part" — *sob* — "at all."

"What? But everyone had to be in the school play."

"Everyone" — *sob* — "does. Except I told Miss Rossi that I QUIT."

"What?"

You were devastated because Miss Rossi had given you the part of Mrs O'Brien. A silly old Irish lady, you said. Not a doll. Or a pony. Or even a tin soldier. The only grown-up in the play and ugly. And *o-o-o-old*. You wanted to be Molly *Dolly*.

Mrs O'Brien had only two lines, while Molly Dolly was the lead role and it had gone to Angelina Boyle, the prettiest girl in the class. I could see where Miss Rossi was coming from. At that time, you were about four inches taller than everyone else in the class and growing out of baby prettiness. Dolly, you weren't.

"You said I was the best actress," you cried, making it my fault. "You said I was a *star*."

I held you tight while you sobbed, tried to soothe. When the storm eased a little, opening a space, I said, "Don't you want to be in the play, sweetheart?"

"Not" — *sniff* — "if I'm not Molly Dolly."

"But won't you feel left out, watching all the others practice and perform if you're not in it?"

Your chin wobbled. You hadn't thought of that.

"Y'know, it's not how big or small your part is that counts, it's how you do it. Why don't you and I work together hard to make sure that your Mrs O'Brien is real memorable?"

"But I told Ms Rossi I didn't want to."

"Well, why don't I ask her tomorrow to give you the part?"

"Mommy, you can't. She won't."

"I'm sure she will, if I ask her."

"I *hate* Angelina Boyle."

Star got her part back and, for the following weeks, she and I ran through her two lines over and again, as if we were rehearsing Portia for the RSC. We used our neighbour, Mrs Quinn, as a model. We modified the script, putting an extra word or two into the bare sentences to make them unmistakably Irish. We experimented with clothes, accents and attitude.

By the time the great day arrived and the parents were taking their seats, Star could not wait to get backstage. I took my seat and watched while the curtain went back and each mom or dad scanned the stage until they found their own darling. Star wasn't there, her entrance came later.

Dolls and soldiers and teddy bears came and went around a bewildering plot centred on Molly Dolly's lost teddy and her refusal to do her homework or chores until he was found. But where was he? The action was interminable, designed in time-honoured, school play tradition, to give a speaking part to all. Bored parents fanned themselves with their programs. When, three-quarters way through, Star burst onto the stage, in a lime green evening gown with matching high heels, the audience around me popped awake. Taller than the rest, she walked across the stage and with hands on her hips, delivered her line in a strong Irish brogue: "Now, Molly Dolly, don't you be acting the rascal."

Timing and delivery were perfect. The audience hooted. Molly said her piece and Star delivered Mrs O'Brien's second, final line. "Little girls have to be doing what they're told." Again laughter, not so much for what she was saying, but the look and bearing of her.

Molly said, "But I'm so sad," which was Star's cue to retreat and let Tommy Soldier step forward for his moment in the limelight, but she decided her appreciative audience deserved more Mrs O'Brien than was scripted.

"Children these days," she said, turning to the crowd and throwing her eyes to heaven. "Begorrah!" At which point, the place broke up into a spontaneous burst of applause and cheers.

I cheered as long and loud as any, not caring who saw my

pride. She gave a little bow and retreated, finally allowing Tommy Soldier his moment.

For the rest of the performance, my eyes could only look at her, no matter what else was going on. She held her character all through, except for one small moment where she slipped and let her rosy pleasure and pride surface. That was my favourite moment of the night, better even than her accepting her due of compliments afterwards backstage; or the drive home in the car with her sharing all her thoughts, the purr of the engine beneath her small, delighted voice; or even than tucking her into bed after cocoa and biscuits and receiving a special, solemn hug as I bent to kiss her goodnight, a hug full of gratitude and love and a thousand nameless things.

I can still see that moment now, Star, bowing to your applause. I can see it here, now.

But still, too, I hear: "Oh, Mommy, after you left this morning I dropped my lunch on the schoolyard ground and Mark Libovitz came over and he was going to jump on my sandwich except that Sabrina and Casey and Fred came around in a circle and stopped him and then we went in and we had art first today, Mommy, instead of science because Mrs Golightly wasn't in and Miss Cremona said my painting was good, except not as good as the one I did two weeks ago. Do you remember that one? Oh, look, there's a dog crossing the road. Be careful, Mommy. It was boring during English and I was thinking about that program that we saw last night, with the Monkees, do you remember, Mommy? It was good, wasn't it? Did you like it? I liked the sandwiches you gave me for lunch. I think that's my favourite now. Tuna fish. I used to prefer chicken but I think now I prefer tuna. What was I saying? Oh, yes, after Art, what did we do then? Em… Oh, history, that's it. Miss Cremona came in and she…"

That phase Star went through of giving frantic monologues,

reporting on everything that had happened to her that day, everything she'd thought or felt or seen or heard since I'd last seen her, and whatever came into her mind while she was delivering her report, on it would go, compulsively, breathlessly, ceaselessly into the afternoon and evening, exhausting us both.

"It's okay, Star. Let it go. It doesn't matter."

"But I have to tell you, Mommy."

"Not everything. Why?"

"Because I have to."

"But why? What would happen if you didn't? What's in your head now?"

"Bertie, Mr Malkovich's dog and..."

"Okay." I put my finger against her lips. "Don't say the next thing."

She stopped.

"Do you know what you were going to say?"

She nodded, her two eyes thrust wide, my fingers pressing her into silence.

"Hold the thought. You got it?"

Another nod.

"So hold the thought and let it go without telling it."

"No, Mommy, I want to tell you. I have to. What I was thinking was —"

"No, no, wait a minute. You can tell me in a minute."

Four years since Joseph Plotkin and things were worse, not better.

I took it to her teachers in the end, and from there to the school psychologist, and then another private counsellor. Two years of nobody helping much, while the problem pretended to fade or disappear, but was really only hiding, to mutate and rear up again.

Her relationship with trash was not as intense as it had been, though she still clung to certain useless things with a strange anguish. That now seemed almost harmless next to this compulsive sharing of every single detail of her life. By bedtime, we were both exhausted by the torrent of her thoughts and she would be crying at the idea of going to sleep, because sleeping meant not being able to tell me what was on her mind.

It was clear that Star was trying desperately to hold on to what could not be held — whether it was trash or the events of the day — and I figured it was down to the loss of her father.

And so it went until, in the end, there was nothing for it but psychiatry. Not gentle-sounding counselling but a doctor, with connections to a mental hospital, whose medicine bag included pills and injections and confinement and electroconvulsive therapy and other "cures" that I couldn't believe in, and could scarcely bear to contemplate, except that not to give them consideration meant doing nothing, leaving things the way they were, or taking the wacko route: psychic healing or crystals.

Doctor Amanda Aintree — in her nice professional way — suggested that her father's absence alone did not account for how utterly "unindividuated" Star seemed to be. My daughter, for some other, unspecified set of reasons, didn't seem to know where she stopped and I started.

What Dr Aintree set Star and me to do was simple but, as she said, far from easy. I was to give Star a list of all the things she could do to take herself to sleep and then let her go to bed without me. I was to encourage her to have friends and wave her off with them when they went out together, knowing nothing more than where they were going and an agreed time for her to be back. I was to encourage her to do as much as possible alone but also to keep her routine stable and settled.

She would ensure Star was supported with a weekly session.

"So no drugs?"

"Not yet. Hopefully not at all, depending on how she responds."

We were lucky. Dr Aintree was an exceptional psychiatrist: kind, firm, knowledgeable, supportive, wise. We needed her to be every bit of that as each tiny change led Star into shrieking and sobbing fits of anger and me into a fear that I was beginning to see tipped towards paranoia.

It was exhausting. It left both of us wrung-out and wretched. Star was having her toddler tantrums now, the good doctor explained, and I was feeling classic separation anxiety.

Stay with it.

So we did. Not knowing what else to do, I followed instructions, gripping tight while the rollercoaster of emotions that didn't want us to be free, bucked and dipped.

We'd have made it, I think, if I hadn't answered our doorbell on 11thth May 1978.

Ding-dong. I was preparing dinner when our doorbell rang. One of the things I didn't like about myself at that time was that I always experienced the doorbell ringing as an intrusion. Maybe it's because a double-jobbing single mother is always busy and always has a plan for the coming minutes or hours. That evening, it was the usual routine: dinner, Star's homework, TV, bedtime, Kate 's arrival, go to work.

Zach was gone, back to college, sending almost daily letters. He would be home, soon, for vacation. I had a calendar, like a schoolgirl or a prisoner, marking off the days. In the meantime, I was busier than ever. If he was taking a college education, it seemed like maybe I should, too. I had started to read again, to entertain what my father would have called "notions". I had written to UCSP for their prospectus, and then to the English Literature Department and to College Administration about second-chance degrees.

I had started to swim in a sea of words. When I wasn't working or looking after the house or Star, I was reading. That's why I resented the doorbell. I had been hoping to grab half an hour's reading time between getting Star to sleep, and having to go to work. If Star hadn't been watching, I wouldn't have answered it. Now, as I sit here writing this, wishing with every fibre that I hadn't, I wonder what difference it would have made?

I used to play that "I wonder" game with Zach, imagining what would have happened if he hadn't turned up at Honolulu on our first night. What if I had been on my break? Or if I hadn't run out after him? What if he got fed up waiting outside and left? We might have missed each other forever, I would exclaim, shivering at the thought, though usually for such chats we would be snug under his duvet, enveloped in body heat.

Imagine, I'd say.

Just imagine.

It all seemed so random, so accidental. "I don't believe in accidents," he said.

"Well they happen, whether Zach Coleman believes in them or not."

"Nope, no accidents." He shook his head. "No coincidence or happenstance, no such thing. No freaks or misfits, either. Just things that we don't understand."

"Oh, Zach." He was so sweetly intense. That was the day I gave him the Yeats collection, for our two-month "anniversary".

He was delighted. "*The Collected Poems*," he read, taking off the wrapper.

"That Irish poet I told you about."

"I know. I haven't forgotten." He kissed me. "Thank you."

"You don't have to be nice about it. You think you're not interested but you will be, trust me."

"Read me something. Read me your favorite."

"I don't have a favorite. It's more like I have different poems for different days. I know exactly which ones I'm going to read you, but first you have to get into the right place to receive them."

"Huh?"

"Think of it as watching somebody dance, okay?"

"Dance?"

"Poetry is language dancing. That's the way you have to take it in. Like you were watching a dance."

"Okay, I'll try."

"I'm going to start with the early stuff. His early poems are childlike in their belief in another world, less intellectual and formal than his later stuff, but for me they are magic. The lines and phrases make me feel like I've fallen into a dream... Anyway... Here goes."

I began with "The Song of The Happy Shepherd", the poem I've turned to again and again over the years to keep me writing. "The wandering earth herself may be/ Only a sudden flaming word,/ In clanging space a moment heard,/ Troubling the endless reverie..." I looked up at him as I finished the last line — "Dream, dream, for this is also sooth" — and smiled to see how his eyes were shining.

He got it.

I knew he would.

I moved on to "The Cloths of Heaven" and told him all about the poet's hopeless, unrequited love for Maud Gonne and his multiple proposals and rejections.

"That's enough for today," I said as I finished "When You Are Old". "It's like a drug, you can overdo it."

Nineteen years old Zach Coleman might be, but I was living the whole love drug with him. He had me smiling and glowing about my days. At the time, I thought it was because of what I was receiving, the attentions of this kind and handsome (young) man. Now I know it was the giving that had me feeling so good. When you're in love, you give without even knowing. Later in a relationship, you get grudging again, but at the beginning, you're so willing to amuse, to gratify, to charm, to pleasure.

When I recall that time, I always think of the big bed in his apartment. For every long-standing couple, there is a quadrant of emotional landmarks: the first kiss; the first sex; the first "I love you", and the biggie: moving in together. We were stuck on the second one. The three words were not coming out of me and

I knew he wanted to say it, but was being held back by the reluctance he sensed in me. He knew, with that knowing way of his, that it had to be me first.

Also, he kept pushing to meet Star. "She's the most important thing in your life, so she's important to me, too. I need to get to know her."

"I don't introduce her to boyfriends, Zach. It would be too confusing for her."

A small flinch. He didn't have a history as long as mine and hated to think of me with anybody else.

"Zach," I said, more gently. "In a few days, you're going back to college. You'll meet some preppy girl and that will be the end of me."

He sat up, the sheet falling from his chest, and gripped me by the wrist. "Don't say things like that."

"Hey, take it easy."

"You don't really believe that?"

"I... I don't know... It's what happens."

"What do you think I'm doing here, Mercy?" His fingers tightened, making a mark. "You know I've cancelled my summer trip to Europe to be with you."

"Zach, stop. Let go."

"Don't you know I'd give up college tomorrow for you, get a job, move in with you and Star?"

"I'm not asking you... I'd hate you to do that. It would be all wrong."

"I wish you *would* ask. I want to give you something, I want to give you *everything*. But you won't even give me a meeting with your daughter."

"I will, but not just yet."

"I'll know you're serious about me when you let me meet her."

"I'm sorry, Zach, not yet. If you had a kid of your own, you'd..."

"You're just scared, Mercy, but that's okay. You might know

more about poetry but I know more about us. I'll just have to wait until you know it, too."

"Know what, you crazy man?"

"That we were made for each other. That I'm not just a little boy for you to play with —"

"Is that what you think I think?"

"— And that we are never letting each other go."

Next time, I promised. Next vacation, I would introduce them. In the meantime, while he was away, I would prepare the ground.

Except every time I went to broach the subject with Star, I was at a loss. How to start? Now I was coming round to thinking that maybe the best thing was, actually, for her to meet him when he came back, slip him into our life, no big explanation.

Ding-dong went the door again. I waved goodbye in my head to my reading and called across to Star, doing homework at the table. "Will you get that, honey?"

Oh, what if I hadn't? Would he just have come back another day? Or would everything, *everything*, be different now?

I turned back to the cooker, heard Star's chair scrape back, her footsteps crossing the hall, the creak of the front door and then his voice. "Oh," he said, surprise in his tone. "Hello. Are you Maria?" I instantly recognised the unmistakeable timbre and inflection. "Does Mercy Creahy live here?"

I turned too fast, knocking the pot I was holding. Bolognaise sauce spilled all over the floor. *Creahy*. I was Creahy no longer. Before I came west, I'd returned to using Mulcahy. A surge of blood flooded into my skull. The sticky, tomato mess was oozing all over my shoes and it might as well have been glue, because I found I couldn't budge.

"Mom...?" My name fluttered in Star's mouth. She was at the kitchen door, knowing something was wrong. I couldn't look at her. Out in the hallway, the front door creaked and was closed. He had crossed our threshold. He was coming in. Coming in, to our house.

"Mercy," he said, putting himself in front of me. Blood butted against my temples. He looked bad, I saw that in an instant, though he'd done his best to dress himself up. Gone too far, in fact, with a suit and tie, but the suit was shiny and the shirt was faded and the shoes were bunched and knobbled. And no clothes could disguise the mottled skin and the red-rimmed eyes.

"Oh, God," I said. And then noted, in that detached way that you do, even while you're in shock, how people in moments of extremity always call to either God or their mother.

We were frightening Star. "What is it, Mommy?"

"It's all right, baby."

"Mommy, tell me."

"It's…"

What could I say to her? She was beside me now, looking up at me, the false sophistication she'd adopted since turning eleven knocked off. Tugging my sleeve, eyes full of accusatory questions.

"Mom! Tell me!"

How was I going to find the words to explain what I could see she already knew?

It was her father, of course. Who else but Brendan, returned from the dead to haunt us?

You may call what I said a lie and I know you wouldn't be wrong but it's not that simple. It came as a half-imagined dream of an explanation, the morning after the night I discovered what he'd been doing behind our backs. He's dead to me, people say, when they've truly been betrayed and that was how it felt. Better he would be dead than have to share with anyone, especially Star as she got older, the truth of that sordid discovery, the subsequent arguments, our departure from his sullied orbit.

"Was there somebody else?" That was the question people were sure to ask if I told them I was separated or divorced. A question I couldn't bear. It undid me, made a fool of me and a mockery of everything I thought I knew. My Brendan would not have been able to so tenderly share that weekend with me and Star in that Cape Cod hotel, to help feed her as he did, and put her to bed, then bring me downstairs for dinner, her baby monitor on the table between us along with the candles and flowers and the pre-dinner drinks. To clink a glass of wine against mine — "Look in my eyes, Merce!" — and exchange those heavy, meaningful looks all through the meal that got us both worked up long before we got back upstairs and then, when we did, make the kind of frenzied, wild, all-over love he made with me, with Star sleeping sound and oblivious in her cot beside us, do all that, in that way, while having a girlfriend on the side.

A girl in the office, who phoned our house the night we got back, whose call made him speak in a tone of voice that, even though I was in another room, even though I didn't hear the words spoken, even though the conversation lasted only moments, told me all, as I stood in Star's bedroom and realisation dropped in me and I started to shake, all over.

The call ignited a question from me when I came back into the kitchen, and an admission from him, and then a screaming, wailing, piercing argument that woke Star, and broke us, broke me, broke everything.

Separation didn't describe it, didn't even come close. My husband was dead. Defect of the heart, previously undetected.

That was the truth of it to me.

So why, remembering all this, did I take him back eight years on, when I'd just fallen properly in love with somebody else? That is the question that flays me now.

It wasn't like he'd improved with age. Whatever had happened to Brendan since I'd last seen him in Brooklyn — most of his communications on the matter were long, circuitous rambles that told little and left more than I wanted circling round my imagination — he had become a man incapable of settling on anything for more than a minute. Watching TV meant flicking up and down through the channels; smoking meant lighting one cigarette from the last; telling a story meant losing his place and stumbling onto something else.

The night he came back, he spent telling us an allegedly funny tale about what some guy had done to him in a motel, littered with cussing and swearing, each one followed by an "excuse me". No matter how round Star's eyes grew or how often I said, "Brendan, will you please mind your language", he just excused himself and did it again, as if the apology cancelled out the use of words like "fuck" and "prick" and "mother-fucker" in front of an eleven-year-old girl.

I sat, offended by his careless talk and by the sprawl of him taking up way too much room. And fearful. When he tore a piece of laminate from a napkin carton and started to pick his teeth with the edge of it, I thought: for this, for *this*, I must give up my Zach.

Poor Zach. When I told him he cried. Yes, tears, real ones, forehead pressed against the steering wheel of his car. He raged against me, calling me a liar, a cheat, and a whore. He tortured us both with his imaginings of me sleeping with this other man, this husband, and my assurances that I had no intention of sleeping with Brendan were spurned. What did such assurances mean from a liar?

Trying to hold some dignity for us both, I kept bringing it back to one quiet line: "He is Star's father, Zach." Now she knew about him I had no choice.

It was no good. Zach had made an idol of me and wasn't able for the *real* Mercy's life, all shimmers and shades and blurry edges. His hurt was sharp and certain and pitiless and he said the most outrageous things. He'll learn, I told myself, pulling defences up around me as I looked out the car window. Just live a while longer, dear boy, and you'll come to see it's not so simple.

Though maybe, if you were as good a person as Zach, it was. After he was gone, the absence of him hurt. I missed that goodness of his, and his youth, his caramel smell and the bright metal taste of him in his secret places but mostly I missed the true adoration I'd got used to, that had been turning me into something I wasn't before. I could have cried and wailed and ranted, too, it would have been nice to have had the luxury of that, but I had to be shatterproof glass. Splintered all over, but holding together.

Star would have a father again. Brendan and I would synch our schedules to ensure one of us was always there for her. We would become a family again but a proper one this time. We'd make up to Star for what we'd done.

Except Brendan didn't co-operate. He had lived the easy life for so long that he had become incapable of doing anything for anybody else.

"Honey, no TV for us tonight," he said to me the night after his return.

"Huh?"

I came down at about ten-thirty, groggy, having dozed off beside Star while trying to get her to sleep.

"We are going to that swish new bar down on the waterfront."

"It's my night off, we've no sitter."

"The kid's asleep. She won't miss us for a few hours."

Was he serious? It seemed so. "You go," I said.

"I think I will."

It was 4.30 a.m. when he came home, stumbling and cursing.

I should have sent him packing then but I didn't want to allow that I'd made a mistake. I had lost Zach to take Brendan back. I wasn't going to let him make nothing of that. We were going to make it work.

On we staggered, with me forgiving the unforgivable and

him promising promises we both knew he didn't even mean to keep.

Guilt made him lash out at me. "It's so bad for Star, the way you indulge her."

"It would be better to indulge myself, I suppose."

"Lying beside her every night to get her to sleep. At her age. Never leaving her out of your sight for one minute that you're not at work. The poor child can't breathe."

"Oooh, I'm so bad. I should be the person who can't last two evenings without getting drunk or stoned."

"A man has to do something. There's no room for anyone else in your little hothouse for two."

"Of course, I drive you to it. Like you never touched a toke or a bourbon till you fetched up here."

"God help you when she grows up," he said, his Irish accent strong in his anger. "God help her even more."

I struck back of course, scoring my points, knowing we were both losing the match.

It ended the night I came back from work at the restaurant and found a drunken mob there, three men and two girls, with Star upstairs. The thought of her rising from her sleep and seeing their carry on… I gave them all their marching orders, including him and he went, "happily", he said.

I didn't tell Star that part, of course. I just said he'd had to go away and would be back soon. And then, weeks later, when she missed him less, I told her that I didn't think he was going to be coming back.

But it hurt her horribly, I know. Thirteen weeks he'd stayed for, just long enough for her to get used to the idea of a father and then becoming distraught at losing him all over again. Just long enough for him to wreck our lives a second time, in a whole new concoction of ways.

What a mistake. I see it so much clearer now. What I should have done was bid Brendan good day when he turned up unannounced, stayed with Zach and introduced him slowly to

Star. Let him grow over time into being her father. Zach would have risen to the role and all that happened later would never have happened. With Zach, I could have gone to Europe, traveled the world together, done whatever we decided to do...

Now, I see my taking Brendan back and letting Zach go for what it was: self abuse. I made myself sorrier than any woman should ever be, not just for Star — which was what I told myself at the time — but because a part of me felt more comfortable with my flawed and floundering husband, or with being alone, than being with my sweet and upright Zach.

Brendan, or loneliness, was as much as I deserved.

PART V
STARTURN

The person of the performance that is the most interesting or exciting

STAR

2009

I do call it a lie, Mom. Not an imagining, a mistake, a dream, or an oversight. A monumental, unforgivable lie. Only somebody looking through that big hazy mirror of yours could call it anything else. How you liked to live right up against that mirror, close enough to kiss. It made you so much bigger than the rest of us behind you, didn't it? And so conveniently turned us all back to front, turned the truth you'd rather not tell into a deliberate lie. Liar!

Yes, I'm reading your book. I threw in those first pages that day by the lake and watched them bobbing on the water but it was all taking too long, and so I stopped, and went back to the house and told Shando what I'd been doing, and he told me she'd left him another copy just in case I destroyed the first. So I surrendered to the pair of them and I have been reading and trying to understand, as my husband advised. He's right, he's right, I know he's right.

But here, Mom, I must speak. I know that mirror of yours so well, I can see right through it.

Like that concern of yours that makes you feel so good about yourself, so motherly. That was the burden of my childhood. Oh, you never said it out straight, I grant you that, but I grew up knowing I was the one who was holding you back, who had brought you to small town suburban life, who was keeping you in deadbeat jobs, dependent on unreliable men. If it wasn't for me, you'd be traveling through Europe, reading and writing poetry, dancing in the moonlight on a misty Irish beach with a lifelong soulmate.

As a child, that felt right to me. You were my lovely mother, so much younger than the other moms, so much more beautiful and free-spirited. An ancient kingdom of Celtic mists and shadows seemed just what you deserved. I do remember that.

I remember you singing "Twinkle twinkle little Star, How I love you, all that you are." I thought that song was mine and yours alone and was amazed when I went to school and heard it in other mouths, with different words.

In those days, I would sit on your bed, watching you, adoring every gesture — the way you shimmied into or out of a dress, or twisted your hair into a coil, or kicked off your high heels. I would put them on after you, feel your warmth through my soles. When you'd sit me down beside you to look into the bedroom mirror, you'd point out how alike we were — our long hair down, our eyes the same shade of green, our freckles the same spatter across both noses. I would grow up to be very beautiful, you said, trying to hide your bewildered disappointment that I wasn't, yet.

"Never forget we are of Ireland," you said one day, during these mirror-to-mirror sessions. "Land of saints and scholars and female fighters. Maeve, the warrior queen. Grainnehuile, the pirate princess." I was surprised the first time, because before this, Ireland had always been that back-of-beyond relic, that priest-ridden theocracy, that patriarchal hellhole.

I knew you'd been reading something.

Or met someone.

"Tiny Ireland held out against the Romans first," you'd said, brushing your hair, staring back at me through your mirror. "Then against the English. It kept the Celtic culture alive. In the village where I grew up, they told stories and sang songs that were old when Homer was a boy."

You made me see what you saw: the misted mountains and the rained-out fields. I heard the clash of spears, felt the strange, outlandish alphabet in my ears, tried it out in my mouth. *Maedbh. Grainnehuile. Doolough.* You were fighting hard in those days to remain true to all that. I felt your struggle and the weight I made pulling at your bronze-red hair, drawing you down.

In your book, in your looking glass, there is almost nothing about your "friends", the string of men without whose favour we could not have lived as we lived. Did you really think I was unaware of the tension that was always fizzing beneath your skin when you were lining up a new one? I would fizz, too, as I felt your need. Our house would crackle with the static of your yearning.

Sometimes I knew them, my friend's father, or the man in the deli or, once, one of the teachers in my school, but mostly it was someone you met at the restaurant. You never brought them home but did you really think I had no eyes or ears to notice how all your gestures inflated at the start of one of these affairs? How your clothes mutated, and your voice flew higher, your laughter loosened? How your pupils darkened and you began even to smell different?

I watched and waited, fearful each day when I was leaving for school, fearful each evening as you left for work. What if this guy did what the others had failed to do, won your love, swept you away? Would you bring me with you or leave me behind? In the end, it would collapse, suddenly and completely. Then we'd have our best times. I loved those post-lover weeks when you were sated, when you'd read to me and tell me stories, when you were back to me and we breathed ordinary air again. Until the next time.

Enter my dad. He was hopeless, I won't deny it. Even as a twelve-year-old bowled over by surprise that the father I'd had given up wishing for had risen from the dead, I could see he wasn't good enough for you. He wore denim jeans and jackets and a long grey ponytail. He was puffy and pale from drinking and too much time indoors. He rolled his own cigarettes with a sweet-smelling tobacco that once, when I smelled it twenty years later in another country, brought him right back. His shirt buttons strained over his stomach, he didn't wash often enough, his manners were bad.

But I *liked* him. He had a lovely smile, that said, sorry for getting it wrong. He taught me to play poker. He introduced me to old movies, actresses like Barbara Stanwyck and Katherine Hepburn. He told me I was going to be a "smasher", that the boys would soon be lining up. He was full of words like this, words I'd never heard, and the Irish lilt in his voice was much stronger than yours.

And yours was stronger when you were with him. The night after he came back, as we got the house ready together for dinner, I knew that, for once, your thoughts were the same as mine. We were going to be three now. You would have help and everything would be easier. He would feed us and mind us now, smooth out the jagged edges of your longing. Together, we'd become what we should be; a family, and you wouldn't want to go anywhere else any more.

I gave thanks as you lit incense — *nag champa*, the only one you allowed —and let your hair dry loose, walking barefoot around the house, in a white dress, humming. I gave thanks as we ate dinner together, the two of us listening to his stories, trying to laugh in the right place. And, after I'd been sent up to bed, I left my door open and gave thanks, all the way into a sleep lulled by the sing-song of your Irish voices, one deep, one light, in the darkness.

. . .

It was a hot, hot summer that year, the winds blowing down from the canyons, shrivelling the grass. The TV showed fires burning to the south, the hills seemed to smoulder and the wind smelt burnt. In the supermarket, a man fell over a trolley, looking at you. You often invited looks, only to stare back at the victim with eyes fixed and disapproving, until he'd grow awkward. That day, the man in his confusion stepped backwards, to be felled by a low trolley behind.

I didn't like you doing that with my father nearby. It was wrong now; there was no need. And then you said: "Men!" in the disdainful voice you kept for that word, and turned away with a sideward glance at my father, a glance that almost knocked me down, too. The brackets either side of your mouth included him in your scorn.

Dad was looking back at you, laughing at the other guy with one of his pulpy smiles. Oblivious. He didn't know what was ahead, not yet, but I did. There and then, I tipped out the hope chest I had started to build in my heart: a chest full of summer camp and a bicycle, new clothes and Thanksgiving dinner, and all the taken-for-granted things that girls with fathers knew. It hadn't even begun and already it was over. After twelve years as Mercy Mulcahy's daughter, I could spot a dead man walking.

Not long after that day in the supermarket, you brought me out onto the screen porch. It was dusk, the blue of the evening turning black, not wanting to leave, a lingering hope. I looked up at the sky — *twinkle twinkle* went the stars — while you told me he had left us again, but that this time he wouldn't be coming back. Up, up and away I looked, away from what you were saying but mostly from the look of judgment in your lime-green eyes that would wither any living thing.

PART VI
STARSHELL

an explosive projectile designed to burst in the air and light up an enemy's position.

PAULINE

CHRISTMAS EVE 1989

itness Statement of Mrs Pauline Whelan: 29.12.1989
As dictated to Garda Joe Cogley, Rathdrum Barracks, Co Wicklow.

Just after 1 p.m. on the day in question, (24.12.1989) I went to look in on Mr Martin Mulcahy as I had been doing for the past number of years, ever since his second wife died. More recently, I'd been hired by the Mulcahy family — namely Mrs Mercy Maria Creahy, née Mulcahy — to give nursing care five times a week. I visited at 11.45 a.m. approximately.

I found the victim in good form, considering his health status, though perhaps a little more tired than usual. He complained of a number of ailments, but that was not unusual, and he also had many other complaints, many of which were imaginary in nature, including that somebody was feeding him poisonous concoctions, trying to "do away with him". He accused his daughter, and also his granddaughter, Miss Maria Creahy, newly arrived from America, and also Mr Zach Coleman, lately of Santa Paola, California, who had been staying in the house.

He often made accusations of this nature and I did not, and still would not, take them seriously.

After seeing the patient, I spent some time with Mrs Creahy, as was customary during my visit. We had lunch and talked about many subjects, including the care of her patient. She was tired and under strain. Her father needed constant care and she was very devoted.

She told me that Mr Coleman had left some hours earlier and would not be returning.

I left the house at approximately 2 p.m. and went directly to my own home at Doolough Upper, Co Wicklow.

MERCY

1990

*T*o Doolough Stores today, to stock up on provisions. I
left the house early, while Mass was on, so the roads
and shop would be quiet. The village, which I visit as seldom as
possible, feels small and closed and sealed tight, much as it was
when I left, which was much as it had been for decades before,
but I did like the lanes that took me there. I searched for spring
in the hedgerows, found it in primroses and snowdrops.

Doolough Stores is one of those shops that used to be
common in the Irish countryside, stocking the most unlikely
items alongside milk and bread and newspapers. Should you
find yourself in need of a tea towel or fish bait or a gas stove,
Wellington boots or string or a plumbing U-bend, a tyre repair
kit or feather duster or drawer liners, you would find them in
McFadden's, among thousands of pounds' worth of other stock,
all snuggled together under a blanket of dust. My needs were
more everyday: milk, orange juice, bread, tomatoes, potatoes,
dried pasta, sugar.

As I was gathering them together in my basket, the bell
tinkled over the door. "Good morning, Pauline," boomed Mrs
McFadden. I turned and yes, it was my friend, her too-blonde
hair lighting up the dull morning.

"Hello, folks," she said, her big, open smile including Mrs McFadden, Deirdre on the other till, the two other customers and me, too. No peering, prodding eyes from Pauline. "Lovely day."

It was, in fact, another dreary grey morning but, to Pauline, every day was lovely. At the till, as I took my change, she came across to me. "Are you walking back?"

I nodded.

"Hang about for a minute or so," she said. Mrs McFadden was watching us, without seeming to. "I'll walk back that way with you."

"Sure," I spoke quietly. "I'll wait. Take your time."

"Lovely," she said, in a loud voice, deliberately, so the others would hear. "I'm finished for the day, so would you like to come back to the house for a cup of tea?"

"I'd love to," I said, equally firm. "Thank you."

I didn't just mean for the tea but for showing our Doolough audience that at least one person believed in me.

Pauline and I had gone to the National School up the road together, where I was the sergeant's daughter and she was one of the Breens, the seventh of eight girls and a brother, the boy that Mr and Mrs Breen had kept on trying for. "If Josephine had been a boy, they would have stopped then and I wouldn't exist," she told me one day in school, all solemn-eyed at the thought. Eleven of them lived — I can't imagine how — off a tiny patch of land and a couple of pigs that Mrs Breen, who also worked as a cleaner, used to fatten for the local bacon factory.

"I'll have coffee," I told her now that we were all grown up, sitting not in her mother's gleaming kitchen or my father's squalid one but hers, chatting about inconsequential things like her children being back at school and the end of the winter. Just like her mother, Pauline loved to clean. The oak table, on which I was now laying my cup and saucer, was as scrubbed as the hospital she'd worked in as a ward sister before becoming District Nurse. The oven and all its racks gleamed inside their glass. The undersides and insides of everything were as pristine as the sides that were up or out. Her movements around the kitchen, too, were just like her mother's. Almost sharp, bringing a little more energy than necessary to each action. *Tap-tap-tap*: the coffee into the container. Pat it down with the back of the spoon. Splash the water from jug to pot. Click the coffee canister shut. Flick the kettle switch.

Her efficiency made me feel tired and inadequate as the room filled with the aroma of percolating coffee and we enjoyed an idle, easy conversation. I pushed away the question I wanted to ask, to bask for a minute or two in these moments, to pretend that we were what we appeared to be, two ordinary friends having a coffee.

Before I came back to Doolough, it was Pauline who looked after my father, visiting him to monitor his vital signs and make sure he was getting the care he needed, a role she continued since I'd arrived. Only she knew how tough those months before he died were and she'd monitored me, too. "It doesn't have to be like this, you know," she'd said to me one day a week or two after my return, when I was complaining of being unable to get out for a walk or a drive. Looking after my father had brought me right back to when Star was a child, to how it felt to be constantly tied to another's needs. "I could organize some respite care."

I shook my head. "He wouldn't take it." And I would have felt guilty if he had. Perhaps if I loved him more, I would have been at ease with doing less.

Now I was going to further draw on her good nature. I reached across her kitchen table for a biscuit and said: "I was going to call you, Pauline. I wanted to let you know that my lawyer is going to ask if you would appear for the defence."

The cup stopped on the way up to her mouth. "Really?"

"You don't have to."

"I don't know what it means."

"To be a character witness. To say that you think me of good character and why. To talk about what you witnessed while you were nursing my father."

"Oh."

"Like I said, please don't feel that you have to. Think about it and you needn't even tell me what you decide." I pulled a business card from my jeans pocket. "All you need to do is let Mags — that's my lawyer — know."

I changed the subject then by telling her about a man from the Right to Die Society who had called me out of the blue, saying they wanted to take up my case. According to him, I could be a role model for the thousands of people who care for the terminally ill. Carers were the ones who knew best about what was right for their charges, he'd said. Certainly, they knew better than the courts, or than the doctors who wanted to keep the patients alive, against their own wishes.

"Oh, my heavens," said Pauline. "What did you say to him?"

"When I could get a word in edgeways, I told him I didn't do it."

"Do you ever wonder," she said, "whether those people aren't right?"

A prickling sensation crawled up my back. "Is that not against your religion, Pauline?"

"It is, I suppose. But when you see the things I've seen... It would be hard to say certain people would be wrong if they decided to go down that road."

I topped up my coffee from her pot, unable to meet her eye, uncertain what was being said. "I wouldn't let Dr Keane hear you saying that, Pauline," I said, in a jokey voice. "He might think you did it."

"Oh, he would never think that." She laughed.

She was right, he wouldn't. None of them would. Not of her. But they thought it of me.

MERCY

1980

*S*o we settled back into life without Brendan. After a while, for Star, it was as if the interlude had never happened and I was happy I'd done the right thing. I got a promotion and, as Dining Manager at Honolulu, I worked a split shift around lunch and dinner, which allowed me to get home to Star in between and save on the cost of childcare during term time. She and Ginnie, her school friend who lived next door but spent far more time round at ours, looked after each other while I wasn't there. They were on the rim of adolescence, sometimes high or low or beside themselves with feeling, but sometimes still childlike, cocooned in whatever thought-free moment they were in. I enjoyed spending time with them.

I'd overcome my scorn of managers now I was one myself and found that their life wasn't as easy as it looked when you were on the other side. The increased wage, now called a salary and paid monthly instead of weekly, still wasn't enough to support me and Star. Without the help of some friends, I couldn't have managed but our lives were more settled than they'd ever been. Empty and largely uneventful, and I can't say I didn't long for something more, but settled was what we both needed at that time.

One afternoon when I arrived home from work, a package was waiting for me in the hall. Star and Ginnie were in the kitchen, making flapjacks for the school fair. I immediately recognised the handwriting. My heart clenched, as if an ice hand had thrust itself inside and squeezed.

Star had come out to say Hi, and was staring at me staring at the letter. "What's the matter?" she asked.

"Nothing."

"Is it that mail?"

"It's nothing."

"Aren't you going to open it?"

"Maybe later."

"Who's it from, Mommy?"

"Honey, have you and Ginny finished your homework?"

I whooshed her back to the kitchen and took it up to my bedroom. It was a book: *Words Alone Are Certain Good*: *WB Yeats, Religion and the Occult*. By Zach Coleman. And inside, this inscription on the flyleaf: *For my first love, Mercy Mulcahy*. Below, a quote from Yeats, writing about Maud: "*I will not in grey hours revoke the gift I gave in hours of light*."

Zach forgave me? He was coming back to me? Could it be? The room started to spin. With him at my side, I would be able to cope with Star. With anything. With him, all would be well.

I sat on the bed and when the room came to a stop, opened the letter with shuddering fingers.

Dear Mercy,

I hope you are well. I can write that sentence now — and so I can write to you (don't worry, just this once).

I wanted to send you a copy of my book (enclosed). I teach English Lit. now at UCLA and this book is based on my MPhil. In it, I try to show how Yeats combined the myths of ancient, heroic Ireland with a belief in Western magic to create a new mythology and a new religion.

That all his writing, including the poetry, was devoted to disseminating his belief system.

Will you read it? I'd like to think you might try. Will you enjoy it? I doubt it. I'm not sure any layperson can even finish it — but I wanted you to have a copy because it was you who introduced me to WB.

Also, I wanted to say to you that I've come to think of him as being so like you, in the way that oppositions tormented him and at the same time spurred him on.

Perhaps none of this is of any interest to you. Then how about this? That famous line he used to describe Maud Gonne: "I had never thought to see in a living woman such great beauty." That's just how I felt all the time when I was with you, Mercy. Are you still beautiful? Still breaking hearts?

For a long time, I have to tell you, I did not wish you well. I wanted something to come along and hurt you like you hurt me. You killed our love, so how could I not hate you, even if, in the doing, you killed a part of yourself, too? But now I am grateful to you — and I wanted you to know that.

And to know how my work benefitted from knowing you. Whatever I might have studied, it would not have been Yeats's magic and poetry had I not known you — and now the influence of Eastern philosophy on his beliefs and poems is opening up another world to me. He, and all the writers you introduced me to, have led to a thousand good things for me, Mercy, so for that, too, I am grateful.

I hope it worked out for you with your ex but I suspect it didn't. Maybe that's what you really wanted — to be alone? I don't know. This isn't coming out right, I really didn't want to go over all that — otherwise I'd have written long ago. What I wanted was to tell you that I am, at last, over us. And now that I am, what I'm left with is gratitude.

I'm not providing an address, Mercy, and I won't write again. There's no going back for us, I do know that. I just wanted you to know that I'm at last able to hope that it worked out for you and your husband and your little girl, who I suppose is not so little any more.

Be happy.

Zach

Not so little any more, no.

I went back downstairs in with stockinged feet, looking for the shoes I'd discarded on the way up. In the hallway, I stopped in the doorway, where the girls couldn't see me, for the pleasure of listening to them, hoping it would settle me, the camaraderie of their voices around their joint effort, their little fuss over measuring sixteen ounces of oats, the homely clunk of their baking utensils.

Ginnie was complaining about her mother and Star was laughing at the story she was telling, the latest tale of her absent-mindedness. Then Star spoke about me. "When my mom gets cold," she said, and I could hear the roll of her eyes, "she puts a sweater on me."

I was so shocked, I gasped.

"Mom? Is that you?"

"Hi, girls," I called in a breezy voice that implied, I hope not too emphatically, that I had heard nothing, nothing at all. "Just getting my shoes. I'm heading out for a walk."

It *was* nothing, I see that now. Nothing but the sound of separation, of a child stepping away from a parent. What was more everyday and, for Star, more necessary? I could tell Dr Aintree she was cured, finally detached.

I took my shock up the hill, towards Turner's Point, the highest outcrop on the coast near us, two miles from our house. Some yards west of the public viewing point, I found a small pathway, concealed and overgrown. I followed its winding way through grasses and dry spiky shrubs to a flat shelf of rock jutting out over the sea, a natural viewing bench. The sky made a high domed ceiling of blue and, ninety feet below me, the swoosh of the waves closed over a small beach. And again. Over. Again.

I sat and cried a new outburst of tears. Each bout had its own root and rhythm and today, it wasn't silently weeping into my pillow, or swallowing and gagging while turned inwards towards a supermarket shelf, but out-loud sobbing in the outdoors, scraping off the scab over the wound of Zach's leaving it raw and bloody again.

The tears were also for Star, pride in her, self-pity for me. Relief and loneliness all erupting into each other.

The detachment in Star's voice was exactly what Dr Aintree and I had been working for. What I hadn't expected was that hearing it would be so hard. Soon, in a few years, she'd be gone. I was going to be all alone, with friends, yes, but no family. Why, why, *why* had I let Zach go? What, what, *what* might have been?

I saw it all again, the life together I'd unspooled so often in my imagination, the life I would have lived with him. The two of us, a couple, in love. Him a proper father to Star. Star well adjusted, settled by his quiet calming presence in our house.

After a long time at this, I left my rocky perch, promising myself I'd come back again, and often, and retraced my steps back along the little pathway. As I walked, I cultivated my regrets, brooding over the unfairness of life and why Zach should have saved us from me. I turned into a conveyance of thought, dead to the day around me, as he argued back in my head, insisting that my choices were my own.

Half way down, I caught myself, stopped in the middle of the path, remonstrating with him, telling him what he should have done. Pathetic. A crazy old biddy talking to herself: that's what I'd become. That was what lay ahead. Star was going to outgrow me and Mr Broken-Hearted had already outgrown me.

"I can't, I can't, I can't live without you," he'd wailed, in the car, clutching his hair, all but banging his head off the steering wheel. Yet, here he was, not just living on but thriving. *He* wasn't in floods of tears on a rock. He was happy. He had enough happy left over to be grateful.

Grateful. God, I could hate him for that.

MERCY

1981

*Y*ou will agree that my passage through life thus far has been chequered: an absent mother, a menacing father, a feckless husband, a dearly departed lover, a troubled child. It's not self-pity, I hope, to say any one of these events could be considered unfortunate, but I've come to know that everybody suffers, that if I didn't have all that big stuff to worry about, I would have fretted more over the small.

Zach's letter did me a favor, making me finally sign up for B.A. courses at UCSP, availing of a funding program especially designed for single mothers that gave me a fees waiver and a small stipend. I had been drawn in by the English and American Literature course but had begun a Women's Studies component that was turning out to be far more significant for me. My literature lectures always reminded me of my old Biology teacher, standing in front of the class having dissected a rabbit, pointing out the parts. I know we need critics, just like we need doctors, but the act of dissecting a poem or story makes me feel faint, like something is being violated.

Women's Studies was teaching me what I needed to know, awakening me to politics and economics as well as literature, bringing me to all of life and making sense of my part and place in it.

My classmates who were mostly, except for my friend Marsha, fifteen years younger than me enjoyed the camaraderie of UCSP's small campus, but I had to juggle classes and assignments with work. My small scholarship fund just wasn't enough. When I read back my diaries of that time, I wonder how I managed it all, oscillating between gratitude and grief, in a perpetual time and money squeeze but knowing I was lucky to be able to do what I was doing.

I have a list in front of me that I drew up for my course, part of the personal development work that our Director of Studies deemed essential, the personal being, in the slogan of the time, political. I was to enumerate all the things I had in my life that I liked and made me proud. I started off thinking it wasn't much to show for ten years in Santa Paola — a modest three-bedroomed house (two-bath); a six-year-old — but instead of my usual standpoint of pondering what I didn't have, and trying to work out how to get what I wanted, the task was to stop and appreciate what I already had.

So I listed them, all the things I was grateful for. The new Philips record player. My Remington typewriter. The rug on my easy chair in the hall, my favourite thing to wrap round myself. The hall itself, that I had turned into a kind of study, where I could do my course assignments in the fading light of the Western sun. The towers of books and records in rooms all over the house. My yard full of flowers. My vacations in Mexico, in a beachside hut lent by a friend. My friends. My daughter. The exercise worked, made me feel better. The people that most people took for granted — father, mother, husband, lover — might all have abandoned me, but Star and I were doing okay.

As I read the list now, I see it was an important moment for me, an important memory. Golden, actually. I look back on that short period in my life the way my father's generation used to look back on the pre-war years up before 1914, suffused in sepia tones that shade out so much. Far from being a tranquil, rosy time, Edwardian Britain and Ireland boiled; the army mutinied; labor unions learned the power of the strike and suffragettes burned and starved and threw themselves under racehorses. You'd never know any of that to listen to the harker-backers writing about the life they remembered before The War came in and ruined their idyllic days of tea and roses on the lawn.

I refused to hark back. I also feared to look too far forward. Maybe that's why the time now seems so golden. I kept myself marooned in the safety of the present.

Just the smallest while later, I would be remembering with wonder that the me who sat so tentatively dispensing her pride on the things she loved, she would seem so poignant, all unknowing of what lay just ahead, waiting in ambush.

Star's Adolescence.

Oh, yes, capital A.

It arrived sudden and complete, like a light switch turned off. One day, Star and I were on the same side, tackling her childhood problems together; the next, I was fumbling about, unable to help. Worse, I had somehow, suddenly, became the enemy.

Photographs of Star as a young girl always show her with a golden tan, dressed in whites and blues and pinks. Once we get to her teens, it's as if the pictures have reverted to the days of black-and-white photographs. She stopped growing at fourteen and, during that year, a tall, skinny, golden-haired child turned short, as her school-mates passed her out. She began to put on weight and dyed her hair the blackest possible shade of black, cut and gelled it so it stood up straight from the crown, except for bangs that were so low I wouldn't have been able to see her eyes, if it weren't for the kohl rim around them.

She started wearing what was to effectively become her uniform: black lycra T-shirts with a wide elasticated belt pulled tight so her flesh bulged above and below, bulges that grew and shrank, multiplied and melted, depending on what stage she was on with her latest diet. A skirt not much wider than the belt. Chunky boots and pantyhose in — what else? — black. Clothes that simultaneously called for, and shunned, attention. A body that wanted to claim space and also to disappear.

And beneath, a devouring drive that I called "It". It wanted to eat but she didn't want to eat but it wanted to eat but she didn't want to eat but it wanted to eat but she didn't want to eat but it... The fatter she got, the more comfort she needed, and so the more she gave in to what she didn't want to do and the more she loathed herself for not controlling It. At times I felt it would give her no rest until she was entirely smothered, but much of the time, I too stifled my knowing, told myself it was classic teenager stuff — bad crowd, drinking, smoking, overeating — and I was being the classic worry-mom.

Hadn't I done all this myself in my own way, learned and grown from it? Wasn't this sort of self-fracturing essential for a child to crack open and mutate into a functioning adult? Hadn't we already come through tough stuff? If I stayed vigilant in the wings, doling her enough love and care and attention of the right kind, she'd be okay. Sooner or later, she'd be back in a shape that fitted us.

Underneath, I was frightened. Food, the staff of life, had become a dangerous substance for Star. To see her standing at the kitchen counter — throwing down four or five slices of buttered bread while waiting for the toaster to pop — was frightening. To find her picking something out of the trashcan that she had earlier tossed away in self-disgust was frightening. To see a suitcase crammed full of empty biscuit wrappers and potato-chip packets felt like finding an empty syringe.

And when she was out with her friends, were there drugs, too? Food was the home habit, but out of the house, she was vacuuming up great quantities of cigarettes and alcohol and, I suspected, speed or worse. In the sixties, drugs had been about exploring our psyches and our perceptions. For Star and her friends, it was the opposite: they just wanted to get "out of their minds".

At night, I'd lie in bed and hear her stumble in, the unsteady fall of her feet just like her father's.

By this time, she was bringing only one friend home. Only Ginnie was willing to abide by my house rules of no drugs, no alcohol. She and Star were linked by music, being two members of a four-girl band called Vixen. Ginnie's stage name was Venom and she wanted Star to take one too.

"Something anarchic, something frenzied, girl, instead of that hippie-dippie handle."

Star refused, saying two names were enough for anyone.

Ginnie — Venom — was another big girl. Her approach to people was to find a theme and keep a running riff on it. With me, it was scoffing at my generation's music. Pleased to be communicating at any level with somebody who was important to Star, I held up my side.

"You kids are still listening to our songs," I'd say. "Can't see that happening with any of your lot."

"Wait and see, Mrs M. It's only the best from any era that lasts."

"So who will last, Ginnie … sorry, Venom. 'The Cloquettes?' Can't see it."

"Yeah, I've heard that when you get to a certain age, you don't see too good."

Star snorted.

"All I'm hearing in your music, Venom, is just the same note, over and over," I said. "Anger, anger, anger."

"Anger is *the* energy, Mrs M. It's the only sound that makes the complacent bastards sit up and listen."

"Yeah, Mom." Star curled her blackened lip. "Don't talk about things you don't understand. Go listen to some" — she looked at Venom and they simultaneously spat out their grossest insult — "disco!"

Then they collapsed into giggles at the line they'd obviously prepared to use against me. Not only was I held responsible for the musical and political shortcomings of my own generation, but also those that were following, crumbling our sixties' idealism into glitter-dust. Our generation had done its best to change the world — a lot more than Star and Venom's seemed set to do — but we didn't understand what we were up against in a world that didn't want to change.

We thought we were on an inexorable move forward; now we were finding out that action brings on an opposite reaction. Tit for tat, ebb and flow, lash and backlash...

By that time, my mind was knotted with such thoughts. A great wave was breaking across North America and it was heady: the civil rights movement had been quickly followed by women's liberation, its bastard child. Unplanned and unwanted by its parent, it was sweeping into kitchens and schools and community halls, finding me and women like me, and giving us what we had never had: the understanding that what felt like private, individual problems were, in fact, socially constructed and widely experienced. And — most important — malleable. We could change them.

We could change ourselves and in so doing, change things for others.

This reading was handing me a whole new way of looking at my life, spinning connections I was only beginning to grasp. As I read and worked on my Women's Studies assignments, a fuzziness I had always carried about the workings of the world was clearing for me. I saw how my experiences — of sex, of work, of money — had been determined by an invisible weave of societal beliefs. I saw how these beliefs had been as binding of me as any law of the land. I saw the potential for my own transformation if I could unpick them. I saw the potential for social transformation in understanding that what was true of me was true for many, if the many could be brought to the same understanding.

But now here was my daughter and her friend — two intelligent, educated and anti-establishment young women — belittling all that, writing us out of the record already, while we were still here.

"Do you honestly think they didn't listen to us in the sixties? We had far more political impact than you guys are having."

"Political impact!" Star sneered. She stuck two fingers in her mouth and made a vomiting gesture.

"Yeah, Mrs M," said Ginnie. "Do you really think you can win a fight against anyone, especially the establishment, with peace and lurve?"

"Ah, girls," I said. "You can't win anything worth having without them."

When Star and I were alone together, of course I tried to help her.

"Darling, should you really be doing..."

"I don't think you really need to..."

"Can't you just..."

"You always..."

I organized a nutritionist. A gym. A personal trainer. Each time she got slim, though never as slim as she was the time before. Then, after a while, she got fat again. Fatter than before, fatter than ever. Naturally, I turned to my Women's Studies course for answers.

I read books that told me food was a language, and fat a metaphor, a message to be interpreted: the desire for protection, maybe. The desire to remain unseen, the desire to rebel against imprisoning social ideals.

I read books that urged girls and women to stop dieting and instead seek to understand the patriarchal culture that wanted them thin.

I read books that explained, graphically and eloquently, how the body has been used as a form of social control through the ages and how a mature economy can only achieve growth by making us feel abject, hungry and isolated from ourselves and each other. Making us hate ourselves from the inside out ensures we will overspend, over-consume and over-indulge…

I came to hate how everything gets junked in America: the food processed and poisoned with sugar and fat; the clothes cheapened; the TV dumbed down; the sex pornified. No matter how much we're given, we never feel sated, we're always craving. They've got us addicted to addiction.

All of this drew Star's complete scorn. "It's a candy bar, Mom, not the disintegration of life as we know it."

I tried not to preach; tried to appreciate that it had taken me thirty-three years of living to be ready to hear this stuff but all the understanding I could muster didn't stop my eyeballs from wanting to roll whenever I saw her reach for another biscuit, didn't stop my foot from itching to kick the refrigerator closed when she opened it, didn't stop my hand from wanting to reach across the table and close itself across her insatiable mouth.

"Whatever happened to 'mother knows best'?" I said one day to Marsha Blinche, a new friend and the most articulate women in my class.

"Forget that. It's 'A mother's place is in the wrong' now."

I laughed.

"It's a pity you've only one kid. If you had more, you could point to her brothers or sisters and say, 'Look at them, they turned out fine, it must be you'."

"How many do you have?"

"Three. Grown up now."

"Three! I couldn't do adolescence twice never mind three times."

"Oh, you can set one against the other." She grinned.

Marsha was another single mom who had come in on the same scholarship programme as me but her children — Dan,

Larry and Kirsty — were all in their twenties, so now she was on what she called "me time". In truth, Marsha was one of those people who had time for everyone and everything, who fit in so much yet never seem hurried. She adopted all the younger women in our class, and me, doling out care and attention and advice — and delicious, homemade cake. She proofread my dissertation before I submitted it and also the revised version that I turned into *A Child Dancing* before I submitted it to journals, seeking publication.

"So well written," she'd told the others in the class, until I squirmed in my chair. I was embarrassed but it also warmed me, I admit it, to have this intelligent woman pressing my vanity buttons. I had never had a true female friend before, something I'd put down to not having enough time but here I was, busier than ever with home and work and writing and essays and a dissertation, still able to meet Marsha for coffee, or have her over for dinner.

I wasn't somebody who blurted in the Californian way but nobody could be with Marsha for even a cup of coffee without spilling a secret or two. A few months into that summer after we'd completed our first exams, I found myself at her kitchen table one morning, hearing her story of having been raped by an uncle when she was seven and then — astonished at the sound of my own voice in my ears — I told her some stuff about my father.

She listened, one ear angled towards me, forehead bobbing in encouragement, eyes on my face the entire time. I cried familiar hot tears of shame and anger and she took my hand and we talked it all through, her experience and mine, knowing from what we had learned on our course that all over America, all over the world, women in pairs and groups were having similar conversations. Feminists, pulling back the silence, the rug of what we called patriarchy, to reveal the slime beneath.

As for Star and me, we were back with Dr Aintree, who said

she could no longer talk to me now Star was a teenager. What happened in their sessions would have to be confidential.

If I wanted to know anything, it would be up to Star to tell. Surprise, surprise, she didn't.

If she wanted to attend, it would be up to Star to keep going. Surprise, surprise, she gave up.

At the beginning, each outbreak of aggression or blame, each rebuff or denial, each stupid mistake, felt like an isolated incident. We'd have a period of peace when I would think we were getting some connection again, but realize that it was only something she wanted, something practical or financial, that was drawing her back. Once I'd given or refused it, along would come the next eruption, this time a little more intense and the dip in our relationship left a little lower than before, until we found ourselves permanently down there, without the energy for any more argument. So far down, you give up imagining how you might rise again.

Poetry helped. I watched television, that was good for passing the time and I read novels, sometimes poor ones that passed time a little better, but also stories that were more than that. The Brontës for passion. George Eliot for intellectual fervor. Jane Austen for wit. Toni Morrison for compassion. Henry James and Alice Walker for their, each very different, outsider's eye. But stories took time to digest. When I needed a quick hit of consolation, I turned to poems. The people whose words supported me through all that was to come were John Keats, William Blake, Elizabeth Barrett Browning, Robert Frost, Rainer Maria Rilke, Emily Dickinson, William Wordsworth, Adrienne Rich, Percy Shelley, Eavan Boland and, most of all, WB Yeats.

I lay out their names, a list you'll find in any canon, nothing original or pioneering about it. As I freely tell all here, in the private whisper of mind to mind that is a book, so I want to acknowledge in writing how they helped me. How they were, simultaneously, the roof on my house and the gap in my fence and the bed I lay down on when I didn't know where to go or how to stay.

"Have you ever considered," Marsha asks, "that there might be more?"

Marsha and I were enjoying a coffee between classes.

"More?"

"Locked away? Repressed? I had only the vaguest memories of what my uncle did to me until I went into therapy."

She invited me to go on what she called a rebirthing weekend, a two-day session that used breathing techniques to bring about the recall of lost memories and transformation. "You'll remember something you've forgotten, guaranteed. It might be your birth, or it could be some other grief or trauma from way back when."

"Marsha. I'm Irish. A feed of booze and a two-day hangover: that's our idea of therapy."

"You don't even drink," she said.

"You know what I mean. I'd rather let sleeping dogs lie."

"Even if they're yowling inside?"

"Is that what you think?"

"You tell me," she said, and looked at me too hard over the rim of her coffee cup.

A saw-toothed silence sliced down.

""Hon," she said, very softly. "If you want more pain, that's what you'll get."

Over the weeks that followed, I found myself thinking again and again about the word she'd used: *Rebirth*. The idea appealed but the procedure Marsha described made me nervous. She offered to come with me, to be the partner that every participant had to have during the session, to look out for them.

"Like a second in a duel," I said.

"Not a bad metaphor. It *is* like a duel, the better part of you will be slaying a weaker part."

"With breathing!" I laughed.

According to Marsha, she had been a mess before this rebirthing. Chronic pain in her lower back. Disappointed with Danny, her boy, and generally with the hand life had dealt her, negativity eating her up. This description of herself bore no resemblance to the woman I knew and admired. Negative was the last word you'd use for Marsha, whose slightly protruding teeth were always rushing towards a smile and when they did, every part of her was gathered into that beam of white, eager teeth, brilliant as a photographer's flash.

She was the most engaged person I knew, in her work as a classroom assistant; in her voluntary activities for the hospice that had eased her mother's death; in her exercise routine, swimming and yoga, both daily; in the projects she was forever taking on for the needy, fundraising or second-hand clothes collecting or event-organising. All this, not to mention the degree she was cruising through, and yet, somehow, when she was with you Marsha was, always, totally with you, giving you full attention and when alone, apparently complete. Not fretting over her children, not restless for other places or experiences, not mourning lost love.

I went to her rebirthing weekend not for the reason I told her — that she'd give me no peace if I didn't; I knew if I genuinely asked her to back off, she would — but because I wanted something of what she had managed to find for herself.

The procedure was to sign in on Friday morning at The Rebirth Center and stay until Sunday evening, accommodation and meals included. Our facilitator was a woman called Frankie in a pink tracksuit and we were sixteen women and two men in loose, comfortable clothing, each with a partner, all of us believing we had been mistreated — the word to use was "abused" — as children.

Marsha sat on the beanbag as I took off my shoes and lay

down beside her on the mattress. Frankie ordered us to close our eyes and a soft male voice came across the sound system telling us to relax, to breathe softly. Some new-age music started up, Celtic-style pipes.

"Breathe as though your breath is liquid," the voice said, smooth as olive oil itself. "Let your breath make a noise in your throat as you breathe in and out."

I did as he said. Now that I was here, I would do whatever I was told to do. The lights were slowly dimmed, then extinguished to full darkness that deepened even more as I continued to breathe in this very deliberate way. Sensations of numbness, a tingling rose in my limbs and face. The music changed. A drum sound entered and the beat picked up.

"Now breathe fast," ordered a voice, female this time. Frankie? I didn't think so. "Breathe as though your life depends on it, getting as many breaths inside you as fast as you can."

The drum sound became louder. Lights flashed on and off and the heavy drums rose another few decibels and now wild music was pouring in on top of the relentless beat. Distress came welling up in me, brimming over, drowning my heart. I heard a prolonged shriek.

Now all sorts of cries and moans were thickening in the room, adding another layer to the strange music. I knew Marsha was there beside me, that I could ask for her hand, or for a drink of water, or to help me get up and leave — Frankie had said we could do that any time — but I'd moved into a different world, with new and urgent rules that made hand-holding or water or escape irrelevant. I had to keep breathing hard and fast, breathing like a madwoman, had to … wanted to… I felt the distress inside shape itself into a loud scream. This time, definitely me.

Time warped, folded over. At one point I broke to ask for a tissue with which I dried my eyes and into which I blew my nose, then matter-of-factly I returned to the breathing, in and out, in and out and the breath in time pushed a memory up out of my center. I had come here expecting my father, but what I got was my mother. Specifically, her funeral. Her body in its coffin in our front room. The room hot, so hot, and me, my face boiling red from being closed in for too long. A fly was crawling up her face from her lip towards one of her eyes, the one that was not quite closed, that had a small opening at the inner corner.

I couldn't take my own eyes away — if I did, the fly was going to crawl all the way there, his skinny legs were going to touch the innards of her eye. The thought made me panicky, but around me, everyone saying how well she looked, laid out in her Sunday-best suit and high heels.

"She's dead, for God's sake," I wanted to shout at them. "Why are you talking about how she looks?" But I couldn't have said or thought such a thing then. I was only three when she died.

Now I'm at another funeral, much later. I am a teenager. I have taken off my new and scratchy jacket. As I pass my father on the way to the food table, he catches hold of my arm.

"She's as flighty as a feather, this one," he says to his brother, Uncle Benny, sitting beside him.

"I can see that," the uncle replies. "What's your name?" he asks me.

"Mercy."

He laughs, says to Daddy: "It was a blue mercy, all right, when you married the mother."

Daddy pulls me down onto his knee.

"What's this?" he says, lifting my arm. He points to the down forming in my armpit, starts to laugh. Uncle Benny laughs, too, loud and false: *ho ho ho*. I spring from my father's grasp and run off, with their laughter chasing after me.

I found myself screaming: "I cannot do this, I cannot do this, I cannot do this." The ache in my chest hardens and swells, a boulder in danger of bursting. I am clutching my rib cage. Marsha, growing worried, calls Frankie over to check, but I'm fine, apparently. I'm aware of these events but it's as if they are happening behind gauze. I'm in a different pleat of time.

Next day, after the deepest night's sleep ever, we sat in a circle in a sun-lit room and wrote down the memories that the process had "resurrected" and then shared them with each other. Nobody — including me — got to the end of their story without crying. I hated it, this crying in a room full of strangers, but I had given myself over to what was happening. It was bigger than me; I didn't understand any of it.

Did I really remember my mother's funeral when I was only three? Why did I feel responsible for her death? Why was I mixing up that day and the other funeral? I hadn't known what Uncle Benny meant by a blue mercy, and I'd looked it up later in my small school dictionary and, when I didn't find it there, in the big blue book at the library, The Oxford English Dictionary.

Frankie wasn't giving us time for introspection. Once everybody had spoken, she launched into a long lecture with slides and graphs. It was not our experiences that had damaged us, this explained, but our repression of the appropriate response to those experiences. When suppressed, anger or sorrow causes toxic amounts of endogenous neuro-chemicals to accumulate in the brain.

On the talk went on, adding science talk and psychological proofs, culminating in Frankie handing each of us a tennis racket with which we were going to do an "anger detox". Holding the most painful part of the memory in our heads, we were to take our tennis rackets and beat our anger out onto the beanbags.

Any questions?

"What if we don't feel any anger?" I asked.

"Honey, I saw you and your tears. You are angry, believe me."

"Am I?"

"Anybody here think Mercy isn't angry?"

Everybody looked awkward, stared at the ground.

"What happened to you yesterday, Mercy, didn't come from nowhere. It came from deep inside you, a part of you that knows more than the surface you. So why don't you ditch the tears and give in to a good old tantrum instead?"

We were each assigned a beanbag. Frankie and her assistants came up behind us, encouraging us to beat harder and faster. Then we were sent home with a list of suggested activities to do whenever we felt anger rising.

I have that list still. *Select one of the following*, it says. *Pound on a bed with your fists and yell. (Use a tennis racket to spare your fists if you prefer).*

Take a pair of jeans, hold it by the ankles, and whack the hell out of your bed.

Tear up a phone book. Yell while you tear. (Put on work gloves to avoid paper cuts.)

Yell, scream or shriek into a pillow in the closet.

Pound on the wall, or hit a punching bag. (Put on heavy gloves.)

Throw things at the wall. (Not random things: safe objects, like pillows.)

Take pages out of a magazine, tear them in half, and throw them around the room.

Do a dance of anger.

Stomp your feet when you walk.

Kick a rock down the street.

NOTE: The use of knives or dangerous weapons is to be avoided.

One spring morning, Star made a pronouncement over breakfast, her official breakfast, the cereal and fruit she shared with me before moving to a day of resisting, then succumbing to, doughnuts or pastries or muffins or rolls or pancakes or blinis before moving on to potato chips or corn chips or fries or sweets or chocolates or … or … or…

"You know, Mom," she declared, after a week of being

particularly obnoxious, "we need each other. We're the only family we've got."

"Is this Ginnie's latest theory?" I asked.

Ginnie, Venom, had declared she wanted to be a psychologist when she grew up. She and Star made an odd couple, Star in her outsize black, bovver-booted outfits and piercings, Ginnie half a foot higher, turned in towards her, talking. Always talking. Venom had opinions on everything and was becoming particularly wide-ranging on the subject of my shortcomings.

She had developed a nasty streak, become a cynic and was, like all cynics, hurting hard and taking it out on those closest to her. Venom was supremely good at pretending to be on Star's side while actually undermining her. A benevolent controller, Marsha called her.

"I thought you'd approve," Star said. "You would if it was anyone else who said it."

Perhaps I'd have been more enthusiastic if I hadn't felt that next week she'd be quoting her saying the opposite.

"It makes sense," she said, shovelling a heaped spoonful of cereal into her voracious mouth. "With no aunts, or uncles or grandparents, no other family, is it any wonder that we're too much for each other? After all we…"

She spoke on but I wasn't listening. I was stuck on those two words: *each other*. Each other? What had I done to you, Star, that weighed, even in the smallest way, against your insults and aggressions and rejections? Made your food? Washed your laundry? Paid for your education and the extra-curriculars that you decided to skip, often as not? Tried to protect you from a father who was never going to do anything but hurt you?

Each other: that stuck in me, irksome and impossible to leave alone, like a sliver of food between the teeth that the tongue can't shift. I thought I'd welcome her saying such a thing. Instead, I found myself getting up and going over to the sink to rinse my bowl so I could turn my back to it. I wanted to deal her back a slight, an insult, an act of disrespect, just one in return for the countless numbers I'd swallowed.

I thought of doing one of her favourite tricks, covering my ears and singing *la-la-la* so I couldn't hear what she was saying. I thought of — somehow I know this would be the worst — ignoring her, changing the subject, pretending I didn't understand that this was her big effort.

You'd want to be a saint, an outright saint, to resist.

How had it come to this, thinking such twisted thoughts about my own daughter? Plagued by a tension that had become a living component of my body, a perpetual acid that was corroding what was left of the fragile ropes that held us in place. Whenever we got to this point in our communications, I always experienced Star's size, and the ugly spikes of her black hair, as an attack. Her attempt to be as different from me as possible. It panicked me to think I could no longer trust myself to do the right thing. To be … not a saint. Let's face it, you didn't have to be a saint, just an ordinary tongue-holding, time-biding mother.

That day I withheld only by staring out the window and not letting her words in. Bits filtered through: that I needed to back off and let her be who she was, stop fretting and nagging, give her space. That, again, we were too much for each other because we had no other family.

I let her speak on and on and let her finish and, when she was done, I said, "Okay, honey. Fair enough. I'll think about what you've said."

But that was wrong, too.

"Is that it? Is that all you're going to say?"

The items on my counter-list, all the things I felt she did wrong, banked up behind my teeth, banging to get out. But where would they take us? Only down a pathway we'd already worn away: me trying to help her see how she created her own misery. She was right, something needed to change.

That's when I, not knowing what I was doing in choosing

this less-traveled road, not knowing all the difference it would make, the terrible places it would take us, turned round to her.

"Star, if I tell you something will you promise not to be mad?"

"Go on."

"No, you have to promise."

"I promise."

"Really. Will you promise to look on the positive aspects, like Dr Aintree said?"

I'd been thinking a lot about Ireland. A version of my thesis — *A Child Dancing: Yeats's Love Poetry To Iseult Gonne* — had been accepted by a small publisher in Dublin, for inclusion in a book of essays about overlooked women in Irish literary history.

Since hearing this news, I'd got it into my head that Yeats might be leading me back. Back to the home I'd escaped from as a teenager on the back of a Honda 100. Back to my father, my mother, the mess of my origins. That I was going to have to sort all that out if I was ever to feel safe in this world. I'd learned that freedom, which I'd always valued so highly, could be yours only from a place of safety.

London. Paris. Dublin. Just the names were enough to send a shiver of excitement through me. And Star saying that, about not having any family, felt like another sign pointing me towards Europe.

Now that I was finishing my women's studies course, I could just about manage to make it happen. It would mean working a double-shift twice a week, taking on any other overtime that was going, then seeing if I could wangle three weeks off.

"Mom, for God's sake, tell me. You're scaring me."

"We do have other family. You have a grandfather. He's in Ireland. I'll take you to see him if you want."

Five months later, under the false, bright brilliance of San Francisco Airport, I'm watching Star heft her bulk down the long corridor towards a transatlantic flight to Dublin. Trying not to notice her too loud breathing. Averting my eyes from the waddle holding up the weight of her backpack.

I thought I was intimately, overly, sensitive to every pound of her flesh, but here, under the relentless lights, her fat feels like an onslaught. The back of her head banked from ears to neck with flesh, held taut as far as the chin by the skin of her skull but from there settling in rings. Her breasts now an indiscriminate pillow of flesh, captured but not contained by her bra, overlaying duvets of flesh above and beneath. Each of her thighs now the size of my waist.

You thought an end point had been reached, it seemed to scream. Hah, were you ever wrong! This will go on and on! This will get worse and worse!

What was wrong with me? All I could see was her fat, her walking her fat walk down the airport corridor, feet splayed. Toting her fat suitcase onto the check-in platform, perspiration breaking on her forehead. Most fat people wear fat clothes — loose, baggy, indiscriminate — but not Star. Tight layers that ignored her bulges were her style. From the knees down, she was encased in lace-up boots, the spiky, metal-studded kind. I understood the intention: is there anything more poignant than fat feet in high heels, bulging through their straps?

We boarded the plane and loaded our carry-on cases in the bins above our heads and I saw our air stewardess eye Star's hips with anxiety. I managed to show nothing of my anxiety or relief as she managed to squeeze herself down between the armrests. We fastened our seat belts.

I hadn't told her anything about my father, of my fervent hope that he was going to have mellowed with the years, become what Yeats once called "a comfortable kind of old scarecrow". I would tell her some of it, as little as possible, now. Didn't kids almost always like their grandparents? Even when — maybe especially when — the parents didn't?

We leaned back in our seats, silent, as we waited for take-off.

PART VII
STARCROSSED

(of a person or a plan) *thwarted by bad luck.*

MERCY

DOOLOUGH 1982

I'm drifting upwards, through murky lake water, curving like a fish through the loops of previous risings. Strands undulating as I circle through them, round and up, up and round. I'm holding my breath until I break the surface. My eyes open. I am awake.

Awake in Doolough, for the first time in eighteen years. Light leaks in at the edges of the curtains, but early light by the look of it. No more than five or six a.m., I reckon, pulling my wrist out from under the covers to check. Yes, 5.42 and the sun is up already. The Irish summer night, lengthening now that it's August, but still short.

I hoist myself off my pillow to look around. It's all so familiar and why not? I woke in this room for sixteen years of my life, and little has changed. The wooden ceiling and rafters, the big mahogany wardrobe and dressing table stand out, sharp and new, such ordinary furniture by vibrating with significance and strangeness. This must be how it feels when the bandages are removed after a cataract operation, when you see again as if for the first time, but also remember what you used to look at before. Both at once.

The air is as familiar as the room: a chill in the atmosphere that I now know is always there in Ireland, indoors and out, summer and winter. Doolough Lake. The liquid of the lake is in the air, and so is the clay of the mountains, the breath of the woodland, and the unfeasible green of the grass.

I slide from the bed and pad, barefoot, across the chilly floor to pick up yesterday's clothes. Suddenly, I cannot wait to be gone, to grab a slice of this early damp morning and make it mine. A quick brush of my teeth, then I look in on Star. I want out, but I don't want her to feel abandoned, not on our first morning. I stand over her in the dim light, listening to her breathing. Deep and even and likely to stay that way for hours. I scribble a note, leave it beside her head on the pillow. Then I tiptoe down the stairs and out the back door, down the pathway through the trees, towards the lake.

Doolough Mountain oversees my path and the ring of mountains that surround it. Ballinedin, Cloughernagh, Carrrigasleggaun, Slievemaan, Lugnaquilla. Old friends: I never let myself miss them in California, until now that I see them here, blue hills whose distance seems to sigh the presence of bigger, more mysterious matters than anything I might care about.

This morning, I feel it again, the comfort they used to give me in childhood. I become aware of the birdsong and the sound of it makes me skip along the wood-path into a tunnel of trees. It's spongy underfoot and everything is soaked. I pick a sprig of pine and a shower of dew, or yesterday's rain, spatters my head and shoulders, making me laugh. The lake when I reach it is impassive, its quiet water lapping in the old way. Flitters of the dream I was dreaming come back to me. The fish. The feeling of being fished.

My father used to bring me down here in summer sometimes. Fly fishing, of course, the only kind that warranted the name in his book. Coarse fishing was for boot-boys; any "eejit" could do it. Fly fishing took skill because a fly weighs almost nothing, so how do you propel it twenty or thirty feet into a lake? He showed me how: a complicated combination of the weight of the line, the flexibility of the rod and the casting action that send the line into a perfect horizontal "U" behind your back, then forward onto the water.

"The whole thing is in that pause between back" — he cast the line behind — "and forward. The rod flexes behind — see? — and gathers the energy. Like that. Here, you try."

I tried. I failed.

"Stop snapping at it like a fairy wand," he said, but not crossly. Down here he was a different Daddy. He showed me how to hold my wrist unnaturally straight. He showed me a variety of flies. He showed me how to tie knots. He showed me how to "play" a fish. Then he showed me how to do it.

He caught a trout. It jerked and bounced at the end of the line. I had never seen an animal fighting for its life before. As it was unhooked and priested on my behalf, I fought the impulse to cry and, as soon as I got back home, I went up to my room and sobbed for the fish. Even then, I think I knew that I was also sobbing for me, for my mother and, yes, even for my father.

Concentrating on those square feet of water brought my father an ease he never had anywhere else. You don't succeed at fishing until you calm down and accept what weather and water offer. You are in the hands of the unknown, of things that you can't see. But even down here at the lake, he was still himself.

As he was yesterday, on our return to Doolough. We were shown in by Rose, his new wife while he stood at the fireplace, in the very place he used to stand eighteen years ago, waiting with the same bald, blotched head, same thick neck, same trousers pulled high over his paunch by metal-clipped braces, same hefty posterior warming itself by the fire, no care for how he blocked the heat. I had expected the serge navy trousers of his policeman's uniform, the cap on the mantelpiece beside him, medallion shining but, of course, he was long retired by now, dressed in civilian garb.

The furniture and décor were just what I had left behind, only a few accessories and the new bulky television in the corner were different. And, of course, the new wife. She was an O'Leary from Carrawood and I found out afterwards that he had advertised for her in the local paper. *Widower, Garda Sergeant, own house and land, seeks wife.* And it was she, I knew, who would have added the few bits of color and comfort that had found their way in. She welcomed us in: gladiators into the den.

My father looked up from stuffing tobacco into his pipe, rested his eyes on me for a second, then moved them across to Star, to give her the full treatment, from crown to feet and back up again, with eyes that hadn't blunted with age. "Well, well, well," was what he said. "Look what the cat dragged in."

The trees draw in around me as I shiver. The sky is growing lighter as the sun climbs up from behind the hills. The lake is a mirror this morning, allowing the mountain to admire itself. So very quiet, as if it was waiting for me all this time, and now it is hushed and attentive. I sit on a log and listen to its lap-lap-lap, as I did when I was a child. I breathe deep, sucking in air, as if I could suck its peace in through my pores. The lake is blameless.

Such a thing for him to say. Oh, what had I done? How could I have forgotten what it took to leave and lock that door on him.

His refrains from the long length of my childhood come colliding towards me, down the tunnel of time.

How would you like to be packed off to the orphanage?

Oh no, that wouldn't suit you, no, because ones like you always know what side their bread is buttered.

The nuns wouldn't put up with your carry-on for a minute, they wouldn't be long putting manners on you.

And now: *Look what the cat dragged in.*

"Would you listen to him?" Rose had cut in, all bustle and distraction. "And he was so looking forward to you coming."

"It's good to see you, Daddy," I said, anxious like Rose to move us off the insult. "You look well."

He looked the same. Exactly the same. How could that be, eighteen years on?

He didn't answer me.

Rose said: "Come in girls, come in now. You must be dying for a cup of tea."

Tea: one shilling and six. Butter: two shillings. Eggs: one and eight. Sausages...

"Could I have coffee?" Star said.

Rose's hand fluttered to her chest. "Coffee. Oh, dear. Do we have coffee? Do you know, I don't think we do."

"Then tea will be fine," I said.

"No, no, let me check. There might be a jar at the back of the press."

"Really, there's no need..."

"But, Mom," Star whispered, as Rose disappeared and my father bent to put coal on the fire so he wouldn't have to talk to us. "You know I don't drink tea."

"Try," I hissed back.

Rose seemed kind, very like what I imagine my mother to have been. He must have had a nose for that kind of woman, the ones who would take what he doled out. The sin of my leaving was still rigid in him, hard and hot as the fire-iron he'd started to clatter round the grate. Somebody was going to suffer, it was only a matter of time. I feared for Star, who had no idea what it was like to be treated so. What had I done, bringing her here?

"I'm awful sorry now about that," said Rose, coming back in. "I never thought of coffee. We don't take it at all. Will you have a glass of minerals ... em ... Star? I got some in especially for yourself."

"Soda," I explained to Star. "That would be lovely," I said, smiling at Rose.

Star folded her arms, stretched out her legs and yawned, making me tense. He wouldn't like that. In his presence, young people sat up straight. Rose returned and we sat to tea, the two of us upholding most of the talk. The length of the journey. The days Star and I had spent in London. The size of London and the busyness of it and how did anybody manage to live there at all. How you couldn't beat a musical for a good night out. The journey from Dublin Airport. The beauty of Wicklow.

A few times, we tripped into silence, the clink of spoons and tap of cup onto saucer growing loud in the room, but we made it safe to the far side of tea. Daddy — still silent — went up the fields and Rose saw us upstairs.

"My old room," I said, as she led us in.

"Your Daddy thought that would be nice for you," Rose said, but I knew it was she who had had the thought.

Same windows looking out on the front drive outside. Same dressing table. Same bed. Could it actually be the same bedspread? The only thing that had changed was that there were now two big mahogany wardrobes in the room, not one.

"And Star," she said, leading her on. "You are here, next door to your mam."

I put my bag on the bed and opened one of the wardrobes. It was full of clothes that smelled of mothballs and the past. Women's clothes. One dress wrapped in cellophane — jade blue, my favourite color — stood out. A memory tumbled into my brain that I'd never known before: my mother, bent for days over her sewing machine, working on this dress. Also: wearing it, my father by her side. His neck, too red, bulging over a white collar and tie. Her in this dress, the shock of her bare shoulders, her hair piled on top of her head, looking like somebody else, her half-nakedness frightening to me though she was smiling.

"Oh now," she'd said, as I started to cry. "What's that about?" She was laughing down at me and up at my father. Happy? Happy with him?

Was it real, this memory?

"That old wardrobe was brought in from the other bedroom,"

Rose said from behind to me, making me jump. "I hope it won't be in your way."

"Of course not."

"That's a lovely dress."

"It's not yours?"

"No."

I looked down at it, then back up at her, the ghost of its owner hovering between us.

"You should bring it back to America with you; get a bit of wear out of it."

"Oh, I couldn't."

"Why not?"

I looked at it. Indeed, why not? It was beautiful: a tight, strapless bodice covered in tiny, worked detail over a full skirt. The sort of detail you rarely get in dresses now, and far too beautiful to be left to rot here. But where would I wear such a dress?

"Just don't say anything to your Daddy," she said, dropping her voice to a whisper. "You know how he likes to hold onto everything."

So that was how she played it, us against Him. Fair enough, you'd need some survival strategy to live with my father.

"All right then, I'll take it. Thank you."

"Not at all. So tell me, have you everything you need?"

"I'd love a shower," said Star, coming in behind us.

"Oh, dear, I'm afraid we don't have one of those."

"You don't have a…?" Star's face would have made me laugh but for poor Rose's discomfiture.

I cut in. "Maybe a bath? I'll show you the bathroom."

"A bath?" said Rose. "Dear me, yes. Of course. I'll just need an hour to heat up the immersion."

It had become clear that mealtime was the only time we were going to be spending with my father or Rose. Their life was going to go on as usual, with no concession to us. Fair enough, that suited us, too. I wanted Star to come with me to Dublin, to hear me speak at the book launch. I wanted to take her shopping and to visit the capital city I'd hardly ever seen myself, do all the sightseeing, touristy things with her we'd enjoyed in London.

To have had Daddy and Rose coming along, sitting in the back seat of our hired car, would have been awkward, so if they wanted to stay put, so much the better. It left Star and me free to explore wherever we wanted.

Except Star was refusing to come to my book launch. My moment of glory wasn't exactly scintillating for a fifteen-year-old, I did realise that. For anyone, really. It was only a small essay in an ancillary volume by a subsidised press, but it was publication, recognition that what I had to say was worth hearing by somebody.

"Who will I talk to? It will be full of whiny critics and up-their-own-ass professors." She shuddered.

Star loathed critics ever since our local paper's music column savaged Vixen, with a line about their particular sound of fury signifying nothing and picking Star out for special opprobrium: "The drummer was a big — let's be honest, fat — girl in spandex and combat boots, with a sense of rhythm as uneven as her sense of fashion". It wasn't that harsh, compared to what could be said, but Star was so sensitive.

I tried another tack. "But what will you do here, while I'm gone?"

She shrugged that jerk of her shoulders that was almost a sneer. "I guess talk to Rose."

That's what I'd found her doing quite often these days when I got back from my solitary drives or walks, but if I came in and settled down beside them, Star always slipped away.

"What on earth do you two talk about?" I asked. Daddy, I suspected, from the few snatches I had managed to overhear. "I didn't think she'd be your choice of company."

"I feel sorry for her."

Star knew how I felt about my father. On the plane across, realising that she had an image of him as a kind of twinkly Dan Rather figure, I began to brief her as to what she could expect but, in the telling, I had somehow ended up in tears — nerves at the thoughts of meeting him, I guess — so that she had to call the stewardess to bring me Kleenex and a glass of water and we'd both been shaken by that. Since we'd arrived, we'd had more than a few whispered exchanges about his carry-on, and silent communications with eyes and eyebrows behind his back. Up to that moment, we were forming a bond of sorts around his perverseness.

"It's natural that I'd want you there, Star. Surely you can see that."

"Granddad said he'll take me fishing."

"If you don't go to Dublin with me."

"Yes."

"Where?"

"Down by the lake."

"And what did *you* say?"

"Nothing. But I wouldn't mind."

And that was it. After all the tirades and tantrums, of being the best I could be, of keeping what shouldn't be said unsaid, that was the sentence that made something implode inside. I teetered, but only for a moment, before letting rip. I told her she wasn't going fishing with him, now or ever. I told her to stop being such a self-dramatising, nasty, selfish fat lump. I said… Oh, I said it all, I said far too much, I said things that should never be said.

Just one sentence about him was all it took to undo all those years of careful forbearance.

"Ladies and ladies," I said, beginning my talk, for there wasn't a single man at the book launch. A titter broke, a small wave around the room. Looking down from my podium at the faces turned towards me put a nervous wobble into my voice. "In 1889, the year that WB Yeats recalled first meeting Maud Gonne, he was moving away from the influence of older men that had been so predominant in his life. Men like his Pollexfen grandfather and uncles, the old Irish Fenian John O'Leary, the magician MacGregor Mathers and, of course, his father, were ceding their place in his life to a number of strong-minded and unconventional women. These women were, variously: emblems, muses, providers, literary and mystical cohorts, mentors, friends, and sometime sexual partners."

There I stopped, blank, a string of panic knotting my throat. My eyes floated back to a couple of kindly faces near the front and I remembered what I wanted to say.

"Of all these women, none was more important to his poetry than the Gonnes and it is them I'd like to talk about tonight, most particularly Iseult Gonne, whose influence is so often overshadowed by her mother. Maud Gonne, the radical Irish revolutionary, the celebrated beauty, the unattainable muse, would —I think — have loved to know that we are here tonight, discussing her. Iseult, her daughter, would hate it. When I started my research, I…"

On I went, talking to a room of strangers with nobody I cared about there to hear me. Before I'd left for Dublin that morning, I had checked in on Star who was sleeping with her head under the duvet, like a bird with its head tucked under its wing, only her quiff showing, collapsed across the pillow.

"Star," I'd called, gently.

Silence.

"Do you want breakfast before we leave?"

Silence.

"You are going to come, aren't you? Please come, darling. We can talk in the car."

Silence.

I went in, sat on the side of the bed. "I'm not even asking for me, Star. I know what I said yesterday was wrong and I am so, so sorry but I'm not asking you to forgive me, only not to let it stop you coming with me today. Today is a big day for me, the biggest day in my life since I had you. I'd love you to be there and I really think that if you don't come, you'll regret it later. Don't let a row stop you. Star? Please…? Star?"

But no.

After my speech, there was a wine reception at which most people, except me, knew somebody. We stood around, eighty or ninety of us, holding long-stemmed glasses between our fingers and our copies of *A Child Dancing* under our arms, saying what we hoped was the right thing to each other. I can do small talk — restaurant work is training school for it — but it always feels more like performance than connection to me and, that night, I had had enough performing on the podium. I should have liked to be with people I could really talk to, ask them what they really thought, and tell them how I really felt. Star or Marsha or — stupid thought — Zach, instead of these strangers coming across to congratulate me.

And then I was tapped on the shoulder. I turned around to a pair of dancing, aquamarine eyes that I recognised immediately, even though I hadn't seen them for years. I had expected the habit and wimple she wore then but it seemed she'd ditched them. She was dressed in civvies, sensible navy, but an ordinary skirt and jumper.

"Sister… Auntie … Catherine!" I said, delighted. "You came!"

"Came? Of course I came. Best invitation I've had in years."

I hugged her, taking a moment to settle the emotions that leapt in me at the sight of her. This was my mother's sister, long-time principal of a girl's school in Dublin. When I knew I was coming back, I'd written sending her a photo, and inviting her to the launch.

"So, the prodigal daughter returns. And…" She cast her lovely smile around the room. "…on a wave of glory."

"Not exactly glory," I said.

"Now don't go making little of it. I don't like when people play down their achievements. It's a fine book. Very interesting work. Very important work, excavating all those untold stories. Tell me about your Iseult Gonne…"

And we were off. No small talk now. We had so much to tell and ask each other.

After the launch party broke up, we sat in the lobby drinking tea, still talking, talking… She knew so much about me and my past and nothing, it seemed, was out of bounds. Towards the end of the night, not even the woman who had been lying, silent as dust, in my past.

"I remember trying to talk to her after she got engaged to your father but she wouldn't let me broach it. It wasn't until the day of the wedding, when we were getting ready, that I got a chance to ask her if she was sure. I made light of it, saying something like, 'This is your last chance now, Martha, to change your mind'."

"What did she say?"

"That he was a guard, with land and prospects, and that she knew what she was doing."

She hesitated.

"Go on, Sister."

"I don't know if I should be telling you this but it's always burnt a hole in my mind. She said to me, 'Isn't a bad marriage better than no marriage at all'?"

"Oh, God."

"She was twenty-five and her time was running out. That's the way it was, then. Marriage was everything for a girl — job, status, home, the lot. Women weren't allowed to work at much else, remember."

"Unless you became a nun." I smiled.

And she smiled back, a smile that was happy for her and sad for her sister. "It was after Martha's wedding day that I knew my own calling."

The next day, driving back down to Wicklow, I thought about

Sister Catherine the whole way, how she'd probed, but gently: careful as a cook checking a soufflé, how much I'd told her. Funny how life works, I thought, driving up the lane at Doolough and parking the European car with its awkward gearstick and handbrake and clutch. If Star had come to Dublin with me, I wouldn't have been able to speak half as freely with her there.

As I walked into the kitchen, lunch was being served but as soon as I crossed the threshold, I knew something was wrong. My father looked like a towering tyrant and Star like a frightened child. The smoke of anxiety I remembered so well from childhood immediately swirled up in me. I stopped, afraid to speak, knowing any word or action would unleash the menace. "Oh, here she is," he said. "In time for the food. And arms swinging, of course."

I looked at my hands and forearms, not knowing what he meant.

"Not so much as a loaf of bread to contribute to their keep."

Our keep? We had brought presents when we arrived. A book, handkerchiefs, whiskey for him. Flowers and chocolates for Rose.

"Nothing but complaints from the moment yez arrived. Coffee, how are you. And showers. It's far from that you were reared but in you come with your notions and your nose in the air, snooting around the place."

Star's eyes were opening white circles all round her irises.

"And all your talk about America, America. If America is so damned fine, what are yez doing here?"

His face was swelling, like a red party balloon. I tried to keep my voice calm. "Are you saying you want us to go?"

For the first time in my life, I held his black gaze. A *throb-throb-throb* began to beat in the space between my eyes but I didn't drop them, and I wouldn't have, even if I'd had to stand looking into his hatred to this day. He was the one to break off.

His eyes sank to contemplate the toe of his boots and I felt my heart surge.

From the side, Star said, "Come on, Mom."

"What about you, Rose?" I said. "Do you want us to go?"

Rose looked from us to Daddy, panic-stricken. He put his hand in the air and flicked his wrist, a wave that dismissed us or her, maybe both.

"You can leave her out of it," he said. "It's nothing to her; yez are not her people."

Star stood up, a loud scrape of her wooden chair on the tiles. "Let's just go, Mom."

"That child needs the strap taken to her," he said. "In more ways than one."

"You lift one finger to her," I said. "And I'll call the police."

"I am the police, you little fool."

"Not any more, you're not."

"Oh God, oh God, oh God," wailed Rose. "Stop. Let's all be friends."

"Come on, Mom."

My father let a guffaw. "Would you listen to them? Should they stay or should they go? It's our house you're talking about, or have you forgotten? Go on. Away with ye. The free hotel's just closed its doors."

Star was in my room, waiting for me to finish packing, when Rose came in.

"Oh, no," she said, seeing what I was doing and Star's case, already packed, on the bed beside us. "Please don't leave. He doesn't mean it, honest to God he doesn't. You should have heard him before ye came. Come back and let's sort it out. Or let him sleep on it. He'll be grand in the morning. We'll try again tomorrow."

Star looked at me as if to say, *don't you dare.*

"I'm sorry, Rose. I left here because I couldn't put up with the likes of that. I'm certainly not going to let him turn it on my daughter."

"Oh, this is terrible, just terrible."

I zipped my bag closed. "I'm sorry."

"I better go back down, so," she said.

"Of course. Goodbye, Rose. Thank you for everything."

"He's not as bad as he makes himself out to be."

"I know," I said.

Star snorted.

"Did you take the dress?"

"Dress?"

"Your m... The blue dress, from the other wardrobe."

She saw from my face that I hadn't.

"Have you room?"

"Yes."

"Then please," she said, leaving to go back downstairs. "I want to think of you having it."

I did what she asked, stuffing it any old way, then we hefted our cases down the wooden staircase and outside to the car, feet crunching on the gravel. We hovered around for a bit but nobody appeared.

"What should we do?" I said to Star.

"Let's just go," she said.

I thought of the last time, sneaking away by night with Brendan. "No, I'd better say goodbye. I'll regret it if I don't."

"What did you ask for if you didn't want my opinion?"

I pushed open the door, and stuck in my head. He was in his seat at the head of the table, where we'd left him, his back to the door. "We're off then," I said, my voice grating with falsity. "Goodbye and thanks for having us."

"Goodbye and good luck," he mumbled.

Rose moved towards us.

"Stay put, you!" he growled at her and she stood where she was.

"Goodbye, Rose," I said, a sort of apology and left.

As I drove away, I looked back through the rear-view mirror at the big, old house that was Blackberry Lodge. My vision was split. I saw the house as it was now and also how it seemed to me when I was small. The years tumbled into a chasm along with all the years I should have had — saying goodbye the first time, returning afterwards every year or two for a visit, to warm hellos and sad departures, observing the changes in the place, little on little, year on year, giving me smaller pangs of loss. Bearable pangs. Shakespeare's sweet sorrow of parting, not this wrench that somehow must be endured again.

"Are you all right?" Star asked.

"Not really. But I will be. You?"

She nodded. "I am now."

A moment of accord. A silver lining. Next to what went on in that big old farmhouse, our little three-bed in Santa Paola seemed a model of family feeling. At least now she understood what he was like and why I kept her from him. It wasn't quite the reunion I'd hoped for when we were setting out but it was something. A bond of sorts.

"*Go up and hide in your rooms and wait until tomorrow,*" Star said in a silly voice, a bad imitation of Rose. "*When he's had his sleep he'll be a pussycat, a little lamb. Is she mad?*"

"I know. Poor thing."

"How does she bear it? He's absolutely awful to her. And she never says anything."

"I'm sure her answer would be that she loves him."

She did, poor Rose, but only because she did not love herself. She was able to live with my father, to — in Star's words — bear it, because beneath his bad behaviour, she sensed the torments that drove him. She was more attuned to his suffering than to her own.

PART VIII
STARSTREAM

a systematic drift of stars in the same general direction within a galaxy.

STAR

CHRISTMAS EVE 1989

*W*hen *my grandfather died, he didn't go easy. It was the first time I ever saw anyone dead and I was appalled by it, the way his body twitched and shuddered in its resistance the way his breath scraped in and out of him. "The death rattles," Mom called it, and I hated the ghoulishness.*

Once, as he slipped in or out of consciousness, he called for his own mother. "Mammy!" he'd yelled, a shout that was prayer, entreaty and accusation, all in one. Mom saw my face at this, said: "You take a break for a while."

"Are you sure?"

"Step outside, get some fresh air. You don't need to be here all the time."

"What if...?"

"Don't worry, I'll call you."

He was lying still then, except for the sound of his tortured breath, in and out. I didn't know whether he was awake or asleep. Sleep had become a thin, worn blanket for him, it was hard to tell the difference.

When the time came, Mom called me in but still he clung to life. On the bedside locker beside him was his jug and tumbler of water, a box of tissues, a roll of mint sweets, the pill box, half full ... Mom smoothed some petroleum jelly on his lips and I moved my breath to match his:

in, out, in... Steady now, not as jagged as it had been earlier, but louder than was natural, and rasping and slow. So, so slow. I felt as if whole minutes were going by between breaths, waiting for him to let the air in or out, so I could do the same. In. Out. In. Out.

Until his stopped. The sound of this silence brought me back, out of the daze the slow repetitive breathing had induced. He made another, different sound, something like a dog makes when it's startled, a growl deep in the throat, fear and menace together: Grr-uh-uh-uh. Mom took his hand and held it as a shudder shook him, from core to skin. How could she bear it? The same sound again — grr-uh-uh-uh — and one more inhalation.

I waited for the exhale, waited and waited, then I knew it wasn't coming. She realised it at the same time and released his hand. She laid her forehead down on the bedcovers. He was gone and it was so strange, how it was still his own face, yet there was nothing of him left in it.

"Mom?"

She lifted her head and her eyes began to clear. I could see her coming back into herself from a long way off, remembering I was there, almost like she was remembering who I even was. "He's dead," she whispered.

"I know."

"I'll go call Pauline." She stood up, brushed down her jeans, like she was brushing off crumbs. "She'll know what to do next."

STAR

1983

*C*hekhov says that writers lie most often at the beginnings and endings of their stories, but where I am most tempted to fictionalise, to improve and alter and just make it up as I go along, is here, right in the middle. Good stories demand reverses and turnabouts, so I'd like to be able to say that, after our trip to Ireland, Star's bad behaviour improved, that our moment of connection as we fled my father's house heralded a new way of being together but no. The turbulence and tribulations continued and — as life is always flowing in one direction or another — because it wasn't getting better, it was getting worse.

I was reminded of how it was when she was a small child, the way I'd just get on top of one phase as she was already in the act of launching herself onto another. Always trotting behind her, trying to keep up.

No longer out till 3 a.m. but now five or later or, sometimes, not home at all. No longer just refusing to pick up her things or help out in the house but calling me names for daring to ask. No longer finding "Cow!" or "Idiot!" released her ire, but moving onto "Bitch!" and "Retard!" and "Fuck off." It was the drink and drugs talking, I knew that, but it didn't make it any easier to hear.

You shouldn't stand for it, people said.

No child of mine would speak to me like that.

It's disgraceful.

I knew it was disgraceful, I tried not to let her away with it, but it was what I got anyway. Reason, sanctions, kindness, punishment: none of it made any difference if Star decided to play the tyrant.

Spoilt, I was told.

A bully.

Selfish.

And yes, all of that was true, but it was not the whole truth. Other words described what lay beneath. Lost. Troubled. Lonely. Confused.

I saw less and less of her, as she spent more and more nights with friends. Along with worries about her welfare, there were financial burdens. Soon, if she managed to get the grades, she was going to start college. She was going to be launching herself upon adult life, leaving home and living without me. The thought crammed me with fear. I was so uncertain of her ability to cope — no, so certain of her *inability* to cope — that I had to visit a doctor and get chemicals to put in my own body each night, so I could sleep.

For some reason my daughter had a very fractured sense of self. She felt the need to armour herself with fat and belligerence to get through life. But why? Yes, she had to grow up in "a broken home" but it wasn't as broken as some of the ones I'd seen with a father still in situ. Did that really account for what was going on?

"You're barking up the wrong tree," said Marsha one night over a late night glass of wine. "She's had nothing but love in this house. It's not you, it's society.

"Huh?"

"Our toxic, sexist society has cheapened and degraded sex. Girls are falling apart all over the place."

"But isn't that our fault, too? Our generation threw off our tops and danced around maypoles in the People's Park." *Drop the hypocrisy*, we'd cried. *Make love not war. Let it blossom, let it flow.* Oh, innocent us.

"No, Mercy. Don't confuse sexual freedom with sexual exploitation."

"Pornification."

"Exactly. Porn's bad enough kept in its place but it's been moved out of fantasy fodder for men, and turned into a paradigm for women."

"Paradigm. Jeez, Marsha, this isn't Women's Studies class."

"You think of a better word, then."

"I know she's doing things she's going to regret," I said, trying to bring the conversation back to Star.

"Of course she is, poor love. And telling herself she's finding freedom all the while."

"Oh, Marsha."

"I know. It's terrible. People who work with child abusers call it 'grooming'. Using porn to convince their victims what they want to do is dandy-o. Well, that's what our society is doing to girls. No two kids come together now without a woman-despising, porn-driven blueprint of sex already in their heads from MTV and the rest. Star is a victim of that. Don't tell me she isn't."

Could this be right?

"And that girlfriend of hers, too."

"Venom?"

Marsha nodded, vehemently. "She looks like Bambi Woods."

"Who?"

"You know, *Debbie Does Dallas.*" A famous porn flick of the time.

"No, I don't know," I said. "And frankly, my dear, I'm shocked that you do."

I knew what she meant about Venom, though. She had kept her pugilist-punk name but had adopted a completely new look — peroxide hair and false eyelashes, low cut tops and push up bras, polished nails and frazzled eyes.

Marsha was still talking. "Don't tell me it's any coincidence that this is emerging in the wake of the women's movement. It's like the woman-haters are saying, 'You want out of the kitchen? Okay, honey, get into the bedroom then. Here, look at this magazine, at this TV show, at this music video. This is what you're good for'."

"Oh, Marsha."

"It's true, Mercy. And it's damaging us all, men as well as women."

"Marsha, please."

"Sorry, I'm ranting. I know. But I hate to see you beating yourself up about poor Star when you've done everything — *everything* — a mother could do."

Calling all mothers! Some advice for you. If you have a little girl, don't be the kind of mother who says: "All I want is for her to be happy." No, no. Want her to be top of her class. Want her to become Chairman of the Board. Want her to marry a millionaire. Want something negotiable, so she has room to rebel. If all you want is for her to be happy, the only way she can separate from you is to be miserable. Tortured even.

Dr Aintree said that I had to turn my attention from Star's life to my own. Worry might be the mother's lot, but it was not to be indulged and my fretting was bad for us both. I resolved to take myself in hand. Inspired by Marsha and by my reading, I had a plan. "Words alone are certain good," as WB had put it and I decided words were what I'd turn to, to fill my empty nest. I was going to become a writer.

In the meantime, I needed a day job that would leave me with enough time and mental space. Weary of working for others, Marsha and I took a leap into business together and opened a little coffee house down near the boardwalk called Better World Café.

The name and the concept was Marsha's. The café would be a hub, a place from where we would encourage what she called "meaningful and creative connections" as well as good food. Our coffee would be imported directly from a non-profit project run by a friend of hers on an ex-plantation in Kenya. Our food would be mostly vegetarian, without announcing itself so. Our staff would be valued with a share of our profits. Our tables would be dressed in (recycled) paper tablecloths with a big light-bulb outline in the middle labeled "Big Thoughts and Ideas" to write within. Our napkins would be smaller versions of the same, labeled "Neat Thoughts and Ideas."

We'd provide colored pens and pencils and cover our walls with thought-provoking and inspiring pictures and quotes. We'd also provide, twice a month, a cultural event: a poetry reading, or music, or storytelling. "The great thing about being on the boardwalk," Marsha enthused, "is that we won't just be speaking to the converted. People will drop in, all unknowing, for a cup of coffee and leave with so much more than that."

I look back now on our audacity and smile. We hadn't a clue what we were getting ourselves into. Over that first year, we had so many crises, especially with staff, but eventually we settled down with Stella and Toni on the floor supporting me, and Mercedes and Laine in the kitchen, helping Marsha turn out her delicious breads and cakes and soups and salads.

Now the crises have all dissolved, it's the daily small sensations, sometimes so small as to seem almost like nothing that come back to me here at my desk in Doolough. By leaning back and closing my eyes, I can smell Marsha's mushroom soup, my favourite, bubbling in the urn. See again the glint of a good Merlot in one of our lovely glasses. Hear the sound of our customers talking and laughing, in what was for many of them the happiest hour of their day.

Small moments that I used to rest in, that helped me believe that yes, everything was going to be fine, maybe everything was fine already, before being thrown again by a brainwave flitting up to the surface, cutting through my peace with worries about Star and why things were the way they were. Stop, I would admonish myself. Return to the sunlit murmur of now, the clink of two classes, the froth on a coffee mug, the shine of dressing on the salad you're serving. Beware the voice in your head. Don't live by it. Be careful. Pick up that finished plate. Smile at Stella. Tidy up the newspapers into the rack. There, that's better.

We only seem to be planted in time. Wherever you are now, stop what you're doing and look around. Observe those people not so far away. Know that no matter how intact and how present they seem, just behind the face, there's a fissure, a separation filled with the crackle and fizz of regretted pasts and anticipated futures.

August turned to September, bringing the annual hoops of fire to the hills. In the middle of scourging heat, we found that Star had secured herself a place in college. Not just any college, UCLA.

I sat on her bed watching her do her final packing. She was scared, I was scared and neither of us was admitting to it. *Snap, snap*: she closed the clasps on her suitcase and looked around her. Clothes in piles, all over the floor and on every free surface. Another struggle I'd relinquished.

"Don't change anything while I'm gone," she said.

"I'll have to clean it."

"You're not to."

"Star, if I don't, we'll have vermin." I picked up a broken cookie from the floor and a glass circled with stale milk. "You're not supposed to eat up here, remember?"

"Jesus, Mom, can't you drop the nagging, like, ever? Even when I'm just about to leave home?"

"I may have to do some fumigation, that's all I'm saying. But I'll keep it to a minimum. You're right, let's not fight."

"Only if you promise not to throw anything out."

"Nothing. I promise. Pinky swear."

We picked up a suitcase each and went downstairs. At the front door, I put my arms around her. One thing about loving a fat person is they're so nice to hug. I sank into her and, of course, broke the vow I'd made to myself and started to cry.

"Mom, don't."

"I'm sorry." I let her go, blew my nose. "I'll miss you, darling. Write to me as soon as you land."

"What will you miss, cleaning up my mess?"

"Star, honey, come on now. You know I don't know what I'll..." The sentence wilted into the shrug of her shoulders and her turn towards the door.

Had she overheard what I had shared with Marsha the night before: that I looked forward to coming home in the evening to peace and tranquility after work, instead of another unnecessary drama? That I wasn't sure whether I'd miss her more or less once she was away than I had for the past years while she was right there under my roof? Was she sensitive because she knew that I was only in part, really in quite a small part, crying for what was ahead and mainly for the loss of all we'd already missed, all those years we would never get back?

I followed her out to where she was waiting beside the passenger door of the car. The morning sun was shining at us through the tree in Mr Connors' front yard, throwing our shadows in front of us, Star's all spiky-headed and bulky and serrated along the leafy ground, mine barely there beside her.

STAR

1984

*C*learing up. Sometimes, most times, was a satisfactory winding down ritual to the working day, but when you're tired, it's hard to face. At Better World Café each evening, two members of staff — one front-of-house, one back — stayed behind to leave the place spotless for the early start next morning.

Marsha and I made it a maxim not to ask them to do anything we don't do ourselves, so tonight was one of the nights that she and I worked together after everyone else was gone home: mopping out the floor, dusting down the shelves and ornaments and pictures, emptying the vases of old flowers, clearing out the newspaper tray. We ticked off the routine tasks in our habitual, silent minuet. The ceiling fan whirred its song of secret loss and I knew Marsha was about to sound me out.

We both knew it, though I hadn't said anything yet about how I was feeling and all her talk so far was about takings and stock and the day's doings. Yet I knew that as soon we sat opposite each other at our favourite table down the back, cup of tea or glass of wine in hand, it would be my turn to talk and hers to listen. Which was exactly how it happened. And in the middle of talking, of telling her everything, or almost everything, I surprised myself by saying that sometime in the future, I would love to go to Europe again, to do it properly this time, and she said, "Why don't you go now?"

"I couldn't. How would you manage here?"

"We're doing okay, you know that. We could hire someone to fill in. How long would it be? Six months? A year?"

"Oh, six months would be enough. More than enough."

"Well, then."

"It would bring our profits down."

"We've plenty of profit, Mercy. What's it for, if it doesn't let us do the things we want?"

"You're serious."

"Why not? Star's well settled in college."

Now I had no excuse not to, I had to ask myself was it really what I wanted? I searched myself. It seemed it was.

"So long as you don't go leaving us for some sexy Frenchman," Marsha said.

"*Mais, non!*" I indulged my atrocious French accent. "*Je te promets.*"

"And you have to send me a postcard from everywhere you go. I'll put them up where all the customers can see them."

She made it sound so easy.

"Are you sure, Marsha? I can't help feeling it isn't fair."

"I'm going to want to head off myself some day soon. Do it, so I can have my turn and you'll hold the fort then, for me."

That was the clincher, as she knew it would be.

"Will you go to Ireland?"

"Oh, yes." Sister Catherine had sent me a package of places to visit and things to do "next time".

"See your father?"

"No. No daughter, no father, no family visits, just me, experiencing the places I want to see. Maybe I'll write about it as I go." I was getting excited as they came spilling out, all these wants I hardly knew I had.

She had a gift for true friendship, Marsha, for knowing what you needed and helping you to get it. I hadn't expected, in my thirties, to make a new, true friendship and, in all my life, before or after, it never happened to me so thoroughly again. We make so much of romantic love and not enough of friendship so I would like to put it on paper here that Marsha has meant as much to me as any lover, even Zach, and far more than my hopeless husband.

Marsha is always saying "I love you" to me, but I am Irish and of a certain age. We don't say such things face-to-face, not easily. I hope I've said it enough in other ways but, just in case I haven't, Marsha, I say it here.

My trip to Europe was a multi-layered pilgrimage and Marsha had persuaded me to take my time. My route was mapped: In Britain: London and Edinburgh. In Ireland: Dublin, Sligo, Coole Park and Thoor Ballylee. In France: Paris, Étaples and Paris-Plage where my father had been stationed, Colleville-sur-Mer, where WB Yeats proposed to Iseult Gonne.

It was during this time that I also launched myself upon another journey, writing about my life as if it were a novel. Instead of telling readers my opinions about what happened, I'd just let them see and hear and taste and touch and feel what happened for themselves.

Just! From a series of hotel rooms, with their desks turned to face the window, I launched myself, uncertainly, at the task. Slowly, over the weeks, as I traveled around London first and then Ireland and then France, ideas and imagination yielded to the pen. I took blind turnings, followed dead threads of enquiry, but stayed there, remembering and recording, though I often felt like jumping up and away from the anxiety it created in me. I didn't write about any of the places I was seeing; my grand tour of Europe was from the inner landscape of memory, as I created an alternative world out of events and emotion I had never explored before.

I spent my mornings wrestling with words and in the afternoons, after a short nap, I headed out at around 3 p.m. into the streets and bars and cafes, the museums and theatres and art galleries, the attractions of culture in the cities. Or else into the woods and seashores and mountains, the attractions of nature in the countryside.

I had grown fast during my college years but I have never felt such an explosion in capacity and possibility as I did in those days in England and Ireland and France, shuttled between my memories in the mornings and the place I was visiting in the afternoons. The effort of recording the past made every meal and every excursion, every sunrise and sunset, every art gallery and performance, every lake and tree, seem more significant. I pitied the poor tourists who could only arrive and stand in the Tower of London for an hour before moving on, with only a postcard to hoard. I had all the days I wanted. I could return to any venue every day for a week if I wished.

Had I traveled more earlier in life, I might not have been so intense. Being alone was also part of it, the attention I had time to give from a position of solitude but mainly it was the writing. It rose from the same place as the willingness to drop out that had taken me away from Ireland and all around America with Brendan. That wanting to live at the extremity of life, to tear through to some elemental truth in the hope of saving ourselves … and others, too. On the outside, it looked very different, a heading-for-middle-age woman alone in her hotel room putting words on a page, but the drive that propelled it was the same. The very same.

Not that it was easy. Often the thoughts of my failed relationships — with Brendan, with Zach, with Star — assailed me, and both past and future both looked broken. When nothing seemed worth the energy it demanded, I'd accept the attentions of the men in whatever hotel I was in, even though sex-to-go usually turned out to be too much trouble for too little reward, and the ones who wanted more were worse. I'd return, with relief, to the kinder, far less demanding notebook and pen.

Those were the days before email and easy transatlantic calls. To keep in touch with home, I wrote letters, supplemented with a weekly call to Star from freezing phone booths or noisy hotel lobbies. She was doing well, she said, and I worked hard to accept her reports at face value and ignore the speculating voice inside that questioned what was *really* going on.

It was in one such Parisian phone booth that she told me her big news, her voice bouncing out of the telephone receiver. "Mom, I have to tell you. I've met someone."

The words took hold of my insides and squeezed. *Don't love him*, hissed the inside of my head. *You are mortgaging your life. He will hurt you.*

"That's wonderful, darling."

"Isn't it? Oh, Mom…"

Normally our weekly conversations entailed me describing what I'd seen or experienced, feeling that without my babbling, the conversation would collapse. "Well, well," I said. "Tell me all."

"His name is Shando."

"Mmmm. That's unusual."

"He's a Buddhist."

"Oh."

"What else? He's twenty-five." (Twenty-five? But, my child, you're not yet nineteen.) "And he's a yoga teacher." (Yoga? How could he expect to support a wife and family with *yoga*?) (*Wife and family*? What sort of nonsense was I thinking? This was just her first boyfriend, for pity's sake.)

"We met a good while ago, before you left for Europe, but I didn't want to say anything till…"

"Are you" — my voice was as casual as I could make it — "seeing a lot of each other?" Tadpoles of rain swam in wavy lines across the glass of the booth.

"I guess."

She was sleeping with him, this twenty-five-year-old. This father figure. This stranger was now intimate with her body. Just thinking about that — not going so far as to imagine it, I couldn't even imagine imagining it — brought on a glut of panic. Oh, my Star, be careful.

"I don't know what else to tell you, Mom. He's a really sweet guy."

"That's wonderful, darling." It didn't sound any more convincing the second time.

There was a silence, in which I felt like I could hear her eyebrows draw together. I took a deep breath.

"I hope he's not making you neglect your studies."

"Oh, Mom, for goodness' sake! But listen, guess what, I've lost weight. I don't even know how. He's always cooking."

Love, my darling. Filling up that space you used to cram with food. Filling up the space I couldn't fill.

"Shando means 'New Way'. It's a Buddhist name. He's a —"

"Oh dear, honey," I said, cutting her off. "There go the pips." The warning sound that we had just sixty seconds left. I was lying. I couldn't bear to hear any more. Fear, or some more loathsome feeling, was rising in me and might reveal itself.

"I'll call again on Saturday," I said, in my breezy voice. "Have a great time with … er … Shando. Tell him I said hi."

"I will. Thanks, Mom. We're going to…"

I put the receiver down on her voice and stood staring, my hand still on it. If he was putting healthy meals in front of her and making her happy, I should be pleased. I *was* pleased. I was. I repudiated the negative thoughts that were springing up in me like weeds. Any guy able to see beyond her body shape to the darling girl beneath couldn't be all bad.

Or did it mean that he was dysfunctional, too?

No.

Stop.

Star had her first boyfriend. And high time, too. It was a good thing.

A good thing.

I stepped outside the phone box, into the rain. The street lamps shone above, their orange glows diffused, a row of blurry suns. I bent my head and pressed on towards the restaurant. I was hungry and my table for one was waiting.

STAR

1990

I want you to know, Star, that for years I resisted writing like this: the autobiographical, confessional, first-person narrative so beloved of Freudianism and feminism. The insistent I. I-I-I-I. It still feels self-indulgent, but nothing else will do. This is the only literary home that has room for us both and my father, too, the only method that allows me to reach into our secret spaces.

Whenever somebody started to tell Henry James an anecdote that ignited his storytelling instinct, he'd stop them before they were finished, saying, "Don't tell me too much." I know why. He wanted the freedom and insight that can only come from the imagination; too many facts would constrain, inhibit his ability to tell the deeper truth.

I understand. Truth above facts is my motto now as I sit in this bedroom in Doolough, before the window that throws a greenish light across my hand, working through this reworking. The weather has finally improved, the cloud cover broken into high columns of white fluff marching across a blue canvas outside the window. The thread connecting now to then, me to my father, Star to Zach, is twitching strong and I am running after it, taking dictation.

With no daughter, no job, no father to call me away, I'm able to write whenever I want for the first time since those days on my tour of Europe, and the writing is repaying that commitment. I use the tools of fiction — selecting incidents, re-ordering time, plotting and orchestrating, representing speech, winnowing the chaff words and chopping and changing others — because I want the truth of fiction. But I also want what is known to have happened to be as accurate as I can make it.

Pulled between my father's diaries and letters that stand in the territory of what was, and my imagination, which cares more for what might be, I cross and recross the frontier, like a demented double-agent, knowing what I hope you did not know but what I fear you did know all too well: the double-barrelled story you and I have carried through our lives.

My father seems to have suffered none of my difficulties in writing about his life. His childhood seems to have always returned to him in clear, bright lines. Marbles in his pockets, games on the streets, dinner on the table, "devilment" with his brother: a happy boy, by his own account. It's idealised, it has to be — he grew up in a tenement house in what was then the poorest city in Europe — but I can feel a truth in it, remembering how, when he recalled those early days, his words softened, his sentences lengthened. It was like he was leaving out a breath. And so I can imagine that as a boy, he was different to the man he became, the man in the later diaries, the man I knew.

The small books told me things like he cut back the ditch at the bottom of the garden on Friday, July 16, 1924; that rain prevented him from finishing the job the next day; that he wrote poetry, sporadically and badly; that he never forgot the war. He kept them diligently, a new one for every year, though only five —1924, 1925, 1937, 1951, 1960 — have survived.

The entries in the large book, the one started in France, during the war, were much longer and he added to it all his life, in spurts. One break between entries, from 1926 to 1937, is almost eleven years long. Anyone else would have started a new diary but not my "waste-not, want-not" father.

It was against regulations for him to keep a diary, or any record of his macabre duties, what it felt like to be summoned by the whistle to jump up and out across open grass, rifle cocked, part of a line that included Irish, English, Scots and Welsh, Australians and Indians, Africans and Canadians, all faithfully or resentfully trudging through their duty into a wall of death.

Between flinging himself up and over, to the moment of his return to the trench, fragments of detail stayed with him to be noted in his notebook later: floating limbs, torn away from their trunks; forsaken helmets or gas masks; heads with exposed teeth grinning beneath the hollowed out sockets of evacuated eyes; rats who always made away first with the eyes and lips, the softest tissue.

Mule was his family's name for him and the quality that gave him that nickname stood to him, as again and again, he leapt out and hurled himself forward at the well-armed enemy. *Rat-a-tat-tat*. Around him, clusters of hot bullets burst into shins and knees and thighs and hips and stomachs and chests and necks and cheeks and eyes and brains and hearts.

Men fell beside him, and before him and behind him, urged on by their captain, "Come on lads. We'll be all right," while all around they saw the different ways trench warfare could kill — instantly and cleanly, or by concussion and drawn out agony; blown apart by direct hit or sliced into segments, mangled by bayonets, bullets or bombs, in some cases sent up by their own side, missiles that fell short or long. The explosions tore at the earth and the skies, as if trying to bring down the heavens.

Somehow, through it all, my father was missed. Forward he marched until given the order to retreat, then back across a carpet of the dead, their flesh plucking at his boots, their smell thick at the back of his throat. And next day out to do it over again. And the next. And the next.

Day after day, fired by rum and adrenaline and shouts and

curses, he hurled himself over the top, offering his body, the only thing he owned, to be hacked like a blade of grass. Day after day, on and on for months, knowing it was happening in all the other regiments, too, gouging place-names onto the map with soldiers' blood. Places I visited in 1984, on my war tourist trip through the killing fields, now cleansed: Ypres. The Somme. Passchendale. Salonika. Suvla Bay.

Through all this, the Allied front slid forward only five miles on its wave of blood. Then, a lucky injury. His leg was broken by a piece of shrapnel and he waited out the rest of the summer in a hospital bed. His journal recorded how he found God. A harsh disciplinarian God, the *one* that was fashionable at that time. A God who believed in discipline, like a Sergeant Major or Head Corporal, who held out no promises of rewards in this life, only bliss in the next, for the dutiful.

His journal filled up with prayers to this new God. That, when his time came, it would be in the form of a bullet somewhere vital. Heart or head, please. Not dismemberment. Not pulping. Please, God. He didn't pray any more to be spared. He expected now to die to be sent back to die.

On the third day of March 1990, I was once again at my desk and having a good writing day. I have mornings when I wake, frozen by worry, unable to know which foot should go in front of the other, but if I can find my way to the desk, I know I can type my way into a day that worked.

I was in the middle of a sentence when the telephone jangled beside me, making me jump. It was Mags Halloran, my lawyer, whirling in to chat. How was I doing? The date for the trial had come through, rather earlier than expected. She needed to see me. When could I come up?

I felt like someone slapped out of sleep but I managed to answer. I was doing fine, fine. Yes, I would come to Dublin. Tomorrow? All right then, tomorrow.

I replaced the phone in its cradle. I was Mercy Mulcahy again, back in my father's bedroom, with the chair under me, the old mahogany of the desk smooth under my fingers, the tips of the trees outside the window and, beyond them, the boughs and budding stalks of other branches and, through them, shards of grey lake water. The lake is only visible from the house in winter and then only in slivers. In another few weeks, the leaves would be fully out and the water and all around it would be hidden from view for another nine months.

I was here, back in this strange limbo between my old life in Santa Paola and whatever lay ahead. Maybe home to California, with or without Star. Maybe into an Irish jail. I needed to clutch hold of the two sides of my mind and draw them back over the fissure Mags had opened.

In my writing, I was looping back towards where I'd started: the events that spun me across the Atlantic Ocean, to take care of my father. The time had come. If I was to fight for my freedom, I was going to have to tell all I knew. To allow Mags to point up other possibilities. To let life decide.

The two sides of the arguments went on and on, slicing each other to ribbons and the writing which had seemed so powerful before Mags's call was diminished, revealed as a poor sticking plaster on a gaping wound.

My double vision that disorientated me. I have come to know there is no what-might-have-been, there is only what-is. What a lot of suffering I would have saved myself if I had known that then.

STAR

1986

"*M*om…Oh, Mom."

I knew at once, the second I heard her voice coming down the transatlantic wire.

"Darling, is it…?" Her boyfriend's ridiculous name stuck in my throat.

"Oh, Mom, I want to die. Just die."

So, it had come to pass. Already, he had let her down.

"Darling, don't say that. Of course you don't."

"I do, I do. I don't think I can bear it. I just want to die, that's all."

Panic gripped me. "Star, listen to me. Don't do anything, just wait. I'll be home on the next plane. I'll ring tomorrow with the details."

Once I had made the decision, loneliness vanished and I began to instantly think of all the things I would have liked to have seen and done in Europe. I had been here yet I hadn't been here at all. I had walked the streets, crossed the bridges, gazed at the churches, admired the art, eaten in the restaurants, explored the war fields but, too many times my mind had been full of Daddy and Zach and Star, and my needy sulky self, ever seeking something that might satisfy its submerged longings, had only half-noticed what I was seeing.

Why did I not write about what I was seeing as I traveled? That would have forced me to pay attention. It frustrates me now, as I sit here remembering, to have so few details to draw on. The sun rose and set on me there for so many days but I retain so little. It's a sin, the sin of omission. The sin of preoccupation. Had I known that the trip was to be cut short, I would have visited France before England, the war memorial at Étaples before Paris. I would have moved considerably faster, been less distracted, done more of what I wanted to do.

Held beside Star's need, however, these objections were nothing. It never occurred to me to stay on, to leave her to recover alone. Other mothers might dismiss their children's love affairs with an indulgent smile but Star was too insecure to cope with rejection. The tremor of her voice on the telephone had been like a finger jabbing into a bruise, reviving the days after Brendan left. I hated to think of her stumbling around that dark well, straining to break out while drawing the walls in around her. Oh, I remembered. I remembered.

Fear. That was the sensation firing me as I packed my bags and hurried a cab to the airport. My big little girl, so needy and yet so fragile. My only prayer was that I would be in time to save her.

I went to her student dorm. Unwashed dishes stacked themselves on the table, along with three half-empty glasses of milk, one with a solid yellow head on top. Dirty clothes lay in heaps on the floor and over every flat surface. Sprawled across the bed, face down in the recovery position a paramedic would put you in if you'd had an accident, lay my unkempt daughter, her ample, duvet-draped bottom facing me.

"Star, it's me."

"Oh, Mom, you came…"

She sat up, she held me, she let me pull her close. A hot spurt of tears stung my throat. I sent forth thanks to this Shando of hers. For the first time since she was — what age? In how many years? Oh, too long to remember — I was being allowed to fully, properly hold her. I felt her soft shoulders under my fingers, sunk my chin on the pillow of her neck.

"My poor darling," I murmured. "My poor, poor darling."

After a time we separated, though I held onto her hands.

"What happened?" I asked.

"He dumped me."

"Why? Did you guys have a fight? Maybe —"

"No, no, no fight. Just … he doesn't want me. Too fat, probably." She detached herself from my hands, pulled a pillow over her face and wailed into it: "Knew he wouldn't. Knew it from the start. Out of my league."

"Oh, Star … honey … don't…"

I made her get up and dressed and brought her out for dinner and she told me everything over a plate of food that she fiddled with while she talked, talked, talked, like she used to talk years ago, when she was afraid to let me go. I brought her to my hotel room and she spent the night in my bed and, next morning, I encouraged her into the shower and then onwards to her lectures.

To my surprise, she obeyed. She didn't know what else to do. By the time she came back to her room in the afternoon, I had it sparkling clean, everything in its place and a bunch of sprightly daffodils in a new vase on the table. "You shouldn't have," she said, shrugging her book bag off her shoulder.

I brought her to dinner that evening but again, she barely ate. At the end of the meal, she said: "Mom, I want to give up college. I want to come home."

"What about your degree?"

"I'm not studying anyway. I cut two classes today. I can't concentrate. I can't stop crying."

"You'll get through it, sweetheart. You're not going to be like this forever."

"You don't want me, either."

"Don't be silly, Star. It's not that."

It would actually have been one of my own motherly fantasies. Star asleep in her bedroom, home with an illness. I'd actually imagined it before. Nothing serious. A flu or suchlike. Nothing that a few days in bed and a little tenderness wouldn't fix. I'd bring her books and magazines, the kind I despised but she liked. I'd set her up with lots of pillows and the TV remote control. I'd fix her lemon remedies and a little food, nothing heavy on the stomach. Soups, custards, plenty of fluids. "You do know it's not that, don't you?"

"Yeah, Mom, sure. Whatever."

I left her a few days later, though a big part of me wanted to stay. I left her with money and presents and a promise to take a phone call every night. It felt like the right thing to do, though both of us were scared. So I arrived back to Santa Paola, months early. Marsha was disappointed for me but pleased for herself, she said. She had missed me.

I slotted back into my life, everything the same, except a nightly phone-call from Star. She was not coping but she was managing to force herself through her days, often giving me a hard time on the phone but always calling again the next night. We hadn't been this close in years.

And so we went, most days mostly the same, until the day I discovered that Zach was back in Santa Paola.

Early one Wednesday afternoon, during that lull time in the café between lunch and afternoon coffee, I headed out for my break. I had two chores to do that day: to go to the library to exchange my books and to Brown's Healthfood Store to get my vitamins. Both were on Ocean Avenue, close enough to walk, so off I swung, out into the sunshine with my book bag over my shoulder, heavy but not weighing me down.

For sixteen years now, aside from my one long trip away, I had lived in this college town— population 50,000 — swollen in term time by the student population to almost double that, basked in its sunshine (325 days a year is its boast), tended my house, earned my living, raised my kid and lived out my life.

Here was where I knew best; here was where I was best known. I was Mercy Mulcahy, the Irish woman. I lived on Westcliff in the smallest house on a lovely road, almost in view of the ocean. And, in that little house, it could be said I'd lived the life I'd chosen sixteen years before after we lost my husband. I'd negotiated its spaces and filled it with islands of homely furniture. I'd been nurtured by its books and music, comforted by its cushions and rugs.

Here I was, one half of Better World Cafe, one of the minority of the town's businesses that were run by women. Nice place, and the food was good, if you didn't mind things a bit hippy-dippy. I was also Mrs Mulcahy, single mom, mother of Maria, more commonly known as Star. Such a sad case, that girl. The town remembered her as a girl, riding her bike along the boardwalk, or strolling the stores with her friends, such a pretty little thing before she put on all that weight and started wearing those awful clothes. Drink and drugs, it was said. An eating disorder? Possibly, yes. And my, so aggressive. Remember her walking down this very street with young Ginnie Cooper? One hand held inside their leather jackets, some sort of affectation. Stomping like a pair of off-duty soldiers, angry eyes up front.

Tough, raising kids these days, especially on your own.

That's what the best of them said and those who said worse didn't bother me, not any more. I was steadied by the presence of my neighbours. Their "Hi, Mercy" or "Afternoon, Mrs Mulcahy!" or "How is Star?" was a small, everyday gift and reminded me of what I opted for when I moved here. Domesticity, suburbia, a place where I could fight free of my past. A place where I, and my daughter, could feel safe. I held onto those small connections, valuing what I still had, though so much was lost.

Freedom and safety aren't external, I knew that by then. A house and a good job won't keep you safe; a trip to Europe doesn't set you free. *I wish, I wish, I wish*...Those dangerous, soft-footed words still formed the backing track in my head. I never said them aloud, not even to Marsha, because I didn't believe in them any more, but I was still thrown forward on them, tossed up the road that day on their swoosh and slice. The draw of desire, the prodding push by the rod, the wand, of I...

To the library, where heads looked up as the wooden double-doors swung closed behind me. We are lucky in Santa Paola with our old-fashioned library. Here too, I was well known. It was quiet today: no students from the high school, too far from exam time. I didn't have to ask for my books. Jenny saw me and bent for them behind the counter. I always rang ahead, a relic from busier days.

She slid them across the polished wood. The new Edna O'Brien, especially ordered. *The Bell Jar*: I was rediscovering Sylvia Plath. A "how-to" on writing fiction. I fished in my bag for my library card, grateful as always for the gift of free books. Tonight, after we closed the café, I would take them home and choose which one to read first. The O'Brien, I reckoned. I could do with an injection of her luscious, over-ripe sentences, her sense of the hidden dilemma within the obvious conflict.

I would turn the key in the lock of my front door and sit immediately down at the work table I have set up in the hallway, leaving the book in its bag, delaying the pleasure of reading until after I have written something myself.

I thought of it as a room now, my hallway. Big enough to take an easy chair alongside the work table, another telephone table and the big blocky bureau in the corner, where I kept my accounts. It faced west and was the place to sit at that time of day, to catch the evening sun. Tonight, I would work until I grew too tired or hungry, whichever came first. A break to eat would mark the end of work for the day. The O'Brien would come out of the book bag and be taken to the kitchen and laid in on the pine table while I prepared supper. Bean stew brought home from the café, accompanied by a robust chunk of bread and a glass, or possibly two, of red wine (never a third). The bright new cover of the book would gleam in its plastic library jacket, catching the light from the lamp overhead.

Food warmed, I would sit and open it. Page one. A new story.

After eating, my reading would continue in the living room. It would be dark by then and I'd put on the reading lamp in the corner. Plumping the cushions, I'd sink down, pulling a coverlet around me. After I'd read my fill, I might watch the late news, hear more about the worst recession since the Great Depression, the nine million Americans now officially unemployed.

Watch is the word, with all the distance that implies. I wouldn't be drawn in by these news stories as I would with the books, Edna O'Brien's or my own. I'd let the TV information wash across me because I feel I should. In Better World Café, earnest students or activists debate the details of the latest news with passion and rigour and Marsha, who is always skipping with feeling over some injustice or another, comes out of the kitchen to join in, with her always intelligent, always probing opinions.

I join in a way that facilitates them to do the talking. To me, the unfolding of political events feels inconsequential. I know millions of people are affected by these decisions but they don't feel real. People enter and exit the world and their own life story unfolds and they bring it to fulfilment. Or not. How they do, or don't, seems to me the only news worth telling.

I admire Marsha and all the others who do care about "real life". I provide a place where they can work out what they think and share it with each other and make a difference, in the way they want. They are so taken with their own thoughts they never notice I don't really have any to offer.

After the news, I would prepare for bed. Tidy the house, iron whatever I was going to wear the next day, undress and go through my night time routine. Cleanse, exfoliate, tone, moisturize, tweeze, brush. Tonight was Wednesday, so I would also manicure. Shiny and polished, I would take myself to sleep with some final reading, another chapter of the O'Brien or a different book, something lighter, or maybe the Santa Paola Sentinel, which comes out on Wednesdays. Then to sleep, in time to get eight hours before rising at seven.

That's what I thought was ahead for me that evening. Instead, I left the library and walked on to Brown's and bumped right into Zach.

As soon as I walked in, I saw him. His eye-catching back, tall and broad under a white T-shirt. For a second, or maybe two, I didn't realise. Then the knowledge dropped inside me, like a weight being dropped from a great height. It was him. He was pointing towards the meat. I drew nearer. Yes, it was his voice, saying: "…and six slices of chorizo".

"Zach?" I said, from behind his back.

He stood shock still for a moment, frozen, before turning around. A splinter of something as our eyes collided. I felt it again, what I had felt the first time we met. His intense presence, even stronger now he was older. A word from my Catholic childhood floated into my mind: Charismatic.

"Well, well," he said, voice breezy. "If it isn't Mercy."

He wore a smile that said, I am pleased to see you but I am just as pleased to see this chorizo I am being handed. You are no more special than anything else.

Instantly a thought rose in me: You can drop the nonchalance, my friend. You are mine, I'm getting you back. The sensations that swirled around that thought flooded my entire body with memory, of what it had been like to be with him and what it had been like to be without him.

I flicked a quick look at his left hand. Naked. Zach would wear a ring, I thought, if he were married.

"It *is* you," I said.

"Me indeed."

"Home for a visit?"

"A bit longer than that."

"Really? That's great."

He turned back to the assistant behind the counter. "And a large slice of Camembert," he said, bestowing his beautiful smile on her.

Mine.

"Your hair," I said. "It's so different." It was short, very short, practically shaven. He ran his palm across the skull and stared at me, as if he didn't know what to say. Didn't have anything to say to me. No, no, unthinkable thought, but words had also evacuated my head. Silence grew and grew like a big, invisible balloon pressing against us.

It was he who rescued us: "How is your little girl?"

"Not so little any more. She's in college."

"No!"

"It's been nine years, Zach."

"I still think of her as a kid."

"Yeah, it's the kids who bring home what nine years means."

I was now facing forty but until this moment, had not found that milestone oppressive. The American obsession with looking younger has always seemed ridiculous to me. All that running and bending, and now all that cutting and slicing, just to pretend you are a few years younger than you are.

That day in Brown's, all such reasoning flew away from me. Under Zach's eyes, I was conscious not only of the lines around my eyes and mouth, the sag that was developing in the skin behind my chin, the wedge of padding that lined the top of my waistband, but also that I wasn't wearing any make-up, that I was in my second-best jeans, only half as flattering, and that my hair color needed a retouch. For the first time, I felt the impulse that drives women under the knife. If, in that moment, a surgeon was to promise that he could restore me to what I had been at thirty — the age I was when Zach and I first met, the age when my skin still glowed without make-up, when my hair was still dye-free and all jeans looked equally good — I might have chosen to believe him.

It didn't help that Zach was not less, but more, beautiful than he had been nine years before. He had filled out in the shoulders and filled out internally too: come into himself.

Looking at him was giving me the strangest feeling, like time was tunnelling in around us from all sides, cutting out the girl behind the deli counter, the two people now standing in line behind me, the shop and all the people in it. There was only us two. I knew not to approach him as I would another guy. The light swapping of banter, the game of the tip and parry you play so you don't expose too much too soon, wouldn't do for Zach.

"Would you like to go get a coffee?" I asked.

He laughed. Was that a bitter note? Was he still hurt? If he was, that meant I had a chance.

Mine. Mine.

"Unless you'd rather not. Unless there's somebody else?" I said.

His eyes widened, surprised at my directness. "No, it's not that."

I saw that he had the advantage on me. He'd known this meeting would happen. His nonchalance was prepared.

"Will that be all, sir?" asked the deli girl from a long way off.

"Come on, Zach, this doesn't need to be so hard. Just say yes or no. Your call."

As soon as the words were out, I regretted them. Too blunt. Yet if I played it as cool as him, he'd let me walk away. I played my last throw. "Zach, I'm so sorry about what happened. It was the biggest mistake of my life."

"You think I don't know that, Mercy?"

"Then let's not make a second one."

His silence stared me down, face full of so many saids and unsaids, but drawn, as I'd known he would be, by the truth of what I was saying. Never was sorrow more sincere. This felt like my once-only opportunity to mend what my mindlessness had broken.

"That will be $6.40, sir."

"Please, miss," I said, without turning my head. "Can you give us a second?"

Still he didn't speak, so I had to. I put my hand on my heart. "I forgive myself, Zach. I forgive me even though I put myself through the wringer by leaving you. I can forgive me, here, now, because if I don't, I'd only be doing the same thing all over again to myself. And to you. Zach? Do you understand?"

"Sir, ma'm, I really must ask you..."

"So don't forgive me if you don't want to, Zach, but know what you're doing, okay?" I felt like I was fighting for the life of a child. "Know that it's you making the mistake this time."

Still he stood.

"Sir?"

I took one of the business cards I always carry in my purse and wrote my home number down on the back of it. "Call me," I said.

He looked at the card. "Better World Café?"

"Or call in there if you'd prefer. Anytime. Come and meet my friend Marsha. You'll like her."

He would and she would love him. I could imagine them, having long intense talks about how best to save a world that didn't think it needed saving.

"Sir, I really have to ask you to —"

"Just wait, will you?" I turned on her, hardly knowing what I was saying.

I turned back to him. "Zach?"

"Ah, go on, son," said a man from the line.

"If you don't, can I?" shouted another voice.

"Yeah, man, you crazy?"

"I'm out on a limb here, Zach. Look at me."

He looked, he let himself look. A spark jumped in his eyes, I saw it. Time tunnelled in closer. "Help me," I whispered.

He reached out his hand.

"Oh, thank God," I said. I dropped my basket so I could take his hand, and my feet were stepping towards him. He opened his arms to me and I half-stumbled towards them.

"Yes!" cried the old man from behind, as if it was his arms I was falling into.

Then I was locked against that white T-shirt, my cheek warming against what it felt beneath. His skin, his muscle, his bone. *Mine.* His hand came up to hold me there.

"Don't make me regret this," he whispered into my hair.

"I won't. I promise you, Zach. I promise."

I looked up at him and he was smiling. The people in the line behind us were smiling. The deli girl was smiling. And me, oh, yes, me too. Even my pores were smiling.

Since Zach and I had last been together, he had got God. He didn't call it that and he wasn't aligned with any particular religion or tradition, but that was what it was. After Brown's, I brought him back to the café, enjoying the look on Marsha's face when she saw me swinging in with him, hand-in-hand. She sat him down in the corner table to share a pot of green tea and some get-to-know-you-time while I fixed up the tables. Then she insisted I take the rest of the day off.

We went straight to my house, I knew he'd appreciate that, and I wanted to underline that I knew it had to be different this time. I showed him around. The west-facing entrance vestibule where I like to write. The open-plan kitchen and dining and sitting room at the back, opening out onto the yard. Past Star's closed door, forbidden territory, with its black painted walls covered in posters of Richard Hell and Tom Verlaine, the Sex Pistols and the New York Dolls, all cut and pasted into enormous, explosive collages. Closed in there too, were my photographs of her, too painful for me to see as I went about each day. Each time she left, I put them away, together with her smell of smoke and despair, until she was coming home again.

"Star's room," I said. Zach nodded, and I knew all our memories of me not introducing him to her were rising in us both. This time, all would be different, he'd see.

I showed him the bathroom, which needed decoration and the spare room for guests where Marsha often stayed if she'd had too much wine to drive home. All these delays were a sort of commitment to our destination.

"This is great," Zach said, almost wistfully. "I can see your life since we parted, here, all laid out."

"Settled and boring."

"Not at all. You're so rooted now, compared to before." He smiled. "Solid."

"Solid? Charming. Makes me sound like a kitchen table."

I put my arms around his neck and gave him the full-on kiss I'd been planning to give since Brown's. No more holding back, I was going to be all his now. I smelled the tang of him as our lips met, his own, unmistakable essence.

"I think it's time this table was laid," I whispered in his ear, which made him laugh again.

Then he grew suddenly serious. "Mercy," he said, with a small frown. "I have a lot to tell you."

"We've a lot to tell each other, Zach. But we've all the time in the world to tell it. First…" I kissed him again.

"Mercy, Mercy," he whispered into my hair, and again, after we'd slid each other's clothes away and tracked pathways along each other's skin with fingers and lips and were reaching to pull the nakedness of each other in close, he said it again, "Mercy, Mercy," only louder this time, as if I was in danger. Or maybe *was* a danger. I don't know.

I was determined that everything was going to be fine. With my ambiguities and reservations out of the way, happiness would be ours, that day and forever, all the coming days.

"Stop," he said.

I lifted my head. "What is it?" Excitement was thrumming through me.

"Stop for a moment. Listen."

"To what?"

"Just listen."

I laid my forehead in the soft hollow beneath his shoulder, stopped the forward press of my desire. I could hear the thumping of my pulse, birdsong outside the window, the ventilator in the bathroom, two kids shooting hoops next door, a car driving past and the hum of my own blood, pressing against my temples… And yes, the silence wrapped around each of the sounds.

"That's better," he said and he kissed me again, with cooler, gentler lips, a kiss that lasted on and on and on until again, I was lost to sound and to anything except touching and being touched. I drew him down and we were together as we had never quite been together before, heartbeats knocking hard on each other's ribs. Two floating souls touching through heaving flesh.

Afterwards, after we'd slept a while, we talked and he told me about the years we'd been apart. Some of it — his academic appointment and his publications — I knew. Now he told me what lay under all that achievement.

"After you left me, I didn't want to live. I blamed you for the way I felt. And at the school there was all this wrangling and competition, first for tenure, later for advancement. I found myself anxious all the time."

"How anxious?" I asked, from the pillow beside him.

"Horribly, horribly anxious. Then, one night I woke with a feeling of intense horror. Everything felt so utterly without meaning. I hated the world and what I hated most about it was me. I lay thinking what I'd often thought before — how could I bear this struggle any longer? Only death could bring me peace."

"Oh, Zach."

"I hope this isn't too heavy for you?"

"Um... no."

"I hated myself. I thought myself the most loathsome person in the world. Why had I said such-and-such? What did so-and-so mean? I would remember you and the awful things I said and the tragedy of what had happened and —"

"Oh, Zach."

"I'm not telling you this to make you feel bad. It wasn't about you, really. I can see that now."

"But Zach, I was —"

"No, Merce, just listen for a bit. I have to tell you this. I lay there, thoughts churning, until I thought I would drive myself out of my mind."

He laughed and then kept on laughing, too long.

"What's so funny?"

"That's what I did," he said. "Which was precisely what saved me."

"Sorry?"

"Out of my mind."

"Zach, I..."

"Bear with me. A thought that kept flashing across my head as I lay there was: 'I can't stand myself any longer.' I had had this thought before but now, for some reason, I became aware of the illogicality of it. How could I not stand myself? Was I one person or two?"

He sat up on his elbow. "As I tried to solve this puzzle, I felt — actually felt — my mind stop its endless bettering. I was awake, still wide awake in the dark room, but I wasn't thinking. A moment of peace. Then..." He paused, dropped his eyes, hesitating at the brink.

"Go on."

"Oh, Mercy, I hope this isn't going to sound too crazy to you — as if my stopped mind was an aperture, what felt like a surge of white light came rushing in. My head felt ablaze with white."

I kept my eyes open to him. To turn from what he was saying would be to turn from us. I knew that much.

"I could feel myself being sucked into it. What did it mean? I started to shake, all over," he said. "And then I heard a voice."

"A voice?"

"A voice," he said, firmly, but with a quick glance to see how I'd taken it. "It seemed to come from my chest but it also seemed to be outside of me."

"What did it say?"

"It said: 'Bow to what is'."

Again he looked at me. I didn't take my eyes away. I didn't laugh, or frown. I didn't. I kept my face straight.

"It was The Source."

"The source?"

"The Source of All Things."

Straight. Straight, straight, straight.

"So," he went on, "I let myself go. I fell, a long way, then I felt my heart growing warmer and then it was as if it was opening, like a flower blooming on fast-motion film."

"Sounds like an acid trip."

He ignored that. "I felt peace and wellbeing washing over me. After that, I have no recollection. I must have fallen asleep because the next thing I remember is waking, what felt like hours later, with light, early light coming in through my curtains. Light as I had never seen before."

His face was alight just talking about it.

"I got up and walked around my bedroom, the bedroom I had lived in for years, picking things up, a pen, a tube of toothpaste, a T-shirt, staring at them in wonder. They were so alive. Alive now seemed the most startling miracle."

A third time he looked at me. "Mercy?"

I needed to answer now. I needed to say something, find

words that were not the half-frightened and half-cynical phrases leaping around my head: New Age-nutty-mumbo-jumbo-freakery. Zach had been so special to me. I had mourned his loss to the point of madness; now life had brought him back to me. This was who he was, now. I needed to get beyond my own opinions, respect the heart of what he was saying. As soon as I had that thought, a new word rose unbidden in my mind, from a different source.

I was able to reach across and brush his cheek with understanding fingers and smile a gentle smile into his eyes. "Rebirth," I said. "You had a rebirth."

"Yes. Oh, Mercy, you understand." He reached for me and pulled me tight against him. "You understand."

Zach's explanation of what happened to him that night was that his suffering was so intense that it forced his consciousness to withdraw from identification with the unhappy and fearful self he had become. As a result of which, unhappy and fearful Zach ("my false self") collapsed and he was left with consciousness in its pure state, consciousness that doesn't identify with form and therefore does not suffer ("my true self").

Although he had shifts in intensity of feeling he had, he said, remained in the same state of bliss since his metamorphosis. He'd tried a few spiritual organisations, joined a Buddhist Center for a time, read all the wisdom books — the Bible, the Buddhist sutras, Bagava Ghita, A Course in Miracles, the Tao — researched their traditions. Out went the promising academic career: he no longer respected its emphasis on intelligence and the thinking mind. Thinking, doing, getting, achieving: all these seemed empty to him now. He just wanted to *be*.

"But how can you be without doing?"

"Of course you're right. We have to eat and dress and so on. What I mean is that once I awakened, I realized I needed to change the emphasis, the balance, in my life. Less doing, less thinking, more being."

"Well, we'd all like a bit of that," I said.

"I'm glad to hear you say it."

"I said 'a bit'." Now we were safe, I could tease him.

"Don't worry, Mercy. I'm not going to ask you to join me on my park bench."

"Park bench?" My heart wobbled.

More revelations. Yes, aside from some odd jobs, he had spent much of the past year on a park bench in L.A.

"Like a … hobo?"

"Not too many hobos are in a state of deep bliss."

He must have seen something in my face, because he rushed to reassure me. "These identifiers, Mercy, class and color and creed. Put them away. They're not who we are."

My right foot was sticking out from under the duvet and feeling cold. I tucked it under, wrapped my leg around his. "But how can you afford all this sitting around? Don't you have to work?"

"People ask me questions."

"Say again?"

"People ask me questions and some of them give me money for the answers. Or food. Or other stuff I need."

"What sort of questions?"

"All sorts — Is there life after death? Why is love so difficult? How can I be free? Do I matter? Anything."

"And you've got the answers to all that?" It frightened me, the awesome responsibility of that, the damn cheek actually. "Don't you ever worry you might be getting it wrong?"

"It's not me; it just comes through me. All the questions lead to the same answer."

"Which is?"

He propped himself up onto his elbow, fixed me with those grey eyes of his. "My job … the purpose of my answers is to point the way out of suffering. The suffering we all create by too much thinking."

"You're a guru?"

He took my face in his hands, spoke like it was the most important thing anyone ever said. "No, not a guru. Positively, absolutely not. A pointer, that's all."

I felt I was falling into his eyes, round and down, like Alice, into a place where the things of what he called the outer world (what the rest of us call real life) were floating, freed from gravity. I felt light and loose as the snow-grey flecks in his eyes.

"A group of philosophy students here in Santa Paola have set me in various venues and are charging a small entry fee. You should come along to the next one. See for yourself, Mercy. Put your anxieties to rest."

I didn't feel anxious, it felt more like a state of mild delirium, different to how we were before but containing that too. He was no longer the awestruck boy and he told me a little about other women he had been with, only one of them special. A "beautiful person", but demanding, with a "sparky soul, a warrior spirit". I tried not to be jealous, not to wonder how he had described me.

"What happened? Why did you break up?"

"'She looked into my heart'," he said, quoting Yeats, what the poet had said to the great love of his life, Maud Gonne about another woman. "'And saw your image was there'."

I didn't bother mentioning anybody I'd been with. I couldn't attribute significant qualities to any of them. "Nobody since me?" he asked. "Truly?"

"Not one." And it was true. Nobody worth mentioning.

He liked that. He was still the romantic who wanted what we had to be absolute, still uncomfortable with shades and compromises.

"We won't ever let each other go again," he said and that was just what I wanted to hear.

With the spectre of past relationships slayed, we now had only one problem to face: Star. I told him about her failed relationship, her inability to find a boyfriend, her jealousy of other girls more beautiful and blessed. "Now this. Even her ancient and decrepit mother finding love while she's still heartsore."

"I guess we could wait a few weeks," he said, reluctantly, "Though I—"

"A few weeks won't make any difference. This has been going on for months."

"Then it has to be now."

"You're right."

He looked at me.

"I mean it, you are right. I've moved on. It's never going to be easy — so best done straight away. Just be warned that she will probably treat you as a personal insult."

"Only at first. She'll get beyond that in no time."

I nodded, not showing the doubt I felt. "She's coming back for Thanksgiving weekend," I said, firmly. "I'll tell her then."

"Maybe," he said, "she'll take it better than you expect."

And I, so happy to have him back, so wanting Star to be happy too, so keen to believe all was going to be fine, agreed that maybe she just might.

Zach's event was in Sports Hall Two on UCSP campus had sold out, with a queue at the door hoping for cancellations. It was a strange experience, seeing so many people avid to see him, not just students but people, mainly women, of all types and ages and colors. He had no props or special lighting or any concession to stage management: just him and his words and his calm and radiant presence. He spoke slowly and carefully, in an intimate manner that made each person in the packed hall feel he was addressing them directly, and he had no problem connecting with the questions and finding answers that made sense. Nothing groundbreaking, just the concepts at the heart of all religion, stripped clean and put into clear, simple, modern words.

I was proud of him, agnostic as I was. Affected, too. In that large hall, encased inside a silence so intense you could touch it, a stillness so deep you could hear it, I experienced what I couldn't accept or understand with my thinking mind. Peace was mine for those two hours, came and settled to all of us in that room. That I couldn't deny.

They loved him but it was I who followed him afterwards into the back room, who waited with him while they cleared the building, it was I who got to take him home.

Weeks passed and Star's vacation time came round. On her first day home I told her, with quavering voice and shaky hands, that I had met someone, someone important. She made it just as hard as I expected. A shrug first (why should I care?), followed by a tantrum, supposedly about her bedroom, (I don't care, I don't care!), followed by a slam of her door (see if I care!).

It was wrong of her and not to be indulged, Zach said on the phone, keeping up the pressure from the other side. Now that she knew, they must meet, and soon.

I considered having him over for dinner, but the thought of the three of us, trapped in my small dining room for an entire evening, felt way too intense. So I'd decided to bring them together for Marsha's AIDS Charity Ball. There, we'd be at a mixed table, some solos, some couples, some groups, so Star need not feel conspicuously single. She would have to dance with him and they would be able to talk without me listening. He would be charming and everybody else would love him and she would be unable to resist. And the first, worst, meeting would be behind us.

By the time the Saturday of the dance arrived, the breathing trick that Zach had taught me was failing me. I left the café early to get ready, with a nest of nerves in my stomach. It's just a hurdle, I soothed myself, as I drove up West Cliff hill. Just a hurdle that needed to be jumped so that life can go on. Once Star got used to the idea of me seeing someone, she would take Zach for granted, not see him as a comment on her life, her inability to attract love. We'd become wallpaper on the background of her life, the appropriate place for us to be. That's where we had to get to, and this was the first step.

She was late home, of course. Zach was coming at eight to drive us to the hotel and I had asked her to be back by six. By seven, there was still no sign. I carried on, had my shower, dried my hair, put on my make-up, growing more and more anxious. My mother's jade-blue dress was laid out on the bed, the one Rose had given me. I stepped into it, zipped it up. I'd had it adjusted so it fitted perfectly and I loved everything about it: the color of it and how it flattered my skin and the jeweled detail across the bodice and down my back; the way it bared my shoulders and supported my breasts, showing just the right amount of cleavage; the way it cinched my waist, but not too tight, then flared into fabulous folds all the way to the floor. I knew Zach would love it, too.

The door downstairs slammed.

"Star? Is that you?"

"No, it's the tooth fairy."

I went out onto the landing, looked down over the bannisters. One look at her face and I knew what I was in for. I weighed it up in my head. Which would be quicker: to go through the motions of sympathy and smooth her down, or to be brisk and try to get her to speed along?

I plumped for sympathy. "How was your day, darling?"

"Shit."

"Oh, dear. Sorry to hear that."

"I nearly punched this idiot woman in the library. She's trying to say I owe $32 in book fines because her stupid system didn't record that I brought her stupid books back months ago.

Then there was a traffic jam. It took me fifty minutes — that would be, yes, 5-0 minutes — to get over here."

"That's awful, honey. There's some chicken salad there if you'd like a snack."

"No thanks. I had lunch with Suzy. What was I thinking of, agreeing to have lentil bake just because she's going on some stupid health kick? It's sitting in my stomach like a football since, I think it might come back up."

"Star, you haven't forgotten the dance? Don't you think it's time you —?"

"Is that what you're wearing?"

"Yes, don't you like it?"

"It's lovely. Mine's rotten."

"You liked it a couple of days ago. I love it. It's dead funky."

"Funky? Jeez, Mom, where do you get the words?"

"Anyway," I say lightly. "Too late to change it now. Will you pick up those shoes and things and bring them up to your room on your way?"

Mistake. Her face hardened. "Don't you think you're being a bit pathetic, Mom? Do you really need to try so hard to impress this guy? If he … ahem … loves you, he's not going to care whether there's a pair of shoes on the floor, is he?"

"Okay, Star, okay. Don't pick up. I'll do it."

"Oh great, now the long-suffering-Mom routine. God, Mom, what about me? I've told you I feel sick. That I've had the most horrible day. Don't you care about that at all? No, only precious Zach. Zach. What sort of a name is that, anyway?"

I did everything for you, Star, went the drip-feed in my head, the self-talk I always pretend not to hear. *I did everything for you, but you can't do this one thing for me. You know this is important, you know exactly how important, but — no, not but, so — you can't let me have it.*

I sighed. What was the use in looking for understanding that she wasn't able to give? Self-pity served no purpose; it only made me feel worse. Wipe the ticker tape. Do Zach's trick again.

Breathe in goodness and light, breathe out toxic thought. We had the jitters, both of us, that was all.

She went up and I came down and started fixing my hair, piling it on top my head. It took a long time to get it right and I was only just finished when the doorbell rang.

Ding-dong.

My heart started to thud-thud-thud, so hard it hurt.

"I'll get it," I called.

Cooler air swept in as I opened the door. Zach looked gorgeous, spruced in a crisp, white shirt, the hair he was growing back still a little damp from the shower. He held two orchids, one for each of us. A nice touch.

"Oh, wow," he said, as he looked me up and down.

I did a little twirl so he could admire.

"Wow, wow, *wow*."

"Shhh," I said, thinking of Star, but he pulled me in close, crushing the orchids between us to kiss me. A long, sumptuous kiss. I had never been with anyone — even the younger him — who made me feel the way I now felt. We were developing new, slow-going ways of being together that were connected to a deeper place: a channelling, rather than a dissipating of, desire. Sometime, sometime soon, I felt I might be able to…

Footsteps behind us on the stairs stopped my thoughts and I pulled away from him, fast. I turned and started to say, "Star, this is —", but again, I was stopped.

Something was wrong. Horribly wrong. Zach's smile was contorting.

Star was looking at him like somebody had struck her. "Shando?" she said, her voice thick with shock.

"Maria?" he said, in the same tone.

The two of them — mouths and eyes wide, aghast — turned to me, as if I held all the answers. Then Star began to scream. "Mom, Mom, Mom! What the hell, what the hell, what the *hell* is going on?"

PART IX
STARBURST

a pattern of lines or rays radiating from a central object or source of light

an explosion producing such an effect.

a period of intense activity in a galaxy, involving the formation of stars.

MERCY

1989

*A*fter Zach left, I was in shock. Clammy sweats, flying pulse, shot breathing, the works. For three days afterwards, I couldn't go to work, or eat, or sleep. I didn't know how to proceed. Putting one foot in front of the other was too much for me.

My lover, my daughter, me, my daughter, my lover: a frenzied drum beat round my head. *She* was the "beautiful person, troubled and demanding" he had told me about. He had even told me her name was Maria but there were a hundred thousand Marias in California and I never thought — how could I ever have thought — that Zach's Maria was my Star? He never mentioned her weight or a single physical detail. Her (warrior) soul, oh, yes, and her (sparky) spirit — but not the color of her hair, her age, her family history or any single detail that might have told me that his girl was my girl, except the name that none of us ever used for her.

As for him, Shando was his Buddhist name, taken when he briefly joined a Buddhist Center just before he met her. At that moment, he was at the height of his renunciation of identity. He told her nothing about his life before they met. When he found out she was from Santa Paolo; he didn't do that thing that people do when they find out you're from the same city: "What part did you live in? Do you know so-and-so?" He never asked any of the questions that might have led back to me because he'd left all of what he called the badges of identity behind. Life story, country, gender, skin color: none of these meant anything to him anymore. *Put them away, they are not who we are.*

So, my Zach and Star's Shando were one and the same person. That's what my daughter and I had to grasp hold of. My lover, my daughter, me, my daughter, my lover.

Star coped in usual fashion — by lashing out, in agitation and incoherence, acting like I had set it all up just to hurt her, slamming out the door to stay at Ginnie's. Zach begged her not to go — to stay and talk it through, the three of us together — but not a chance, and I was relieved. I wasn't able to cope with both of them in the same room.

After she left, he sat in the armchair, elbows on his knees, hands clasped between them.

"You do know, Mercy, that this problem is not really between you and Star, but between us and the Source?" he asked me.

"Oh, *please*, Zach, not now."

"Whenever you have a problem, however much it seems to be about others, it's always really between us and the Source."

"Source, schmource… If you mean God, Zach, why don't you say so?"

"The word God has become empty. People use and abuse it. People, who have never come *close* to the realm of the sacred, bandy the word God around. Or argue against it. When they don't know what it is they're claiming or denying."

"Zach, please. This isn't the time."

He held his hands up, fingers spread wide. "I know. I'm sorry. Of course it isn't. I thought you asked."

He too was unmoored by what had happened and was turning to what he called The Source, knowing how it had saved him before. It was a good instinct; it would save him again.

But what about me? I had nothing now. No God, no lover, no daughter.

I spent the next two days reeling around the house. Star went straight back to LA, still not speaking. I persuaded Zach to follow her down, to make sure she was all right, and I spent a sleepless night envisaging him finding a scene similar to that which greeted me when I arrived from Europe.

And then imagining the two of them, together.

I was a string of elastic being pulled between them, stretching thinner and thinner.

Then, at the very height of the crisis, a letter arrived from Ireland, from my old friend Pauline Breen, now Whelan, explaining that my father needed help. He had been taken to hospital with a circulation problem but had discharged himself. *As you know*, Pauline wrote, *he's over ninety now and he's gone down a lot since Rose died. He doesn't feed himself properly and so has lost weight. We've organised 'Meals on Wheels' and I drop in to do his medicals, and as much as I can otherwise, but I know it's not enough. He needs cover in the house or else he'll have to go to a nursing home — but, of course, he won't hear of either...*

By the time Zach got back from LA, I was packed, ready to leave. "Don't do this, Mercy. We have to sit with it, the three of us, and see what it is saying to us."

"It's not saying anything to us, Zach. It's just empty, random, cruel chance and we need to put it behind us."

"The three of us need to meet," he insisted. "We need to talk. The truth is the truth, Mercy. What is, is. That's all we have to work with."

"Even if I could face it, I'm quite sure Star —"

"She is willing."

"Star?" I was unprepared for the spike of jealousy in me when he said this. "Star is willing to sit down with you and me and talk about this?"

"Yes. Very willing."

Could it be true? If she was agreeing, it could only be to corner me.

"I can't," I whispered. "I just can't."

"You're running away again, Mercy, shutting me out again."

"I'm not Zach, I swear. It's just that…"

"You swore to me that you wouldn't do this again. You promised."

My father answered the door to me himself, chewing food. When he saw it was me, he turned, leaving the door swinging open and shuffled back down the hall, sullen on thin, slow, old man's legs. In the kitchen, the television was blaring. A boiled potato was split open on a plate with two fried eggs on top, oozing yellow yolk. He sat back down and began to eat again, as if I wasn't there, watching. He ate slowly, his mouth making loud suckings and swallowings. The veins on the back of his hands were swollen tributaries of blue. He was a shrunken version of the man Star and I had left a few years before.

Two cavernous Os for eye sockets, and two sharp cheekbones jutting through below, all padding gone. I sat opposite him. "Did you get my letter, telling you I was coming?"

His hair was unwashed and the smell in the room whispered incontinence. Yellow egg leaked down the front of his shirt, mixed with older stains. What he needed was one of those plastic bibs that Star used to wear. His long life had made a child of him again.

"Are you going to speak to me?" I asked.

Another shaky mouthful, half of it missing its mark. Beside his plate were several vials of pills in different colors. The room was in disarray, dishes everywhere, dust widespread, dirty trails all over the linoleum.

"They always were pure nosy, those Breens."

"You mean Pauline? She's so concerned for you."

He pushed his eggs around the plate. "I'll never get out of this dump again. I'd like to have got out again, one more time before I died."

"Doolough is lovely, Daddy. Nicer than lots of places." True, but it must have sounded hollow coming from the one who had escaped.

"It would sicken you when it's all you see from one end of a year to another."

"I could take you for a drive. We could go anywhere you wanted to go. The West?"

"Yerra, don't talk soft, girl."

I picked up the dishes for something to do, while he headed off on a list of complaints. Nothing but funerals in this damn place. Maggie Moran yesterday and don't give him any palaver about the afterlife because he doesn't believe in it and neither do the rest of them, which can be heard clear in the way they talk about the dead.

Or else it was the young sergeant going about in the squad car like he was in one of them Grand Prix. Or children calling to the door selling flags, letting on they were for the school or the GAA, but he knew better and he wasn't going to be funding their sweets. When he had exhausted himself, he sat, caught in the ebb-tide of his complaining, one knobbled thumb spinning around the other.

Then: "I tell you one thing you can do, if you want to make yourself useful. You can get a basin of hot water. My corns are a scourge this past week."

He shuffled across to the fire, the only homely thing in the room and took off his boots. A smell of feet leaked out to mingle with the tang of cooking oil and fried eggs. I boiled the kettle, mixed it with cold water in the basin, put in a dash of Dettol.

"There's a towel in the back kitchen and the blades are in the bathroom."

The towel was threadbare and grey and none too clean. The

razorblades were in a pack, double-edged, each in a separate wrapper. I brought them through.

"Here we go," I said, with false cheer. Instead of taking them from me, he raised one of his gnarled feet. "Will you give them a scrape for me? I find it hard to reach down that far these days."

The foot, blotchy red, dripped water into the bowl. His eyes, though rheumy, were as sharp as the blades I was holding. He knew exactly what he was doing. And I thought I did too, as I knelt and took his foot between my hands.

In those days after I returned, I could feel my sanity quivering as I spent days and nights being drummed round the endless loop: my lover, my daughter, me, my daughter, my lover… My whole life seemed to have collapsed into this one string of thought.

Taking on my father, his moods and machinations, provided a distraction. I did my duty by him, no more. And I did it for me, not him. But I did it — and I did it well. With Pauline's help, I changed the parlour into a bedroom and moved him downstairs. At night, I slept upstairs with my door open, so I would hear him call if he needed anything. I slept only fitfully, on the surface, skating across dreams that left me feeling exhausted when it was time to get up. In the afternoons, I'd find myself napping in the fireside chair, falling into an unconsciousness halfway between asleep and awake.

Pauline was my only connection with normality. Whenever she arrived I was shocked to see her red-cheeked smile, so ordinary and nice, breaking the trance that my father and I lived in. Each time I drank a cup of tea with her, I would feel a piece of myself wakening a little into the real time of the outside world. Then she'd be gone and I'd sink again into the regimen of pills and bed changes and complaints and the cooking of mushy, ill person's food.

The other hours, the alone hours when I wasn't cooking or cleaning or caring for him, I spent in my bedroom. Not writing, no spirit for writing now. Just staring, unseeing, out the window, clutching the ledge, as if I was going to spin loose and be flung off the planet.

A few weeks into my time there, Pauline said she was going to have to fit my father for a urinary bag, and asked if I could come in with her to help irrigate his catheter.

"Will it hurt?" he asked her, in a babyish tone I'd never heard from him before.

"Not too much," Pauline said. "Not compared to what you're used to."

"What I'm used to is not good," he said, in the same little-boy voice. I was his daughter, but I was the intruder in their relationship. A voyeur.

"No, I wouldn't think so."

She put her hand on his, wrapped her fingers round his twigs of bone. "You know it's important that you're not in pain, don't you, Mr Mulcahy? You know that's what the morphine is for?"

His head dropped, too heavy on its skinny neck, a lollipop on a cracked stick. Silence. Then something fell on the conjoined hands. A tear. *Plop*.

"You shouldn't suffer any more than necessary," she said, in the same gentle tones.

He nodded. "I'm sorry now. I'm usually better than this."

"You're surely allowed an old cry."

That annoyed him and he threw off her hand. "It's not a girl you have."

She only laughed, as if to say being male won't save you from tears, not in a sickbed. Not even Pauline could turn my father into a good patient but she took no notice of his crabbiness.

"Should I help him wash?" I asked her afterwards, when we were back in the kitchen, having our tea.

"That shouldn't be necessary. There's a rubber mat fixed to the side of the bath and I've taught him ways to sit on the edge and do himself, in stages. He should be safe enough. So no, not yet. Let's wait and see."

"Wait for what?"

"If he starts to stink." She smiled.

I wrinkled my nose.

"I know. But let's not meet trouble half way. For now he's able to do for himself in that department. We should encourage him. It's something to give a shape to his day."

My own days — and nights — were all out of shape. I don't know why but ordinary, everyday things always seem to be harder for me than everyone else. When Star was small, I remember watching other mothers and the careless, expert way they would swing their baby onto a hip, or wipe a cut knee. Pauline was like that with my father but, with me, it's as if an invisible force is always pulling me back or tripping me up.

The fatigue didn't help. And being beside my father day after day, the effort of not remembering, was taking its toll. After weeks of fractured sleep, night and day had melded. I was never fully awake, never fully asleep and my bones were sore with tiredness. Pauline advised me to exercise, to tire myself out physically. "One good night's sleep would get you back on track," she said, and I knew she was right. I would find myself yearning for the Wicklow Hills, as if I was still 6,000 miles away from them, but not doing anything about it. I felt myself trapped in that house, held in place, even though Pauline said she would come and sit with him any time.

One afternoon, I was napping by the fire when I heard — or dreamt that I heard? — the creak of the kitchen door. I opened my eyes. Or dreamt I did. What I saw there was two jean-clad legs. Long. Familiar. I followed them up the torso, all the way to the top, to his beautiful, beloved head. Zach.

I reclosed and reopened my eyes.

Still there.

"You didn't hear the doorbell," he said. "So I came round the back."

I reached my hand up. I felt his arm, flesh and bone. Fear rose in me. He came in close, put both arms around me, kissed my cheek. A waft of his smell and the fear abated. Visions don't smell.

"You're real," I said.

"What?"

"I thought I hallucinated you."

He laughed. His laugh. "You might at least say 'dreamt', Mercy? You make me sound like a nightmare."

He pulled me in close, onto the white cotton of his T-shirt, onto his broad man's chest.

"Oh, Zach, we can't. I can't... Star..."

"Shhhhh. We'll talk later. We'll sort something. Just hold me for a minute."

"But..."

"Mercy," he said, stern this time. "Rest. Stop thinking. You look wretched."

"Thank you."

"We're not doing it your way any more."

"We're not?"

"No."

"Oh, thank God."

I let him hold me, and for a moment I held him hard too, but it was no good. Distress and bewilderment reared back up. My daughter, my lover, me...

I pulled away.

"Look, Mercy," Zach said, sitting back on his heels saying a speech he had obviously prepared. "You need help. I knew it all the way across the Atlantic ocean, I know it now that I have you in front of me. Let me help you."

"But..."

"Later, afterwards, when you're stronger, I will do whatever you say. But for now, just let me help."

"You mean stay here?"

"Yes."

"Daddy would never allow that."

"Allow it? Oh, Mercy, the question is, will *you* allow it? The question is: what can *you* allow yourself to have?"

I thought of what it would be like, having him around here, being a shield against my father. How tempting that was.

"I can't ask him, Zach."

"Leave it to me."

He jumped up.

"But…"

He was gone. Within five minutes, he was back, giving me a nonchalant thumbs-up.

"What? That's it?"

"Is there tea in that pot?"

"Tell me, Zach."

"Nothing to tell. I asked him could I stay and he said yes."

"Just like that? Come off it."

"Mercy, think about it. What else could he say?"

"Anything. He could have said anything. Lord above, if you don't tell me some of the details, I'll —"

"So you can obsess over them?"

"Jesus Christ Almighty, Zach…"

"Whoa, okay, okay, no need to swear. I told him who I was and what I wanted — what we wanted — and he said 'I'm not dead yet. This is still my house.' And I said, 'We know that, sir. That's why I'm asking your permission to move in.' He said, 'What if I don't give it?' And I said, 'Mercy and I would understand that to be completely your right, sir, and we would move out.' So then he asked what would happen to him if we did that and I told him to rest assured he'd be well looked after."

"Ooooh," I said, laughing. "You're good."

"You know, Mercy, it is really very simple." He took my hand. "He has no power, hon. Not unless you hand yours over."

The clock ticked, too loud.

"Think about it: if you did move out, what could he do?"

"I won't, though."

I hoped he wouldn't ask why. I didn't understand it myself, my coming back here. Not being able to cope with our grotesque triangle was only part of it. Something primitive between me and my father was in it, too.

"I'm not asking you to. I love that you're compelled to care for him even though ... y'know. But we could easily move to a rented house nearby, and you could do it from there. Or get him a nurse and just visit."

How lovely all that sounded. Especially that "we".

I used it myself: "We've no money, Zach."

"We'll find the money if you think it's the right thing to do."

I shook my head, regretfully. "No. He really does need live-in help at this point."

"Okay. But if we stay here, you must drop him as a burden, in your head and heart. And I am going to show you how. We'll start tomorrow. For today, just remember: whatever he was in the past, now he's just a sad old man."

"Hmmm. I'd wait till you know him a bit better before you jump to that conclusion." I looked at my watch. "It's time I gave the sad old man his meds."

I strode in, playing brave, but it was all right. He was reading the paper, and kept his attention on it, unwilling to confront. As I went about the small chores of dealing out the pills and the water, of plumping the pillows and straightening the covers, of clearing away the assorted debris of the morning — newspaper, lunch bowl, teacup — I hardly looked at him. I was afraid of what he'd bring up, but also I needed time to think.

A man like Zach wasn't going to want to be around a snivelling wreck for long, I knew that, but I didn't have it in me to pretend to be strong and, anyway, he'd see through such a pretence in minutes. I was happy worrying about this small knotty question, so much easier to think about than the big one at the back of it all. Star. Star. What about Star?

When I went back out, I stood over Zach's fireside chair and said: "I know we're not going to be able to go on like this, like you're a doctor and I'm your patient. I want you to know I will be strong again."

He held his two hands up to me and drew me down until we had reversed our positions of earlier and now I was the one sitting on the floor. He pulled me in, between his knees, and I sat, looking up at him.

"I don't think you get it, Zach. I can't sleep with you again. She'd be there, in the —"

He put a finger to my lip.

"Of course. I understand."

"You do? But remember what you said?"

He laughed. How could he laugh? "No. I don't," he said. "What did I say?"

"You said a relationship without sex was a relationship in trouble."

He sighed, deeply, like I was a puppy who'd forgotten its training and wet the floor. "Poor, Mercy, always so blue. You're getting everything wrong, fretting, fretting... Here's what's going to happen. I am going to live here and help you to get strong again. Then I know — I just know and you, for now, are just going to have to trust — that everything else will work out."

"But how?"

"It will. It already has."

He must surely see that to love me was to not love her, and to love her was to not love me. The bizarreness, the injustice of it all, he seemed to think only a trifle. "Have you seen her?" I asked.

"Yes."

"Is she still angry?"

"Furious," he said, eyes lighting up, as if Star's fury was something wonderful.

Tears, my constant companions, sprang up. "She loves you so much, Zach."

"And I love her, Merce."

That spike again. He let this statement sit there, between us, out and open. Neither of us had the slightest clue what to do with it. After a while he said, "Aside from the anger, she's actually coping with all this rather well."

"Not like me."

"It's harder for you."

"Is it? What about you, Zach? You seem so calm."

"Oh, I'm reeling, too, of course I am. But I'm trusting the Source. This is in our lives for a reason. I trust everything will come out right, if we let it." He tightened his hold on my hands. "That's what you've got to learn to do, Mercy. Trust."

I looked up into his eyes. Electric-grey, overflowing with love.

"Trust," he said again, a whisper this time.

My skin quivered, grew porous, opened. In that moment, I chose him.

Zach banished the gnarled thinking, the shallow sleeps, the hours of staring out the kitchen window, by taking hold of my time. What I needed, he said, was less thought and more practice.

"Practice" as he used it was a Buddhist word, with a special meaning. Our days were to begin with meditation. In the morning, after giving Daddy a cup of tea, but before making his breakfast or organising his medicine, I was to sit down onto a cushion on the floor beside Zach, legs crossed and, for thirty minutes, focus my full attention onto my breathing. When thoughts arose in my mind — as they were certain to — I was to label them "thinking", then bring my attention back to my breath. Especially my out-breath.

It sounds easy, but oh, it wasn't. The first day I jumped up after two minutes, overwhelmed. Gently, insistently, Zach led me back. "You can't do it wrong, so long as you're sitting there," he said. "See the thought. Don't judge it. Just let it be. Then return to the breath."

I sat back down, quieted again, but as soon as I stilled, hurricanes of thought rushed in, firing me with feeling. Rebellion, restlessness, craving, agitation. I remembered how my dentist once burst an abscess on my tooth before the painkillers had kicked in. I recalled my first boyfriend Mossie Mangan, a boy from Doolough with a too-long chin, dumping me when it should have been the other way around. I felt the plug of dread begotten by my father that always sat in the pit of me. I could feel every layer of it. I imagined escaping him, going back home to Santa Paola or onwards, somewhere else, somewhere beyond him. What would such a place look like? It would have a flat, open plain, with the mountains far in the distance, a ranch, a paddock, horses in a corral...

Everything I had ever heard or seen or felt or even imagined seemed to be still in there, in my mind, and I didn't want it, most of it, and I didn't want to be sitting here with it. It could drive me over, send me insane. I might cut off my ear, or choke my father, or step into Doolough Lake, my pockets weighed with stones. On I sat through it all and soon, within days, I felt better. Calmer and cleaner in my head, as if my brain had had a shower. And I was taller inside. Straighter.

Next came what Zach called free-writing. Writing down, fast and by hand, three pages of those thoughts of mine. Whatever arose in my head. Opinion, idea, commentary, story. Nonsense, bitterness, pettiness, jokes. To be placed on the page, as mixed up as it wanted to be.

"Think of meditation as one leg to take you to peace, and this as the other. You need them both to get you there."

Peace? Hah! The words on the page were crazy. But, like the meditation, I wasn't to judge what emerged. The meaning of the words was secondary to the act of writing them. Again, I resisted. I had Real Writing, my book, to be getting on with. Wasn't structured work like that more valuable than these pages of mish-mash? And why did I have to use a pen when my typewriter was so much faster?

"Oh, fast," said Zach, as if speed was a vice.

"But you said to write as fast as possible."

"A fast pen is quite fast enough. This isn't a race. You're after depth, not distance." He pointed to the pages. "Look how much more of you is there than on a typewritten page. Your handwriting is as unique as your fingerprint. An expression of you. That's what we're after."

"Hmmm," I said.

"That's the you that you can count on, Merce. Just do the practice, the rest will look after itself. I promise. The more you're resisting this, the more you need it. Come on, here's the pen. Another three pages today, fast as you can, starting now. Go!"

Again, he was right. As the days passed, I became aware of the different dimensions and different voices inside me. Thoughts and feelings still tore through me but as I observed them in writing, I separated from them a little, they lost some of their power over me. In time, again a remarkably short time, my feelings shrank. I was becoming big enough to contain them.

I would never gain full control of my mind or my heart, that's what Zach taught me. You can't command the ocean, or strap up the wind, but you can observe them, you can get to know them. He gave me a structured way to do this, a way to flex and strengthen my inner self, so I could rely on it. So I could feel free and safe, whatever my outer circumstances.

Meditation and three pages complete, it was time for breakfast. Daddy's first: some porridge or mashed banana or soft eggs. Going into his room was less of an ordeal with Zach out in the kitchen, within calling distance. Once Daddy was looked after, we took time over our own meal, and then it was down to three good hours working on my book. Yes, his regime had got me writing, too.

Break at twelve-thirty. Prepare the soup or homemade

blancmange or whatever slippery concoction was my father's lunch that day and bring it in to him while Zach prepared ours.

And after lunch, a walk. Daily practice number three.

"When Pauline is here," he said, "I will sometimes go with you. But it is important that you often go alone."

Right again. The step-by-stepness of those solitary hikes in the Wicklow hills somehow synchronised with the pages of free-writing now stacking up on my desk, and with the witnessed breaths of my morning meditations, and with the writing that was going in the book. Beat by beat, these "practices" began to give a rhythm to my days. I found myself beginning to smile again, to laugh, to listen to music. I started cooking us some of my favourite recipes from the café. I bought a camera and started taking photos of Doolough, of the mountains and the lake. My father was no longer the only focus of my day. At night Zach and I sat by the fire, murmuring quiet chat, or listening to a music show on Radio Éireann that played songs of the sixties.

With three simple tools — meditation, walking and writing — Zach nursed me back. The way he taught me was the way he followed himself. On the outside, we looked like two simple people living simple days. Inside, we were warriors, fighting a true fight.

Zach loved Ireland. He loved the Wicklow hills, the mystery that hung about the mountain peaks and the lakes. He began to speak of finding a space where he could offer workshops or even retreats which gave rise to an idea in me. One evening, as we sat by the window looking out at the trees, I said to him, "Have you thought any more about a premises for your workshops?"

"I've committed myself to the idea," he said. "If it is meant to happen, it will."

"Do you see it being in the city or the country?"

"Oh, the country, definitely."

"What about here?"

"You mean Doolough?"

"I mean this house. Daddy won't last forever. You could do it here when — after — he's gone."

The location was perfect: isolated and on the doorstep of some of the finest scenery in Ireland but close enough to a main road to take a car to Dublin in less than an hour. The house would need refurbishment but...

"Are you serious, Mercy?"

"I think so. Yes, yes I am." The idea excited me. To see this house come to life again, and used for such a purpose. It would reverse the rot.

"Does this mean that you want to help? Do you see it as something we could do, together?"

That I could not give him. I was with him now because I'd needed him so badly but, as my strength returned, I could feel our time together running out. Even Zach's magic wasn't going to overcome over the problem of Star.

"It's just a thought," I said. "That man in there is a tough old boot. He could see us all out yet."

And then it came: the call I had been dreading and craving. I was in the porch, in search of a rain mac, when the phone started to ring. My thoughts did a quick calculation as they did every time I heard it: 4 p.m. in Ireland. Too early in Santa Paola or LA (I didn't even know where she was) for it to be her. And yet I knew, before I even picked it up.

"Hi, Mom, it's me."

It gave me a moment's vertigo to hear her voice. I backed against the wall to steady myself. "Star. Darling, how are you?"

She answered, crisp and clipped, repeating prepared sentences. She was well. She was taking time out. She was thinking of coming to Ireland.

"Star, that's wonderful. Absolutely wonderful."

"Just one thing. Is he there?"

"No."

"No, not there in front of you? Or no, not at all?"

I didn't hesitate, not for one second. If I did, I knew we were doomed. "No, not at all."

Okay then. She would come. She should be with me by Christmas Eve. She went on, talking about flights and arrival times but I was only half-listening.

"Mom?"

Hearing her was making me lonely for California, for warm nights and beach days, Marsha and the café, the click of palm trees and the dart of lizards and — most of all — the evenings, watching the hazy sun sink into the hazy sea during days when I hadn't known how lucky we were to have only ordinary worries. I asked, "Are you at home?"

"Yes."

"In the hall or the kitchen?"

"I'm in the hall," she said. "Are you listening to me?"

"Of course I am. I just wanted to imagine you there."

"For Chrissakes, Mom. Don't put me off coming before I even leave."

"No, sorry, of course not. Are you —"

"Look, I have to go. We'll talk when I get there, okay? Christmas Eve. I should be there by lunchtime. Bye."

MERCY

1990

*A*nd so we have come round to the beginning. Back to where there is nothing left to do but tell. No, says my mothering instinct. Keep silent. Make something up. Protect. Go on protecting. But I did not write all these words to sully them at the end with a lie. I have to tell my truth, if only to the page.

Or maybe to the police?

My trial begins in three weeks, Mags says. If I am going to speak, it must be now.

I think Mags knows.

I have started to imagine the trial. Star has been called back to Ireland for it, and she has come. As has Zach. I have started to imagine them, sitting beside each other each morning in the courtroom, leaving together each afternoon, side-by-side all day. While I am brought to and from the defendant's stand, alone. Last time I saw Zach, he'd said, "Don't worry about Maria, Mercy. She will be okay. Her warrior spirit will see her through."

Warrior spirit.

Maria.

He knows a different person.

He and I are estranged since that day before Christmas when

she telephoned to say she was coming over and I told him he'd have to go.

He tried to persuade me, told me there was nothing to fear, that to get beyond this thing — this admittedly terrible thing, just as terrible for him and Star as for me — we had to go through it. He didn't know why it had happened, but it had. We had to be open to what The Source was trying to tell us. All three of us. Enough time now had passed for us to be able to sit down together and understand what it all might mean and how to go forward. I should telephone and tell Star so. If I didn't, he would.

"Oh no, you won't."

"You did tell her I'm here, Mercy?"

He wouldn't understand. He wanted me to be better, stronger, than I was.

"I can't," I said, jumping out of my seat, pacing the room. "I can't do it, Zach. I won't do it and you can't make me."

The only way I could cope with the horror of it all was to have only one of them in front of me at a time.

This time, I chose Star.

She wasn't going to be as easy as Zach, but I didn't blame her for being angry. I deserved all she dealt out to me when she arrived. That her mother should be loved by the man who had rejected her was a cruel mischance. That I should take him back, into my father's house, that I should be with him after finding out what he had meant to her: that, she would never forgive.

The fact that I only did it because I was in terrible need would hold no water with Star.

And so she arrived with her anger, her blistering anger that wanted to fire the fields and poison the rivers, that wanted to hurt everybody in the whole wide world, especially me. Only such an anger could have led her into killing my father. She had little time for him but that degree of hatred was something she reserved only for me.

She did it to punish me, perhaps to see me off to prison, so she and Zach could be together.

Or so I believed. Unless...

Unless. Such a small word, so often used, so rarely noticed. Not a word to announce itself, yet as soon as it came to my attention, I wondered why I hadn't paid it consideration before. It had grown in me, without my knowing it, over my months here in this house, through all the writing about her and my father, through the healing time with Zach, so that by the time we got to the trial, it seemed a lever, lifting possibilities many times its size. Unless, unless...

So, Star, let me write down a series of events that have taken hold of my imagination. It is our visit back here in 1982 and I have gone to Dublin for my book launch. My father brings you fishing as your reward for disobliging me. You leave the house at about four o'clock to go blackberry picking on the way, promising Rose you'll be back in time for tea. He brings you to the brambles on the upper field, then down towards the lake. You hardly speak. He is twisted inside thoughts of his own and you are miserable, guilty about not having gone to Dublin, wondering why your grandfather has brought you out here if he is going to be so silent. Not knowing what you ought to know, because you were never told.

You pass through the high field, black and brown cows munching grass and one raising its head to look. The pigeons are loud in the trees as you approach the woodland that thickens round the lake in summer. My father steps into the drowsy mass of green and you, my daughter, follow. Imagine. Imagine. The breeze smells of the earth but sounds, swooshing through the high branches of the trees, like the sea.

Your hair gets caught in a branch and you have to stop to

pick out the pine needles. He chivvies you forward, his nerves always at him. "Come on, come on out of that."

The trunks of the trees draw closer together, the light dims. He stops against a fallen bough near the lake.

"I don't like it here, Granddad."

"Don't you, now?"

A rattle in his voice makes you look into his face and see something. You feel what is coming your way before you know such a thing can be.

You move to turn.

He catches you by the wrist.

You shout: "No!"

He says, "Now, now. Don't be like that."

He pulls you down. Down into a secret that is the drowsy dull light of the lake, and the pigeons cooing, and the wavy wind in the trees, and the ground going from under your feet, and the berries spilling out of the can, and the twig digging into your back...

"No!" You try to shout aloud again and he claps his hand over the sound.

Then it is the weight of him urging down on you. His knee thrusting yours apart. His mouth by your ear, breath wet and hot. The splaying of you open. The burning inside you. The green scum on the edge of the lake lap, lap, lapping. The ferns curling away. And nothing ever again what it was before.

This is what I need to know, Star. Did this happen? Was this part of your mix of motives? If it was, how can I have you further punished? But if it is all my fancy, if the real reason was revenge on me and Zach, how can I not?

And what of Zach? Does he know the depth and capacity of your anger? You won't have told him, I'm sure but he is an intuitive man. Surely, if he suspected what you have done, that would be the end of you and him. And that is what — yes, I'm going to come out and write it, tell you the worst, the very worst — that is what a part of me, a deep-down, low-buried, loathsome part of me, wants.

I want to tell him the truth.

Unless...

We began each morning of the trial with a man banging his tipstaff on the ground and shouting, "All Rise!" Once he had alerted us, the judge followed in, overweight and bewigged, in dark-rimmed, Buddy Holly glasses, with an irritating way of tenderly placing his well-upholstered posterior upon the well-upholstered bench. Settled, he would take a brisk look at me over his glasses, then nod at the counsel and we were off on another day.

Around me, mouths opened and closed, opened and closed, around the same questions over and again. The pump. The pills. Pauline. Zach. Star. Me. My father. Much to Mags's surprise, it seemed to be going our way. She was taking the line that too much of the Department of Public Prosecution's evidence was circumstantial and was doing a great job of persuading the court that I was not the only person who might have done the deed.

As things looked better and better for me, I felt less and less present to all the courtroom chatter. What seemed more real, more important was Zach and Star, sitting beside each other each day. Zach's grey eyes looked at me and seemed to ask me every question under the sun. Star's green eyes looked at me and were blank as a doll's. I saw those four eyes all day in court and, when I was ushered back to my cell, I saw them still. I saw them while I was awake and while I slept.

By day, when I controlled the dreams, I conjured up for myself and my daughter a world where none of this had happened, where we went to the mall to shop, where we enjoyed pizza and ice-cream sodas together, where she introduced me to some nice boy I'd never met before and I was happy for her. An ordinary, normal mother and daughter, what we hadn't been for so long, maybe ever.

I had no answers. I had no words. I didn't even know what to wish for.

What lay ahead for me, if Mags got me off? My heart forever whispering for Zach, the only man I'd ever really wanted. A proper man, strong enough to be gentle. And now the only man I couldn't have.

My blood forever whispering for Star.

I couldn't think about "guilty" or "not guilty" because there was no freedom from guilt for me, either way. The choice between a physical prison or an emotional one? No choice at all. Lover? Daughter? My mind's eye played with one and then the other until some other mouth would open around some new set of words that would drag me back into that horrible courtroom, back to unreal questions for which there were no answers.

Days droned past. The cyst of trepidation inside me solidified.

Then came an exchange between Zach and Star, a small moment that told me what to do. While the prosecutor, Manny Bradshaw, was cross-examining Dr Keane, Star leaned sideways to whisper something in Zach's ear. He shook his head at whatever she asked, then reached across and patted her hand, a small protective pat. She turned from him to hide her expression, so he didn't see the look that crossed her face but I, sitting opposite in the defendant's dock, viewed it straight on. Adoration. No other word for it.

She flicked her eyes in my direction and saw that I had seen. That chased away the blankness of the stare she had been dealing me for days and, as she looked at me properly for the first time since all this had happened, as I stared into those green eyes so like my own, I felt like I was falling into water. They held pity and pity's opposite, her complete scorn.

Whichever way I looked at what Star had done, a finger

pointed back at me. The night before, I'd dreamed she was a baby and I was feeding her a bottle, but when I looked closely it had no milk in it, only dust and crumbled, dried-up leaves. I wanted to go back, that was what I wanted.

My daydreams took me there. Back to the days before she knew either of us had a father, back to when I was her all-in-all and she was my twinkling little star and further back, to when we were even safer, to before I was even born myself, when she was already buried fast inside me, a tiny egg, the whisper of a promise. Her scornful eyes now seemed to beg a question: what would you give to go back? What would you give? It came to me then, all in a rush: the only answer.

In front of me was a pencil. I picked it up and wrote on a piece of paper that I passed to Mags. Her eyes boggled as she read the words and — predictably — she shook her head furiously at me. I nodded, insistent. Calm now. Around me, everyone else in court began to grow restless, knowing something was up. I closed my eyes to their growing unease, the coughs and the shuffling of papers and the shifting of feet. I took a big breath, settled into my new solidity, serene as a mountain. I knew what was coming. I took the time it needed to take.

Then I pushed my chair back and started to stand to make my announcement. Mags pulled at my arm, forced me back down and stood herself. "M'Lord," she said. "I wish to request a recess. I need to speak to my client."

He wasn't impressed but he granted it.

In the inner chamber, Mags slammed the door behind us. "If you're not careful, he is going to throw the book at you for wasting the court's time. I refuse to do what you wrote down in there." She couldn't even bring herself to say it.

"It's what you said you wanted me to do."

"Yes, back at the beginning. Not now. For Christ's sake, Mercy, if you do that, you'll get the absolute worst of both worlds. He'll give you life."

"So be it."

"You can't! I won't let you. It's going well in there, there's a chance of getting you off. Why would you do this?"

"I'm sorry, Mags, I know it's inconvenient for you but..."

"Incon — bloody — venient! It's a damn sight more than that."

"I know it's hard for you. I wish I'd known earlier that this was what I wanted, but I didn't. I'm sorry — but if you don't tell him, I will."

Something in my voice communicated itself. She sat down. Her shoulders slumped. She looked so unlike herself I almost laughed.

"Have you any idea, Mercy, what prison is like? You'll be an old woman when you come out."

"So be it," I said again.

"I don't get it," said poor Mags. "I just don't get it. Tell me why."

How could I explain that my going to prison was the only chance I had to liberate us all? The only way to salvage ... something.

I couldn't, I didn't even try.

"I should never, never have taken this case," she said, flinging her pencil down. "I knew you were trouble, from the first day. Christ! I am never going to forgive you for this."

We went back out.

Mags approached the bench. "M'Lord, my client wishes to change her plea to guilty."

Reporters woke up out of their snoozes and followed their colleagues rushing for the exit. Star's hands flew to her mouth, one over the other. Zach found my eyes and held them and sent me a small smile, the only one who knew enough to know what I was doing.

PART X
STARLIGHT

*Star: A fixed luminous point in the night sky that is a large, remote
incandescent body like the sun.*

Light: natural agent that stimulates sight and makes things visible

STAR

2009

*T*he day she went to prison, my mother was not allowed to see us, so she explained what she wanted in two long letters, seven pages each to Shando and me. I can summarise each of them in a sentence:

Dear Zach,

I want you to work with Star, to take my father's house and turn it into the healing center you've been talking about. Work on it together, be together. That is my wish.

Dear Star,

Your Shando will need your help to make this work, so be there for him. Be together, that is my wish.

It was our wish, too. We were both so fragile after all that had happened, it gave us a way forward but at the same time, I was furious that she had appropriated even this. Now I would never know if he'd have come to me of his own accord. She'd got in even there.

He and I settled down together, with some high-drama moments at first. For me, that is. My husband doesn't do drama. At the beginning, we were so busy, remodelling my grandfather's house, turning Blackberry Lodge into a healing center, with Mom encouraging us at each prison visit to use as much of "that man's" money as we needed. "What better use could it be put to?" she would say, when we'd ask her permission to take another tranche of funds for another improvement.

We knocked walls to make a large catering kitchen. We added a sun lounge on the south-west façade and a dining area at the opposite end and extended the front rooms into a yoga studio and classroom. We called it The Better World Center in tribute to Mom and Marsha's café and we carried over some of their (big and neat) ideas. Marsha came across to visit, when she could, more often after she retired.

At first, we had a struggle to keep going. Ahead of our time in Ireland, we found it challenging to build a clientele and it was years before we won trust among the locals of Doolough. Mom's very public trial and imprisonment didn't help but all sorts of other crazy rumours flew. We were part of a cult, we were witches, we were offering orgies and pagan practices.

Pauline Whelan, who worked part-time for us in the office, would bring us the latest nonsense that was circulating the village. I would have given up many times, but Shando never wavered. "If we stay true to the vision," he used to say, "everything will work out fine." He was right. By the mid-1990s, we were thriving.

And Mom was still in jail. They made her serve more than thirteen years. Thirteen years of avoiding the drugs and sex and dramas that got the other inmates through prison days and nights. At first, her aloofness annoyed the others. "Her Ladyshit," they called her. "Her Ladyshit thinks her shit don't smell." Before long, though, she was the old hand, the lifer watching the small-timers come and go and, as her acceptance of where she found herself settled, the others came to acknowledge it and turn to her with their troubles.

On visits, she would tell us some of the dirty secrets that seeped out from under the cell doors — the punctures and jabs of drug abuse; the sex connections that were a kind of hate; the aggression and belligerence and occasional violence; the self-harmers who broke plastic cutlery to cut themselves; the screw who forced himself on the most hopeless of the hopeless.

She categorised her cellmates into three types: the ones who cried over their parents, the ones who cried over their children, the ones who cried over their men. (Which always set me wondering: which type was she?)

She recorded her thoughts in hard-backed notebooks, filling pages with the details of these days which, from the outside, looked so identical. The particular details of neglect or abuse that led these women to their addictions, or their shoplifting, or whatever misdemeanour had brought them in, came to fascinate her and became her subject. She wrote books that told these true life stories and, with the help of the prison's librarian, who came to be a friend, she had them published to some success.

But still, it was prison.

"How did you stand it for so long?" I asked her once.

"Whenever it got tough, and self-pity started up in me, I would ask myself: 'Can I bear this moment here and now?' I always found, if I went deep enough inside, that I could."

Happy in prison. Her Ladyshit, serene in the face of hostility. That's who my mother made of herself.

Dear Star,

I finished writing Blue Mercy today, finally, and realised that I had to be here, in prison, for that to happen. How strange. Our story is so very strange from start to finish, isn't it, but strangest of all, maybe, is *that coming in here has been a good thing for me. A good thing. I imagine you punishing yourself over it so I want you to know that. It's okay, I'm happy to be here. Happier than I would have been outside. In here, where the outer days are harsh, beset with rules and ugliness, we're supposed to be sitting out our time, waiting for our release date so life can strike up for us again. Not me. The outer world for me has become the lesser half of life. I'm dancing to an inner rhythm now.*

I know you'll find that hard to believe. You've seen the place, the visitor's room is enough. And when you get back here, it's the real Victorian deal, complete with clanging steel doors, hard beds and chamber pots. The others laugh like crows all day and cry like owls all night and hardly know the difference. But it's okay, it's okay.

The practices Zach taught me help. They keep me safe and well and yes, happy, in here. Each day I write, I read, I walk in the exercise yard and I call a halt to my thunderous thoughts by meditating and returning to where I am. If I let these practices slip, I get resistance, fear and struggle again. If I stay with them I get trust, surrender and acceptance. Even joy, sometimes. Yes, joy. Here in prison, I'm free and safe at last.

Star, darling, this is what I hope for you. That you will drop the questions that have no answers and allow yourself to be free. That you will let him show you how. It took me half a lifetime, and Marsha's help, to realise that I was angry with my mother for dying young and abandoning me. Senseless — as if she was responsible for dying, yet that anger ran my life, ruined my life, until I went deep enough inside to see it. Seeing it was the start of my happy ending. I believe reading this manuscript could be yours.

During your visits, we talk about the doings of other inmates, the latest challenge at your Better World Center, the weather — anything, except the complicated, tender territory between us. This book is our hope, the real work of my life but for it to do its work, I need you to read it. So over to you. I can do no more.

Sometimes Star, not too often, I allow myself a small imagining. Not a why-oh-why, or a what-if; something closer to a dream. I am out of prison and back in Doolough and you have read this book. It is dusk

*in summer and we are walking towards the lake. The fading light has
greyed the water. The wildflowers are out — wood avens, honeysuckle,
greater bladderwort — and on the lake's eastern shore, a cluster of
white water lilies.*

*I tell you to keep your eyes alert for young hedgehogs or badgers or
foxes that might be coming out to feed. We go down to the water,
admiring the stillness that makes it look half-solid, like mercury. We
circle round it, pushing through the spot where the pathway knots with
nettles, through the strings of the weed we call Sticky Nelly. The
blackberries are young on their stalks, still green, in places turning red.
I pick fuchsia and show you how to suck the flower for honey. I deal no
reproaches, I let no shadow fall.*

*We stay out until the bats start to appear and then we leave the lake
and turn back the way we came down. I pick another flower, an orchid
for my daughter's hair, and we walk, with me just a shade ahead of you,
through the slow-gathering darkness, back to the house where my father
no longer lives.*

Shando and I used to visit separately, one of us taking out the
old Hiace van we had before we got the jeep, to make the drive
to Dublin and come back and report to the one left minding the
business. She made a great effort for those visits, I know that
now. I suppose I always knew it, that it couldn't have been easy
to seem so pleased to see us, so open to being entertained and
amused, as my mother always was for visiting hours.

One day we had big news for her, news we went together to
deliver. I was so nervous that Shando had to stop the van twice
on the way and approaching the meshed door of the visitor
room, I'd balked. "You tell her," I said. "I'll wait out here."

"Don't be silly."

"It's not fair to her to have to deal with us both together for
this."

He was having none of it. He made me go in and took my
hand in his to tell her the news. She was better than good about

it. The smallest flicker, just for a fraction of a moment, then she turned her eyes to hold us both and said, in her mawkish way, "A new life! How wonderful!" As if she was any other prospective grandmother.

Exactly how Shando had said she would respond (and in case you're wondering, yes, it is irritating to be married to Mr-Right-All-The-Time, especially when he's so indulgent of your irritation). Still holding my hand, he reached across and took one of hers. I blushed blood-red, but the two of them were smiling. We sat there, a small chain of hands with them looking so serene, while my circuits surged into overdrive. It was only afterwards I realised I should have reached over and taken her other hand, to close the circle.

I was so young then, not yet able to grasp what Shando instinctively understood: the depths of my mother's need for reparation. Prison was her penance; she opened herself to it, utterly.

My feelings, as always, were more conflicted. The thought of her locked away from us — from him — consoled me one minute, plunged me into guilt the next. That day, the hand-holding day, resurrected what had begun to settle in me. I began to torture myself again with speculation about what she and Shando said and did during those visits while I wasn't there. I would boil myself up to a pitch where I'd lash out. He'd respond with his trademark calm, which would drive me further into fury. I would storm about his coldness, he would respond with what felt like condescension, and the upshot of it all was the worst thing that could have happened to me: I lost the baby.

It was to be another nine years, two IVF attempts and a long journey into humility before I was pregnant again.

When they finally let Mom out "early" for good behaviour, she was forbidden from traveling to the States. That was the hardest of all for her. She longed to see California again, to drive a top-down Chevy through Ben Sur, to go for a walk at sunset by the Pacific, to admire the soar of a red-breasted eagle, to lie under a moon burnt red by the Santa Ana but it wasn't to be and the stoicism she'd learned in prison stood to her then, too. She traveled instead in the opposite direction, to Spain and Italy and the Greek islands, writing travel books as she went.

Not a bad life, for those few years. And then, the final blow. Breast cancer, diagnosed three short years after she got out. She battled it, as they say and took the treatment but it failed and as she weakened, we had no choice, after all she had given us, but to invite her to live with us at the Center.

And she had no choice but to accept.

Living with her illness in my house added daily guilt to my internal swirl of resentments. I even resented her cancer for bringing her back into my daily life, as if she'd arranged to have tumours gnaw at her just to get to me. Shando worked with me to dismantle these rages, which were really most unfair to her and destructive to me. I did see that, even as I pickled myself in them.

When she died, prison staff and a good contingent of ex-prisoners turned up to the funeral. All sang her praises, told me they'd never known anyone like her.

Imaginative empathy, my mother used to say, in the days when she drew up lists of books for me, prescribing them like medicine: a dose of Dickens, a *soupçon* of Yeats... That was the reason to read. To develop your imaginative empathy.

Ironic, no?

Let me play her trick for a moment and get you to imagine this: a scene from our last days together not long before she died. I wake in the middle of an ordinary night, at around 3 a.m., to the sound of her shifting about in her room down the corridor. I sit up in bed, my movement changing the rhythm of Shando's breathing beside me, and discard whatever dream I've been dreaming. I slide from the warmth of the covers, the chill air pouring across my naked skin. At the door, I put on my robe, slip out and down the corridor. All quiet. I pause by one of the corridor windows, made a circle in the condensation-covered glass to look out. Nothing to see, except Irish winter darkness, blanketing us in.

Often, on blacker-than-black winter nights like these, Santa Paola would come to mind, the warm swirling blue-black sky that's so different there, its smells of laurel and burnt offerings. I flip-flopped down the corridor in my slippers.

Her room was dark when I looked in. "Are you okay?"

"Fine, fine. I just went down for a drink of water."

"Do you need anything else?"

"I'm fine, Star."

You can see we'd swapped roles by then, which neither of us was much good at, though we managed to keep it civilised.

As I made my way back to bed, I did the work Shando and the other facilitators at the Center have taught me. I took my focus off my coiling emotions, onto my breathing. Breathe in … and fill the belly with air. Breathe out … and all the badness with it. And again … in. And … out. There. Everything was fine. No cross words, no harm done.

I slipped back into the warmth of bed and arranged myself around the curve of my husband's spine. His heat transferred itself to me and I kissed the knobbly bone at the base of his neck. If I slid my foot along his shin and kissed him again in a certain way, he would waken. He would turn and our legs would straighten and we would feel the length and center of each other.

I'm sorry but I needed to write that. I have to claim him. For all that you have read in my mother's book, it's important that you understand that he is my husband. *Mine.* And that there's a whole story you haven't been told.

He was my first love and he will be my last, I know that. Even if I wanted, I wouldn't have time now to learn again how to take and give with the mix of abandon and familiarity that only years together can bring. Where, I would have liked to ask my mother, is the poet who's done justice to *that* kind of love, the intimacy that takes years to build? The lovemaking that has within it all the other times you've been together? Yet another question I can never ask.

Years, he and I have shared. Years, as husband and wife, building our Center, getting and staying pregnant, having and raising our children. We have grown into each other. We hold each other up. I am his wife. *I am his wife.*

This, then, was my life before my mother died, before I read her book. In my bed, my husband's heartbeat under my hand. In the room next door, my two children safe in sleep. In the rooms around and below us, our home and work, our life's purpose. Down the corridor, trying to get some sleep, my mother, his mother-in-law. And in my core, despite years of effort, a heart still pumping jealousy and fear.

On our last day out together in Laragh, my mother tried to give me this manuscript. To please her, I'd arranged this day out with the kids, her grandchildren, our two little miracle babies, born through the wonders of science, by then six years old.

We had a good time at Glendalough, strolling through the ruins. Cancer and its treatment had made her frail and she, who had always been such a great walker, was unable to go far but we'd enjoyed the jaunt with the kids skipping ahead of us, along the grassy paths.

Afterwards, I drove the four of us to Laragh and as I drove, I was congratulating myself. Shando had thought it a good idea to have this day out together, and so it was turning out. She was sure to love the water sculpture in the church grounds that I was bringing her to now, a bronze statue of Saint Kevin's arm and hand, the hand in which, according to legend, he'd allowed a bird to nest and hatch its eggs.

In the church car park, I walked round to the passenger side, to open the door and help her down. Frail as she was, she still had beauty. Her tan, faded during her prison years, had been resurrected by her travels so that now, at the end of her life, she looked like a white settler in an African colony, leathery skin against long ashy hair that she twisted into a knot at the crown of her head.

Dean was already unstrapping himself and hopping out. Are all children always in such a rush? My two can never just wait. "The Hand!" he shouted, remembering the water feature, the last time they'd climbed all over it. Since I found this place, so close to where my father was born and bred, we'd come often. But it was my first time to bring Mom and I couldn't help recalling the last time, all those years ago, that we'd come here looking for his house.

Aimee fumbled with her seat belt. Tumbling out, she took up her brother's call. "The Hand! The Hand!"

My mother and I followed at her pace, me feeling too large as I always did beside her. Though I am thinner now, I'm still a chunk of marble to her silken gauze. The kids were trying to climb up already. "Don't get wet, you two," I called as we got close, one of those motherly interjections that everyone ignores.

I sat Mom on the bench and wrapped a rug around her and read the poem from the plaque aloud for her. *Saint Kevin and the Blackbird* by Seamus Heaney. A poem that ask us to imagine the feel of warm eggs in our hand, the beat of a bird's breast against our palm, the scratch of its claws on our skin, to contemplate what it would be like to be that self-forgetting.

"Since the whole thing's imagined anyhow," my mother recited, from memory. "Imagine being Kevin…" She sighed, her legs folded together to one side, like a lady riding side-saddle. "You should learn it by heart, too, Star. Poems have to become the marrow in your bones."

All my life, she'd said things like this and ignored how I ignored them. I saw Aimee was climbing too high, over the ledge. "Aimee!" I shouted, jumping up and going across to them. "Come down. Now!"

She did as she was told and when I got back to the bench,

Mom had her manuscript out of the bag she'd been carrying. She put it in my lap. "I need you to finish this for me," she said, fixing me with a baleful stare.

I refused and she sighed and reached up to remove the grip that held her hair in place at the crown of her head. It tumbled down, the same color as the cloud-filtered light around us, and she folded it over one shoulder, so it fell in a curtain across the place where her breast used to be.

"Star. Please. You *must*."

A thinness had taken over the skin around her eyes. Another person wouldn't have been able to tell, but I knew I was making her tired.

"It's your story, too," she said to me and, unable to give her what she wanted, I called out instead to the children, "First to the car gets to choose the story we'll play on the way home!" Bribery, as usual, worked better than nagging and they jumped down, Saint Kevin's hand forgotten till next time.

If only I'd agreed, taken it from her. Nothing would have pleased her more. I knew it and so, I said no. That's what I live with now.

I never read it, we never talked and so I never got to where I could have said to her, "Why did you do it, Mom?"

Or "Did you do it, Mom?"

She didn't. She didn't do it. That's what the book makes clear.

Not only that, but she thought I did. A thought that would make me mad as hell — the gall of that, the nerve — if I hadn't done the same to her.

She didn't do it. And now that I know, I wonder how I ever could have thought she did.

I didn't think. Blinded by my emotions, I believed the surface story. *I* never wondered, *I* never imagined. Maybe, deep down, so low I didn't quite know it was there, I thought she'd had help.

From the great helper himself. Shando, for pity's sake. That's a measure of how far off I was. I believed her capable of anything and I thought any man, and especially that man, would do anything for her.

What does it say of me that I could so misjudge them both? What does it say of me that I could think him a murderer — even for a flash, even deeper-than-deep down — and still take him as a husband?

He says I am being too hard on myself, that he thought she did it, too. But she didn't, she really didn't.

And so I'm left here, forever trying to re-imagine it all.

Which brings me to the straggliest, loosest thread of all: what precisely happened in my grandfather's house in the years before my mother ran away to America? Her book gives us the scene in the bathroom with Miss September, but nothing after that. She tells us what she told that demented psychotherapist in Santa Paola, but what did she not say? She shows us the rebirthing weekend but again leaves so much unanswered. Always, she is skipping in and around and away from the topic. And then, at the end, it is me she puts beneath him, something that never happened.

He was a tyrant, my grandfather, the slinking sort, always scheming and conniving. My mother searches hard to find the reason why he was the way he was, and the war can't have helped, but does it explain him? Not to me. Our fear of her father and our desire for Shando blinded us to each other and so we got it wrong, all wrong.

It could only have been he who did it. Who else was there? Shan? Pauline? The idea of either is ridiculous. No, he did it himself … and we should have known that, we should have known. Once your head is clear, nothing else makes sense. I can so totally see him, collecting his stash of pills, hiding them where she couldn't find them, salivating over them like a miser over gold. I see him opening the tissue paper or handkerchief in which he kept them, putting them between his wasted lips, his tainted teeth... With what poisonous thoughts? With what mixed motives?

Unanswerable questions.

My life is full of them. I can't turn back time. I can't change the facts. All I can do is offer this book of hers. I changed very little of it in the end: moved the letter from her "boyfriend", added in another letter here, a witness statement there, inserted my own memory of the day Granddad died and a little bit about Dad but anything I did was just to help the story along. Not to claim it back or tell it from my side.

That was the right thing to do, Shando said, making me want to rip it up and start again.

But I won't. I'll finish without having had my say and with the focus not on Granddad or Shan but on Mom, her last day out with me, the kids' sinewy, young bodies running up the hill, four short legs pumping, racing to the car, she and I behind, a gap between us as we walk.

I was thinking: what was the point in this drive of hers to write? Whether that precious book of hers succeeded or failed, or hovered somewhere in between, it would vanish, sooner or later, along with everything else. There are so many books, far too many, and only a fraction survive and then not for long. A few centuries if a writer is really gifted and really lucky, a tiny beat of time on Planet Earth. So I reasoned as we walked back to the car and drove, in drowsy silence, home.

But what if I'd dropped my reasoning for a minute and surrendered to her wishes and learned what we needed to know, while she was still here to know it? Oh, imagine if I had. Imagine me taking a walk with her down by Doolough Lake, looking at all the Irish country things she showed me, seeing them through her eyes, accepting an orchid for my hair.

"She felt a need for reparation," Shando says, as I try to work it through with him, why she volunteered to be punished for a crime she thought I'd committed.

"What a way to do it."

"That was the way that presented itself." His eyes are the color of rain-soaked clouds.

"But…"

"Yes?" he encourages, holding himself still, like I'm some shy animal he's just surprised in a wood, but I don't know what to say. It's too late.

Too late. The saddest words in the English language.

If I said so, I know he'd disagree, and in certain moods, I almost do, too. I see how my relationship with Mom goes on changing even though she's gone and I know it's not over yet. I also that if she were still alive, we would probably be scraping against each other, still. That, too, is true.

Sometimes I can even believe that all is, as Shan insists, just as it should be. That happens mostly down here, by Doolough Lake. I imagine the things I would have said to her if I'd read her book in time and say them anyway. I say them out loud to the clear air and listen for something that the water and the mountains might whisper back.

It's her book, not mine, so I leave you with her word. Imagine. Just imagine. Because, as she had her poet say to me that last day in Laragh, it's all imagined anyway.

THE END

PUBLICATION NOTE

*T*he early parts of this trilogy were first published in 2006 by Penguin Ireland as Lovers Hollow, and subsequently republished by me in 2011, and further developed into a trilogy. This allowed me to give the books the title and treatment I had first envisaged when writing the books.

The joy of that self-publishing experience, and the experience of selling more books than Penguin, made me a passionate advocate for indie authors and led to the formation of the Alliance of Independent Authors.

AUTHOR'S NOTE

*C*ounty Wexford is blessed with an abundance of talented, devoted local historians, and I am greatly indebted to their work, particularly that which acknowledges the lives of women.

ALSO BY ORNA ROSS: FICTION

My novels are family murder mysteries, stories of lies, secrets and the ties that bind,
across centuries and continents

—The Irish Trilogy—

An epic trilogy that follows five generations of women as they move through the momentous
dramas of the 20th century.

—The Yeats Trilogy—

A famous poet, his revolutionary muse, and her confused daughter. What is true and what can
only be imagined?

—Blue Mercy—

A heart-breaking, mother and daughter mystery, with a patricide at its heart.

You can buy my novels directly from me on my website, or on your favorite online store

ALSO BY ORNA ROSS: POETRY

My poetry aims to inspire. It doesn't deny doubt, damage or despair but seeks that secret space where we can also transact with the truth of beauty.

—Chapbooks—

Chapbooks of inspirational poetry: Ten poems at a time.

—Themed Poetry Selections—

Here is Where: A Book of Remembrance Poetry

Allowing Now: A Book of Mindfulness Poetry

Nightlight as it Rises: A Book of Love Poetry

—Occasional Poetry Selections—

Poetry for Christmas

Poetry for Mother's Day

AND MORE

POETRY BOOKS:

You can buy my poetry books directly from me on my website, or on your favorite online store

BECOME A POETRY PATRON:

You can become a patron of my poetry on Patreon.com/OrnaRoss.

My Patreon page is supported by a band of poetry lovers and indie poets who receive exclusives and bonuses from me. It's also where I feature the work of other indie poets through #indiepoetryplease

MY PODCAST

FAMILY HISTORIES & LIFE MYSTERIES

Follow my "Histories & Mysteries"
podcast for more poems, stories and
behind-the-books news

Font Publications is the publishing imprint for Orna Ross fiction and poetry, the Go
Creative! books and the Alliance of Independent Authors author publishing guides.
All Enquiries: info@ornaross.com

 Created with Vellum